Lytton's Diary

Also by Ray Connolly

A Girl Who Came To Stay
That'll Be The Day
Stardust
Trick Or Treat?
Newsdeath
A Sunday Kind Of Woman
John Lennon 1940–1980 (biography)
The Sun Place
Stardust Memories (anthology)
Forever Young

Ray Connolly

Lytton's Diary

Thames Methuen

First published in Great Britain 1985
by Methuen London Ltd
11 New Fetter Lane, London EC4P 4EE
in association with Thames Television International Ltd
149 Tottenham Court Road, London W1P 9LL
Copyright © 1984 by Ray Connolly
Lytton's Diary format © 1984 by Peter Bowles
Printed in Great Britain
by Richard Clay (The Chaucer Press), Ltd,
Bungay, Suffolk
Filmset by Northumberland Press Ltd, Gateshead
ISBN 0 423 01420 X (Hardback)
ISBN 0 423 01370 X (Paperback)

For all my friends in and around Fleet Street

Contents

Chapter One

Rabid Dingo – Shock, Horror

It was well after three when Neville Lytton left the gloom of the Galley Proof, slightly the worse for a lunch of Sancerre and Camembert but much fortified by a considerable goading of the opposition. Stepping out from the white-walled railway arches under which the wine bar burrowed, Lytton congratulated himself upon his two hours mischief-making and, belting his raincoat, headed back across Ludgate Circus and up Fleet Street.

This was, he always considered, quite the best time of day in Fleet Street, an hour or two when the conviviality of lunch appeared to leak across the rest of the afternoon, and he had frequently noted that while sackings were usually carried out in the mornings, pay rises and promotions were more likely to occur between the hours of three and five. Not that Lytton had been the recipient of many pay rises recently. These were, pay supplicants were invariably told, difficult times in the newspaper industry, and with accountants taking long and searching looks at the latest computerized schemes for economies it was not considered wise to raise one's head too far above the typewriter lest some over-eager statistician should discover a new area for pruning.

While it is unlikely that there has ever been a time in Fleet Street when things have not been difficult, there was, that afternoon, a new sense of unease and uncertainty, which, while making for wicked gossip in the wine bar for Lytton, had sent more threatened rival journalists scurrying back to their offices well before their usual two-hour break had elapsed. The threat was called Wayne Monroe.

Outside the *Daily Express* building Lytton stopped and, buying himself the latest edition of *The Standard*, glanced at the front page to ascertain that nothing important had happened while he had been at lunch. The headline of the evening paper was unchanged. NEW BATTLE OF TYCOONS IN FLEET STREET, it read. Reassured, Lytton set off again in the direction of a black coffee and the *Daily News*.

'Hey, Lytton, wait for me.' The voice of Laura Grey pealed through the clatter of traffic.

He stopped and waited. 'Until hell freezes over, if necessary,' he grinned as she reached him.

'Sounds like you had a good lunch.' Laura raised an eyebrow in mock reprimand. She was an attractive, neatly built woman of thirty-five, confident in her own abilities, professional in all her attitudes.

'It could have been worse. I was with a couple of chaps from across the Street, offering commiserations and trying to reassure them that it might never happen. I'm afraid I couldn't convince them.'

Laura reached out and took his newspaper from where he had lodged it under his arm. 'D'you think it's true?' she asked, studying the first few lines as they walked.

He shrugged. Fleet Street was a honeycomb of rumours, most of which were not believed, and none of which were ever preventable. No one had believed that Rupert Murdoch would really gain control of *The Times* until it was too late to stop him: while the notion of Robert Maxwell buying the *Daily Mirror* had been widely ridiculed only hours before his takeover. Now Fleet Street was said to be under siege from a new aspiring press baron called Wayne Monroe, yet another antipodean millionaire in search of that dubious respectability which proprietorship of a British national newspaper appears to offer the foreign born. Whether the rumours were true or not Lytton had no way of telling, and since Monroe had already made it known that his target was the *Daily Post*, chief rival to Lytton's own paper, it was for him of less immediate concern than for the chums he had teased over lunch. 'He's mad enough, I suppose,' he said.

'Barking mad, according to *Private Eye*,' replied Laura as they turned off Fleet Street down towards the Thames.

Lytton laughed. 'I never believe anything I read in *Private Eye* unless I wrote it myself, and then I know it's not true.'

'All the same ...'

'All the same Monroe would have to be mad to want to buy a newspaper, wouldn't he? Especially a lost cause like the *Post*. He was obviously bitten by a rabid dingo when he was still in the pouch.' Aware of a shadow, Lytton looked up. They were passing a loading bay where a bale of newsprint was being winched from the back of a truck into the bowels of the *Daily News* machine room. Putting an arm out he guided Laura around the outside of the truck. 'I wouldn't go under there, if I were you, or you might find one of your better paid colleagues dumping an extremely large toilet roll on your head.'

Laura giggled and stepped out into the road. She had been having what she liked to call a relationship with Lytton for several months (she wondered occasionally what Lytton called it) but had still not become accustomed to the elegant display of good manners with which he dressed every occasion. While some might have complained that Neville Lytton had the morals of a scavenger when it came to journalism (an estimation with which Laura would not necessarily have agreed), no one could criticize him for lack of courteousness. If the knife had to be plunged between the shoulder blades, there was no one in Fleet Street who could perform the act with greater gallantry.

'I had an affair with an Australian once,' said Laura as they reached the pavement again. 'He was very nice. He was a stringer for the *Los Angeles Times* in Cairo. Quite sweet, really. I was there to write a feature on some Egyptian film actress called Nefertiti. It was a freebie and was never printed. I didn't mind. I had a lovely week cruising up and down the Nile with my little Aussie. He used to write me poetry in Greek – at least he said it was Greek.'

They had reached the *Daily News*. Lytton held the revolving door as Laura stepped inside. 'Is there no end to your sordid past?' he murmured, following her into the building.

Together they crossed the marble floor of the lobby. Once it had been a polished and permanent reflection of bulldog entrepreneurial energy in newspaper publishing, but, like so much of Fleet Street, it had not weathered well in recent years and the once gleaming checkered stones were now dull and worn.

'If I could manage a romantic sonnet in the style of Diogenes do you think you might be free for dinner tonight?' asked Lytton.

'I'd settle for a couplet in the style of Betjeman,' said Laura stopping at the lift.

'Splendid,' replied Lytton, heading for the stairs. 'I think I'll walk. I need the exercise.' At forty-five he was vain enough to worry about the soft patch which had appeared recently under his belt. He was damned if he was going to allow it to become any bigger.

Laura watched him go. He was an attractive, tall man, almost a dandy, she sometimes thought, and not for the first time she reminded herself that she was grateful they had chosen each other as part-time, semi-permanent lovers. She had had lots of affairs but Lytton was the first man who, while being extraordinarily attentive when she was with him, had never displayed any serious pro-

12

prietorial rights over her body when she chose to be with someone else. In a word he was not the jealous type, or, to be more precise, he was not jealous of anything *she* might do, which, since she considered herself a woman without ties, suited her very well.

For Lytton, his forty-fifth birthday had been a singularly depressing milestone. Most men reach their menopause at around forty, it is alleged, but Lytton remained as he had always been, a chronic late developer. Forty-five was the killer for him. What am I doing with my life? he worried inconsolably for days, suddenly horribly aware of a thinning pate and bulging jowls.

Despite Laura's frequent companionship, and a job which led him like a dazzled moth from bright light to bright light, he was essentially a lonely man. He was separated from a wife who had been the best friend he had ever had, was childless, and, should the evening not provide a party, he seemed forever doomed to return to an empty flat. Happily in the life of a gossip columnist there are few party-less nights.

Though Lytton's job at the *Daily News* was profligate in its excuses for socializing, it was also extremely frustrating. No man of forty-five should be marooned at number three, Lytton would tell himself in his bleaker moments. But every avenue forward seemed permanently barred. Had he perhaps concentrated earlier upon his career, or at least stuck to one job, then who knows where he might have been, he told himself. But he hadn't. After a dazzling start across the Street at the *Post*, Lytton's career in journalism had been interrupted when one night he had shown more enthusiasm than discretion and turned in a highly amusing, but totally fictitious piece about the '*real* reasons' for a cabinet minister's trip to China. Any normal cabinet minister would have been more amused than angry, but to Lytton's eternal mortification the chap had shown no sense of humour, and decided to chuck himself out of his private aeroplane somewhere above the Royal Wimbledon Golf Course, leaving a note to the effect that he could no longer stand being hounded by that dreadful man Neville Lytton.

At twenty-nine Lytton, who always claimed that his piece was true in spirit if not detail, went, in one bound, from top feature writer and columnist to his local labour exchange. It wasn't that he couldn't have found himself a place on another newspaper (heaven knows, there are stacks of liars in the Street of Shame) but his confidence was gone. He no longer wished to be a journalist, although he did not know exactly what he did want to do.

Travel should have helped, but it didn't. In New York he wrote advertising copy, in Sydney he sold second-hand Rolls-Royces, in Baden Baden he taught English in a finishing school, in Santa Monica he lived by the ocean, developed the best English tan on the Pacific coast and dabbled in real estate, and in Paris he became a film publicist. Indeed it was while at the Cannes Film Festival, helping promote a rather unpleasant Franco-Italian movie about a woman who marries her adopted son, that he discovered the course which was to lead him back to newspapers. When he had been a young feature writer he had gained access purely by hard work and cheek. But now, more than a decade on, he discovered that his university of the world experience had equipped him with a social panache, an address book full of rich telephone numbers (admittedly all overseas, but since money cleaves to money the world over they were more than useful for introductions), and more understanding of the ways of the world than could have been gained in ten lifetimes chained to a newspaper office. In his thirties, as he roamed the world, Lytton had dreamed about being rich: but now satisfaction was what he most craved. And for him satisfaction could best be found with one hand wrapped around a telephone and the other on a typewriter.

Getting back into Fleet Street had not been as easy as he had expected, however. He had been out for over twelve years, and there were lots more youthful men in front of him. But persistence had paid and he had eventually begun again at the bottom of the *Daily News* diary desk wondering if he had not left it too late. For the first time in years he was truly happy with his work, which turned out to have ironic consequences. No sooner did he begin to regain his eagerness and nose for a story, than his wife, Catherine, ran off with another man, leaving him a jar of sugared almonds, a magnum of Moët Chandon (to celebrate what she didn't say) and a frozen pizza.

For at least a week he was shattered. Catherine, fourteen years his junior, had befriended and kept him when he was living in Paris and between jobs and it seemed to Lytton particularly perverse of her to ditch him just as soon as he began to make some progress.

Catherine saw things slightly differently. Like all men who are truly good at their jobs, Lytton was wedded to newspapers, and since a gossip column was to Catherine only one step up from the dung heap, it was perhaps hardly surprising when she took up with a worthy, but slightly dull academic from the LSE. A better organized pair might have dissolved the marriage legally as well as emotionally, but, while marriage had been difficult, they quickly found that the limbo state of separation had much to recommend it. And although Catherine's new man frequently raised the subject of divorce, Lytton had found little difficulty in persuading her that for the time being at least they should not do anything too final. So, in name at least, they remained married, and before very long Lytton found that batchelor life for a man in London in his forties was not without its compensations. If only he could have seen a clearer way forward in his professional life Lytton might well have thought himself a fortunate man.

A familiar figure was crouched by the coffee machine when Lytton reached the second floor corridor. It was Wesley, the messenger on the Diary page, trying to balance seven plastic cups on a small tray. Lytton liked Wesley. The son of West Indian immigrants from Beckenham in Kent, Wesley was, in Lytton's opinion, quite the brightest boy on the editorial floor and he had been consequently disappointed when Wesley had confided that he hoped one day to go into the print. 'If you want to work in newspapers become a reporter,' Lytton had urged. But Wesley was adamant and Lytton had not pressed him further, preferring to leave the issue in the lap of maturity. At sixteen Wesley had a lot to learn about Fleet Street.

Holding the door on to the editorial floor open, Lytton reached down and helped himself to a coffee as they entered together. 'I hope you remembered to get one for me, Wesley,' he said.

'How's the novel going?' Wesley asked, frowning slightly.

Lytton shook his head. 'Like every other counterfeit passport out of Fleet Street, I'm afraid. Extremely slowly.' With a grimace he put the plastic cup back on the tray. 'Are you trying to poison me, Wesley? This coffee's got sugar in it.'

Wesley grinned: 'That coffee's tea and the editor likes sugar in his tea. You've just drunk his.'

'Really? God has a sweet tooth? I'd never have guessed it,' said Lytton and strode away across to the Diary desk while Wesley made his detour towards the backbench.

On morning newspapers mid-afternoon is when the job of making the paper really gets into its stride, and as Lytton crossed the open expanse that was the editorial floor he was aware of a cranking up of energy as sub-editors took their seats for the beginning of their afternoon-into-evening shifts and reporters hacked away at their heavy manual typewriters. By and large the editorial

16

department of the *Daily News* had changed little since the newspaper had been created more than seventy years earlier, save for the cosmetic effects of pastel-coloured emulsion on the walls, carpet tiles to soften the noise of fifty people working in the same office and push-button telephones, which had been introduced when the old system finally became unworkable. In common with other newspaper proprietors, the owners of the *Daily News* had never subscribed to the view that journalists might enjoy modern technology and creature comforts, so while the advertising personnel on the third floor swanned about among fitted carpets, electronic, computerized typewriters and lavatories of pristine cleanliness, the editorial staff made do with conditions designed for a more robust age.

The Diary desk, upon which Lytton worked, was situated at the far corner of the floor, an out of the way place, envious news reporters sometimes suggested, where the glib peddlers of gossip could exercise their powers of creativity unhindered by the hard-nosed realism of the news pages. It was to this desk, over by the window, with fashion on one side and specialist writers on the other, that Lytton made his way, two seats down from that usually occupied by the Diary editor.

'Anything exciting going on?' he asked of Dolly Brown, the girl who sat next to him as he glanced around the desk. He was the last back from lunch and he resented the way a couple of the younger Diary writers were looking at him.

'Only that I had a row with Donald,' growled Dolly. 'He called me a stuck-up cow and a traitor to my class. Can you believe it? And me from a comprehensive school.'

Lytton smothered a smile. Having met Donald only once, at a farewell party for an aging crime reporter, he had gathered very quickly that Dolly's current partner in life would never forgive her for having left him in *The Guardian* newsroom to throw her life away, as he put it, on the trivia and foibles of the super-rich, over-glamorous and essentially unimportant flotsam and jetsam characters who peopled smart London.

'Serves you right for having lunch with him,' Lytton replied. 'You should know by now never to have lunch with the same person you have supper with. You'll have no one to talk about. Who's Henry talking to, anyway?'

At the end of the table a smart, rather handsome, slightly obsequious little man was smiling roundly into his telephone while simultaneously scribbling a shorthand note of the conversation. 'A million,' he was saying, 'and would that be paperback or hardback, Jeffrey? UK paperbacks ... I see ... How much? A million. So many millions. Pounds or dollars? Oh really. And has Robert Redford definitely said "yes" this time?'

'It's Jeffrey Archer doing his shrinking violet act again,' laughed Dolly. 'It's the fourth time he's been on today.'

Lytton shook his head. 'Where would we be without our dashing sagaman? What about you? What are you doing?'

'Chasing a rumour about Rod Stewart.'

'A malicious rumour?'

'I'm doing my best. D'you think he could sue if I described him as being in his mid-forties?'

'Surely he's older than that.'

Dolly laughed. 'Have you heard the news?'

'What news?'

'Never mind, I suspect you're about to hear all from the piebald pundit.'

Striding down the Diary desk came Henry Field, his conversation with Jeffrey Archer completed. As deputy Diary editor he had recently taken to wearing three-piece suits even on comparatively warm spring days such as this, which together with his bow ties and thick greying hair gave him at least the appearance of some distinction. To Lytton, Henry, while technically senior to him in the

Diary desk pecking order, was little more than an irritating pest.

'I've been having a word with our ailing leader, Lytton, and –'

'Nothing too erudite, I trust,' broke in Lytton, unable to miss the chance of a cheap point.

'– and I'm afraid the poor chap's had a relapse,' carried on Henry, oblivious to the interruption and smiling wolfishly. 'His doctor's told him he needs at least a year off, so, being the louse he is, he's decided to take voluntary redundancy.'

At the back of his mind Lytton heard the distinct sound of alarms ringing. He had no particular fondness for the Diary editor (he was indeed a louse, as Henry had described him), but at least he was an ineffectual louse. If he were to retire it was not inconceivable that he would be followed by a termite of singularly more unpleasant proclivities. 'But there's nothing wrong with him, is there? It was only a little nervous breakdown,' he said.

Henry cackled, aware of the effect his news was having. 'Look at it this way. He's been here for twenty-five years. That's a nice little nest egg if he cashes in his pension rights at the same time. He's thinking of starting a chandler's shop on the Isle of Wight, I believe.'

'So for the moment we have no Diary editor,' said Lytton cautiously.

Henry smirked: 'But we do have an *acting* Diary editor. I just thought I'd let you know.' He stopped, smiled again, and then taking his right hand from behind his back, where it had been throughout the conversation, dropped some sheets of copy paper on to Lytton's desk. 'Oh yes, before I forget, old boy, this piece on Patti Hearst . . . it couldn't be sharpened up a little, could it? Something like "Patti Hearst's recipe book for reformed urban guerillas". You know what I mean. See what you can do, will you?'

With undisguised astonishment Lytton watched Henry

stride purposefully back to his desk. Henry was rejecting his copy as though he were a seventeen-year-old *ingénue*. In all the years Lytton had worked as a journalist he had never had his copy rejected for reasons of style. 'Did you hear that?' he asked, turning to Dolly.

Dolly nodded lugubriously. 'I heard it. I don't believe it. But I heard it.'

Lytton picked up the sheets of paper and considered the opening paragraph. It was indeed a particularly silly story he had culled from an American women's magazine on the off chance that it might make an amusing filler on some thin night. It certainly was not worth rewriting, particularly if only to satisfy the seigneurial designs of a buffoon like Henry. With one practised movement Lytton spread his fingers across the sheets of copy, turned them over and neatly impaled the paper on the spike at the back of his desk. 'That should be sharp enough now, Henry,' he said. 'Sorry I missed the *coup d'état*. I must have been out to lunch.'

'You usually are, Lytton,' Henry replied, and stuffing a sheaf of copy paper into his typewriter set about writing his story on Jeffrey Archer. Alongside him, Jenny, the Diary secretary, worked on, seemingly oblivious to the row which was developing around her. A cool girl, she had an uncanny ability of seeing and hearing only those conversations to which she was intended to be a party.

Lytton turned again to Dolly. 'Am I being out-manoeuvred, or am I being manoeuvred out?' he asked.

Dolly groaned. 'For God's sake, Lytton. They'll be screaming for copy any minute and I haven't finished my story. Go and irritate somebody else, will you. Please.'

'Oh sorry, Dolly, was I distracting you?' smiled Lytton, quite unoffended. Opening his *Standard* he looked again at the Wayne Monroe story, and then turned to the City pages for an analysis by Anthony Hilton, their financial expert. 'What are we doing about Wayne Monroe, Henry?' he shouted down the table.

Henry looked pained. 'Treading extremely carefully, Lytton.'

'Why?'

'Because we don't want to get our goolies blown around our ears, thank you.'

David Sellier, a young pretender recently down from Oxford and already as bumptious as only gossip writers can be, looked up from his typewriter across the table from Lytton. 'I'm not saying he's a cringing, slithering coward, but . . .' he started. Lytton ignored him and began punching out the internal number for the cuttings library.

'Could you tell me who has the cuttings out on Wayne Monroe?' he asked. It was obvious that someone would. After a slight delay the information was given him and getting up he headed down the office in the direction of the general reporters. David Sellier, on his way to the gents, joined him.

'What d'you think? Will the frog turn into a beautiful prince when he returns from his ride in the Rover?' David said, looking sideways at the deputy Diary editor as they passed him. In the *Daily News*, promotion always followed being taken in the editor's Rover to lunch at the Savoy Grill.

'*If* he gets the ride in the Rover,' came back Lytton. 'God's getting very choosey about whom he takes in his chariot of hire these days. Frogs, like chickens, don't always hatch out.' And with that Lytton stalked away.

The Wayne Monroe cuttings were spread across the desk of one of the newsdesk workhorses, a worthy chap called Bill Withy, whose greatest talent was an ability to cobble together a reasonably accurate and interesting story on virtually any subject from just a few minutes' delving through the files. Every newspaper has a cuttings expert, a writer who can burrow down into the thick beige envelopes into which each day's papers are filed, story by story. But Withy was more than an expert. His mind was encyclopaedic, his interests limitless.

'Well, would you let your daughter marry Wayne Monroe?' asked Lytton as he came up behind Withy.

Withy looked irritated. He was speaking on the telephone and, not unreasonably, did not care for Lytton's interruption. 'What?' Lytton stood over him. It was obvious he wanted to chat. Withy made an excuse into the phone. 'Look, would you mind if I called you back, something's come up,' he said and put down his telephone. 'Monroe's already married,' he said, turning to Lytton.

'Oh sorry, Bill, were you busy?' beamed Lytton, then without waiting for a reply picked up a handful of cuttings from Monroe's envelope and began to leaf through them. They had been culled mainly from the business pages. 'For a chap who seems intent upon becoming the next press baron in the good old wild colonial boy tradition, Citizen Wayne seems to have led a very uneventful social life, doesn't he?' he said.

Withy took the envelope of cuttings away from him. He didn't trust Lytton, certainly not to cover anything important. 'I don't know about uneventful. I'd say he just likes to keep away from people like you. Wayne Monroe hates publicity. He never gives interviews, never goes on television and never, ever appears in gossip columns. Apparently the only thing he ever talks about is money.'

'He should get on well with the NGA then, shouldn't he?' said Lytton, opening up the picture file on Monroe which also lay on Withy's desk. It was not an exciting collection of photographs. Apart from the usual portraits for the financial pages there was little of interest. Monroe was a burly, aggressive-looking man in his early fifties, with a narrow, blunt, chisel-shaped forehead and a wide and prominent jaw. He looked, thought Lytton, absolutely

22

the right sort of chap to become a newspaper proprietor. 'What's his interest in the *Post*, anyway?' he asked.

Withy shrugged. 'Hard to say, really. It could be prestige, I suppose. He's done everything else. Poor boy, married money, started in construction and then moved on to asbestos. I suppose he's looking for a new toy.'

'But why here?' Lytton pressed. 'I would have thought Brother Rupert's problems had got through even to Australians by now.'

'You know what they're like down there, every one of them out to outshine the other. Wayne Monroe won't think he's made it until he kneels before the Queen for services to journalism.'

'He's hardly likely to get dubbed for his contribution to the spread of asbestosis, is he?' said Lytton, taking a photograph from the file. It showed a very large blonde lady of middle years in a highly revealing evening dress, with cheeks which looked as though they might have been borrowed from a toffee apple. 'And who calls the English poms?' he mused.

'What's that?' asked Withy.

Lytton turned the photograph over and read the caption. 'Mr and Mrs Wayne Monroe, guests of the Lord Mayor of London at the Mansion House.'

'That's Angela,' explained Withy. 'Queen of the Melbourne charity tea dances, they say ...'

'Which sounds a bit like being the secretary of a team seeking re-election to the Fourth Division. She's a big girl, isn't she?'

'Over thirteen stone, I believe.' Withy's little grey computer was spewing out all kinds of information which, while useless to him as a general reporter and rewrite man, was invaluable to a gossip writer.

'Really! A man's been known to smother under less than that.' Lytton was impressed.

Withy tried a joke, a rare effort for him. 'A man perhaps, but Monroe's an Australian. Now d'you mind if I do my story? There's nothing here for you chaps.'

'All the same, any contacts I might call on?' asked Lytton, more out of habit than expectation.

Withy eyed him coldly. 'Come on, Lytton. I've told you all there is. You can't honestly expect me to risk my contacts with you cowboys on the Diary. You'd blow my career in a week if I did that.'

Lytton smiled philosophically and, thanking him, turned to go back to his own desk, pausing a few feet away to compliment one of the secretaries on what looked like a new hairstyle. Surprised at his interest the girl blushed slightly as she explained how she had decided to have streaks added after her husband had begun paying too much attention to her best friend. But Lytton didn't hear her. Through the corner of his eyes he was watching Bill Withy as he returned to his telephone, noting the number, and memorizing the name he asked for. 'Mr Morley,' he heard him say, 'this is Withy at the *News* again. I'm sorry about the interruption. Now what was that you were saying about Mr Monroe?'

'Morley at 438 8000,' mused Lytton, as he excused himself from the streaked secretary and made his way back to his own desk. 'Now let's see who that is?'

A call to 438 8000 gave him the answer. Withy had been phoning Australia House. Mr Bruce Morley was employed there in the trade department.

'If it's all the same with you, Henry –' Lytton began, trying to catch the eye of the man who considered himself his senior.

Henry looked irritated. He was talking to Dolly. 'Just a minute, Lytton ... yes, a very nice piece, Dolly, but I wonder, should we not use the word "piquantly" rather than "ironically"?' He was coming the schoolmaster with Dolly now.

'*Piquant*,' spat Dolly, 'is a diarist's cliché that even Dempster has stopped using now.'

Henry drew himself proudly back in his chair. 'What Nigel Dempster does or does not do is not, I think, the criterion of how to write for this newspaper,' he said, and neatly changed the offending adverb.

'The little worm,' said Dolly as she returned to her seat.

David Sellier tried to take the heat out of the situation. 'Anyone know where Jimmy Young gets his toupées from?' he asked, but no one answered.

Lytton tried again. 'I think I might just have a look at the Rabid Dingo, Henry . . .'

'Who?'

'You know, Monroe, that Aussie who's supposed to be buying our chief rival, the *Daily Post*,' said Lytton slowly and loudly as though speaking to a deaf foreigner. 'I thought you might have heard of him. I'm going to have a little dig around, I think, do a spot of weeding in his undergrowth.'

Henry shook his head. 'I don't think you should, Neville.'

That was it. Henry was now telling him what he could and could not write about. 'And why not?'

'Well, you know, dog doesn't bite dog. All that nonsense.'

Lytton rose to his feet. 'Look, Henry, until Monroe actually buys the *Daily Post* he can't really be classified as a fellow dog, can he? So we can snap away all we want.'

Henry wasn't impressed. 'Well, anyway, he's even more boring than Murdoch, I understand. A calculator with skin. I don't think we want any of that in our page.'

Lytton leaned across the table, the mellowing effect of the Sancerre now curdling. 'Henry, old man, until such time that a note is pinned to that notice board over there telling us that you, Henry Field, have succeeded the now

25

retired Diary editor, I suggest you keep your Grecian little head down before one of us feeds it to the van drivers to be used for football practice when they're on double time.'

Henry remained impassive. 'You know you're trouble is that you're such a bad loser.'

'Quite possibly. But better to be a poor loser than a poor journalist.'

Henry snorted like the thoroughbred he fancied he was. '*Journalist*? Is that what you are? It's a pity I have such a long memory, isn't it? If you pull a few stunts like you used to, Lytton, they'd probably give you the Pulitzer Prize these days instead of the sack.'

With the skill of an experienced diarist Henry had pierced his opponent in a delicate spot. Lytton coloured slightly. There were some moments in his life of which he did not enjoy being reminded. 'You really are a snivelling little reptile. They could skin you for a pair of shoes and a handbag.'

This was even more than the stoney-faced Jenny could stand. Raising her pretty, long-suffering head from deciphering her shorthand she glared contemptuously at the two middle-aged men bickering across her desk. 'If you two old queens have finished ... it's four o'clock, time for conference.'

Lytton smiled to himself. At least he had succeeded in making Henry late before the editor. 'You bastard, Lytton,' Henry snapped, and grabbing his notes, hurried away for the daily ritual of patronization.

'What about Bruce Forsyth? Is that a Crown Topper?' asked David Sellier. Again everyone ignored him.

Satisfied that he had come off better in his exchanges with the acting Diary editor Lytton sat down again and picked up his telephone. Four, three, eight, eight thousand, he punched.

★

26

The one disadvantage Henry Field could see to being appointed Diary editor was that he would be obliged to spend more time with God, Iain Cruickshank, the editor of the *Daily News*, a Scot with a glare and a temperament which might have been stewed in vinegar. Editor for over twenty-five years, Cruickshank was an awesome figure whose daily afternoon conference was uniformly loathed by the fifteen senior staff whose attendance was always required.

From Henry Field's point of view Henry wasn't a bad chap, quite bright really, but Cruickshank never missed the opportunity of getting him by the neck. For his part, being eager to please, and not having the guile to keep his head down, Henry rarely failed to provide a generous target for the ferocious Scot.

'So what unknown delights does Sport have for us to-night?' the editor was asking a stammering Cockney sports editor as Henry entered the conference.

The sports editor cleared his throat as though about to address the United Nations General Assembly. 'We'll be going on the Arsenal home tie against Liverpool. Mac will be doing it for us and Tim Rimmer is covering it for the Manchester edition,' he said in a voice half an octave higher than that which he normally used.

The editor turned sarcastically to his captive audience. 'It always seems to me such a waste of resources to have two men tell different lies about what neither of them saw at a football match,' he chuckled unpleasantly. There was a general toadying of agreement from the assembled journalists.

Henry being the fool he was, could not resist the temptation to curry favour. 'Talk about reinforcing the prejudices of the lumpen proletariat,' he gloated, shaking his head derisively at the hapless sports editor.

The editor's smile faded as his eagle eye turned on the acting Diary editor. Only he was able to make fun of anyone in his office. 'Nonetheless,' he glowered, 'even in sport one can appreciate that there are always two sides to every argument, isn't that right, Henry?'

'Oh, absolutely,' Henry agreed.

The editor stared at him savagely for a moment and then turned to address the rest of the conference. 'By now some of you may have heard that our Diary editor has ratted on us and taken the easy money. I always knew he would ...' He stared around his staff as though challenging any of them even to consider such an act of betrayal. 'And I suppose some people are wondering when I'm going to announce his successor. Well ...' he turned to Henry who, sensing that reward was to follow punishment, began to smile in anticipation, '... I'll let you know when I've made up my mind. Now, Henry, what does the Diary have for us tonight?'

Henry's jaw nearly dropped off the bottom of his face in disappointment. What more proof of his suitability could this bastard of an editor want, he asked himself.

'Well ...?' The editor was waiting.

Henry looked back at his notes and pulled himself together. 'We'll be leading on a very good story about Michael Jackson being asked to play for the President, and then there's a very funny piece about Prince Philip's polo ponies only being fed on a certain kind of oats during the season, and of course we have Prince Harry's first words ...'

Suddenly the editor's hand came down on his desk with a resounding thud, cutting off Henry's litany. 'Wayne Monroe,' he glowered. 'What's the word on him? The Street's going to be hopping with kangaroos before we know where we are.'

The City editor smoothed a crease in his pin-striped trousers. 'The whisper in the City is that Allied are trying to fight off the bid. They've approached Goldsmith as usual, and SOGAT are threatening ...'

Despite his usual respect for a staff member as senior as the City editor, Cruickshank was not to be fobbed off with polite information he already knew. As editor he was isolated, and he wanted to know the feelings of his staff and their friends. 'When I first came down there were real newspapermen around ... real lunatics,' he said. 'Beaverbrook, Northcliffe ... and they had style, inky fingers and titled mistresses. What style has Monroe got?'

The City editor tried again. 'His companies are quoted as being worth over 200 million dollars.'

'Aye, Australian dollars,' scoffed Cruickshank. 'Ah well, I suppose we ought to thank God it's the *Post* he's after and not us.' And with that he turned on the features editor and proceeded to berate him for the dull state of the past three nights' leader pages. When God was in a mood like this, Henry considered, he was the most unpleasant man he had come across since he had been at school.

Bruce Morley was waiting for Lytton at five o'clock when the Galley Proof reopened. He was standing by the bar, a smooth-cheeked corporation man, with a left-over tan from an Australian summer and a line of dandruff in the crease where his suit folded on his shoulders. He was not, Lytton decided, one of nature's born high-fliers.

As Lytton began to make his way across the sawdust strewn cellar, a familiar voice accosted him. 'Hello, Lytton, what'll it be?' Basil Boater stood swaying at the bar, his face the colour of Burgundy, his eyes of claret.

'Ah Basil, sorry to hear about your trouble at the *Post*,' murmured Lytton. Basil was an old friend from when Lytton had first entered Fleet Street and it pained Lytton to see that he had fallen so far.

'No trouble,' came back Basil, with all the false bombast of the ninety per cent proof man. 'We put a rocket up

Rothermere when he came snooping around. We can do the same with Monroe.'

'Of course you can,' Lytton replied sadly.

The Australian swaggered out from between the arches. 'Mr Lytton, Bruce Morley,' he said, holding out a hand to be shaken.

'Watch him, this one's got a smile like a barracuda,' muttered Basil as Lytton passed him. At least some of his faculties were still functioning, thought Lytton, and moved to join Morley.

To Lytton, men like Bruce Morley were specimens to be cultivated, used and then discarded. Their usefulness lay in how much accurate information they were able to sell. Some contacts could virtually make a living by playing one newspaper off against another, selling the secrets of their famous friends or employers, but Bruce Morley's was obviously going to be a short life as a newspaper contact. He had only one story to sell.

'You were saying on the telephone that you once worked for Wayne Monroe.' Lytton pushed right into the conversation.

'And a ghastly job it was too. Three years as a PR for his bauxite concerns.'

'And what kind of chap would you say he is?' asked Lytton.

Morley laughed. 'He's an Australian,' he said.

God save me from these macho brutes from down-under, thought Lytton, but he said: 'Well, yes, but I was rather hoping you might be a little more specific.'

'Tough as a baked wallaby turd,' snapped back Morley. 'If you're thinking of going into bat against old Wayne I hope you're padded up right, because fooling with him is like facing Thomson and Lillee simultaneously. The bastard spits bodyliners.'

'But what about his private life?' Lytton wanted to know. Gossip columns needed facts, not metaphors.

'How much did we agree on?' Morley asked slyly.

Lytton tried to remember what he had told him on the telephone. The figure changed depending on how little he thought he could get away with. 'I think we said a hundred for a lead, twenty for down the page,' he said. For an important story Morley might have got ten times as much.

'Well, never say I told you this, but there was a rumour a while back that the reason he's so keen to pick up a knighthood might be not totally unconnected with his humble origins. Apparently not all of Monroe's ancestors paid their own fares out to the land of the cuddly koala.'

'But I thought most of you Australians were rather proud of your criminal ancestors,' said Lytton.

Morley winced. He obviously wasn't, and even more obviously he had nothing better to offer. 'Well, I think there's a bit more to it than that, Neville,' he muttered.

I hope so,' said Lytton, looking purposely peeved. 'I don't suppose there's a Marion Davies lurking around in some gothic mansion on Boomerang Beach, is there? Someone Citizen Wayne keeps in Renaissance splendour and replicas of David?'

Morley looked at him blankly. 'Pardon? Marion, who was that?'

Lytton swallowed his little joke. After all, there was no real reason why an expatriate Australian, one-time bauxite PR and full-time marsupial rat should be familiar with a movie made before he was born. 'I was just wondering whether Monroe has a penchant for other women,' he asked. 'It isn't exactly an unknown vice in the vastly rich.'

Now Morley understood. 'Girls! You mean does Monroe have girls! Jeez, Nev, even you wouldn't go short with two hundred million dollars as bait.' And he laughed so loudly that Basil, propped against the bar, was stirred out of his reverie by the noise.

The light was fading when they left the bar and the hint of summer had been replaced by rain. Lytton still felt dissatisfied with their meeting. 'What about Angela Monroe?' he asked as they waited in a heavy drizzle for the most elusive animal in London, the taxi: 'You couldn't get me a meeting with her, could you?'

At last Morley earned his fee. 'The great white whale? She's a sweetheart,' he said. 'Very keen on colonic irrigation, but otherwise a real darling. I'll see if I can fix it. Give us your number.'

Laura was sitting reading *Private Eye* when Lytton arrived for dinner. They had chosen to meet at Gebler's, one of the recently fashionable bistros of smart London which occupied the ground and basement floors of an elegant building in Sackville Street, just to the north of Piccadilly. Gebler's, by virtue of its proprietor, food and star-spangled clientele, was the media restaurant of the eighties, and for at least three nights a week Neville Lytton was a semi-permanent fixture.

'If you're still pursuing your Rabid Dingo, I think I might have something for you,' said Laura as Lytton sat down and automatically held up his hand to summon the wine waiter.

'Go on, thrill me.' Laura was a good gossip, but little of what she came up with was ever printable.

'According to a little bird I know, your pal Monroe has been playing the beast with two backs with a lady called Sabrina Wallis.'

'What?' Lytton was astonished. 'You mean the tripe-hound who used to be on the door at the Clarendon Club? She's played the beast with two backs with half the men in London.'

Laura smiled: 'I thought you'd like it. A girl at Quantas told me.'

'There's no accounting for taste, but all the same,

Sabrina Wallis ...' Lytton shuddered. Sabrina Wallis's reputation was awesome. Although stunning to behold, she had never mastered the art of the polite refusal and consequently the stories about her were legion. It was a tip which called for careful substantiating, however. To link the name of a prominent businessman with a lady known to bestow her sexual favours with a near legendary largesse could be a very expensive libel indeed. 'Let's hope we can stand that up,' said Lytton and ordered a bottle of Bollinger.

'What do you think, will Henry Field become the new Diary editor?' Laura asked while they ate.

Lytton winced. 'I suppose realistically speaking he must be the favourite,' he said. 'But since when did realism have anything to do with Fleet Street? I can tell you, though, if he does succeed to the thorny throne I'm going to have to put in for a transfer.'

Laura frowned and ate silently for a few moments. They both knew that Lytton would find a break with the *Daily News* very hard.

Suddenly a man mountain loomed over them. It was Nathan Gebler, the owner of the restaurant, an American of ever-expanding waist, and a mouth only surpassed in its fulsomeness by his arch competitor Peter Langan, owner of one of the other restaurants at which Lytton was a frequent visitor. 'Hey, Lytton, what about that lunatic boss of yours retiring and forgetting to settle his account with us,' roared Gebler so loud that people at tables on the far side of the bistro could hear.

'Oh yes, sorry about that, Nathan,' said Lytton, doubting that the former Diary editor had actually forgotten at all, but had simply decided not to pay his account. 'If you give me the bill I'll pass it on to accounts for you. But I wouldn't hold out too much hope if I were you. You can hardly expect the poor chap to pay bills when he's stuffed full of Valium, can you?'

Gebler burped noisily and helped himself to a glass of champagne. 'Tell you what I'll do. I'll forget about the bill if you guarantee me as many puffs as Langan gets. By the way, the champagne's on the house.'

Lytton grinned: 'Nathan, old boy, I realize that you're American, and that you have different ways of doing things over there, but, you know, you can't bribe an English journalist like that, can he, Laura?'

'We're a crusading and honourable profession,' came in the lady.

'Bullshit,' growled Gebler, and now beaming, set off down his restaurant to chastize some guests whose faces he didn't recognize. For the uninitiated, dinner at Gebler's could be a fraught experience.

Lytton and Laura finished their dinner without further interruption, and, with Lytton's fears about Henry Field's imminent promotion anaesthetized by the champagne, they repaired happily back to his flat, the converted first floor of a house off Queen's Gate. It was not a tidy place. As a man alone, Lytton had become used to comfort rather than style, and although the furnishings were elegant and the lighting tastefully subdued, there was a scattering of newspapers, hand-outs and magazines across the carpets, tables and chairs like a haphazardly-fallen blizzard of newsprint.

'We should have gone to my place, my cleaner comes on a Tuesday,' said Laura, looking around. Lytton didn't hear. He was already by his telephone answering machine, playing back the evening's messages just in case there was anything he ought to know about. There was.

'Nev, this is Bruce,' came the whine of an Australian voice. 'The lady you're so keen to see can be found at Sweats at eight, every morning. All right? Bye.'

'And who is this lady you're so keen to meet?' asked Laura, taking a packet of cigarettes from her handbag.

'Oh, she's just some common or garden, glorious, sun-

34

kissed, blonde beach beauty fragrant with the sweet smell of sexcess,' murmured Lytton, placing one hand on Laura's hip and dipping into his memory bank of film memorabilia.

Laura gave Lytton a long look, then very casually withdrew a cigarette from the packet with her lips until it was cocked provocatively at him. 'Match me, Sydney,' she said, to prove that she, too, was a movie buff.

If possible, Angela Monroe looked even bigger in her orange track suit than she had in her ball gown and Lytton easily recognised her as she jogged from her Saab (a sturdy car for a sturdy lady) to the entrance of Sweats at eight the following morning. At a discreet distance, Lytton, also attired in a track suit, climbed from his car and trotted slowly after her.

Sweats Health Club was a modern pine emporium converted from an old warehouse in West Kensington where fashionable people paid fashionable fees to burn away surplus weight, and, just as importantly, where beautiful people could see and be seen by other beautiful people. While Angela Monroe was pretty, her size prevented her from being fashionable, which was a handicap that, had she been anyone other than the wife of a millionaire, might have proved lethal to her chances of becoming a member of a club which prided itself on having the longest waiting list in London. But money, in any language, is beautiful.

'I wonder if I might join the eight o'clock class,' said Lytton to the sunshine-and-smiles girl in a flamingo-coloured track suit who guarded the Sweats reception area.

The girl viewed Lytton with some derision. He was obviously older than most of Sweats' members. 'I'm afraid –' she began, but Lytton was ready for her.

'You mean Billy didn't tell you about me?' he said. 'Gosh. Never trust a friend to make a booking, eh.' Over the girl's head was a license from the GLC claiming that

William Wansell was a proper person to be proprietor of a health club. Lytton knew Billy Wansell of old, and was not at all sure that he was a proper person to be administering anything other than the South London mafia pension funds. How Billy had finally become legitimate was one of the many mysteries that the Metropolitan Police would be investigating for some considerable time.

The girl was thrown. 'Well ...' she said undecidedly. 'I'm really not supposed to let anyone in who –'

'Of course you aren't,' said Lytton, and then without waiting for her to reply trotted away to the gymnasium after Angela Monroe, calling as he went, 'I'll tell Billy how conscientious you are. He'll be very pleased.'

The gymnasium was alive and jerking in time to some particularly appropriate disco music ('Get down on it, baby, get down and do it, uh huh, uh huh, uh huh') with a rout of narcissists as Lytton entered; two dozen young men and women in leotards and track suits working away at their bodies before a vast wall mirror, while an instructor bellowed advice from a small podium. Lytton viewed in dismay the abundance of energy of the cherry, custard, violet and Lincoln green clad young enthusiasts. Then, sucking in his tummy, he slipped into the back of the class alongside the only other person who did not look like an advertisement for youth.

'Running on the spot ... come on, knees up,' shouted the instructor, eyeing Lytton suspiciously, as though he distrusted anyone over the age of thirty. Lytton lifted his knees higher.

'Now bending from the hips, legs quite straight, fingers in front, to the right and then to the left.'

Lytton's head fell between his knees.

'I'd give a year of my life to have been born with a backside like that,' a woman's voice pined at his side. Lytton looked up. Angela Monroe was staring at the bottom of a girl in ecclesiastical purple who was bending effortlessly in front of them.

'Well, yes,' agreed Lytton. Observing the hind-quarters of the young and beautiful and female at close quarters was not an altogether disagreeable way to start the day.

'I wouldn't need to be here if I'd had enough roughage as a child,' went on Angela, as the instructor bade them all lie on their backs and begin buttock exercising. 'I gave up a beautiful figure as part of Australia's war effort. My shape is Hirohito's revenge. What's your name?'

'Lytton,' came the groaned reply as the muscles in the backs of his thighs began to scream.

'I thought so. I'm Angie Monroe. Bruce Morley said you were looking for me. I don't suppose you wanted him to, but you know what Australians are like. They always like to bowl both sides of the wicket. Anyway, what d'you want to know?'

'What d'you want to tell me?' Lytton replied, wondering why she should wish to help him, and whether he would ever be the same again after another minute of buttock exercising.

Alongside him Angie bounced up and down, her thighs threshing in and out like some huge, orange-coloured baling machine. 'Keep pedalling brother, we've got a lot of calories to lay waste,' she laughed and heaving herself over on to her stomach began a series of violent stretching movements which threatened to wrench her head from her shoulders.

Later Lytton would decide that the keep fit class was probably the longest hour he could remember in his entire life, and with his whole body numb from over-exertion he showered, dressed and then meekly followed Angie into the special gymnasium restaurant, where a track-suited apparition bordering on anorexia served them a breakfast of yoghurt and health foods.

'Now let's see what sort of deal we can do,' said Angie as she watched Lytton struggle with his plate of nuts.

'I don't understand. I thought you knew, I'm a reporter. I write for a gossip column,' said Lytton. Normally victims, and their wives, did not talk about making deals.

'I understand very well, but I want a deal. Come on, eat your nuts, Mr Lytton. Roughage is good for the colon. Did you ever see a constipated chimpanzee? No, neither did I. Bruce Morley says you want some tittle-tattle on my husband and me. Right?'

'Well ...' Lytton was beginning to feel himself submerging beneath the sheer tonnage of the lady's energy. 'Not exactly dirt. Amusing little divertissements, perhaps.'

'Cobblers. You want to catch Wayne with his pants down. Right? Now, why should I give you the dirt on the man I promised to love, cherish, worship with my body and obey until death us do part?'

Lytton opened his mouth and then closed it again as Angie carried on.

'I'll tell you why. This is the deal. Take it or leave it. You help me stop my husband making a complete fool of himself and I'll give you any number of juicy little morsels. All right?'

Lytton grinned. He was liking Angie more with every word she uttered. 'Wonderful,' he said.

'Right, fire away.'

'Well, I did hear an amusing little story about how the Monroes first went to Australia ...'

Angela crammed a handful of nuts into her yoghurt-filled mouth. 'Ah, you mean the old man,' she laughed, sending small missiles of raspberry-coated walnut spraying across the table. 'He was a criminal and he married a tart. Wayne tried to keep it secret from me at first. He was afraid my father wouldn't like the idea of my marrying into criminal blood. Not that he was really a criminal. He picked the pocket of a magistrate one day, and the

38

blighter give him his ticket to Botany Bay the next. He met the old girl on the ship going out. She was quite a well known pro in the Strand, I believe. Good looking, too. They were married as soon as they got out of the camp.'

'That's nice. A happy ending to a shipboard romance.'

'Well, just so long as you don't remember where you heard it.'

'You have my word,' said Lytton, then leaning forward he spoke more quietly. 'I don't suppose the rumours about Sabrina Wallis –'

Angela cut him off. 'My, my, you have been doing your homework. Now let me tell you about Wayne and me, Mr Lytton. In the twenty-five years that we've been married I don't suppose a single one has gone by when Wayne hasn't cheated on me with some chorus girl, dancer or actress. He's got stars in his flies, you see. But we're still married. And do you know why? Because we need each other. Sabrina Wallis may think she's got him by the short and curlies, begging your English pardon, but it'll be big Ange here who'll be taking him for walks when he's in his bath chair. Men are funny things, Mr Lytton. At twenty they want a woman, any woman will do. At thirty they want to make money, it doesn't matter how. At forty they look for a mistress or two, it doesn't matter who. But at fifty they get this wild craving for respectability. They want to be looked up to. Now why d'you think my husband's buying the *Daily Post*? He wants prestige and power, that's why. But I'll tell you something. If he tries to jettison me I'll scream blue murder. I've got stories about Wayne that would make your teeth curl. Besides, since it was my money that started him off I've always made sure that I've got a bigger interest in the family firm than he has.' At last she paused for breath and dipped her spoon into her third carton of yoghurt.

'But you said you need each other,' said Lytton. 'I don't understand how you need him?'

39

Angie shook her head at the naïvety of the man. 'He's my entrée, dear. Without Wayne buying into Fleet Street I'd be just another fat Australian rich bitch from the outback. The biggest bit of action I'd get would be the Earl's Court Anzac Day three-legged hopping race for drunken okkers who can't pay their way home. But if I stick with Wayne, I'll be Lady Monroe in five years, provided he picks the right horse at the next election.'

'You're quite certain he is going to buy the *Post* then, are you?'

Angie shook her head. 'I'm as certain as he is, dear. With Wayne you never know until he knows and by then it's usually too late to stop him.'

Lytton had finished eating. He stared at his almost untouched plate of nuts. 'Well, you've been very frank with me ...'

'All we need do now is give Wayne a gentle little reminder of where his first loyalties lie. He'll come running to heel like a poodle at the first whiff of scandal. Can you do that for me, Neville? Just a couple of paragraphs in your paper should do the trick nicely.'

'I'll do my best.'

'Then I can see we're going to be great friends,' laughed Angie, and happy with her breakfast she waddled off for a session of Slendertone.

Billy Wansell was waiting for Lytton in the reception area with the girl in the flamingo track suit. Once again Lytton summoned up the bluff. 'Billy, how are you, old man,' he hailed, as though meeting an old and dear friend. 'What a splendid place you have here. I've just had a wonderfully invigorating hour.'

Wansell glared at him: 'What about that bit you wrote about me first?'

'Sorry?' Lytton eyed the moose-sized ex-thug with an air of non-comprehension.

'He said he was a friend of yours, Billy,' the receptionist chimed, covering desperately for her mistake.

'Yeah, you called me "a Neanderthal buffoon" and said I ought to go back to laundering Cortinas in Clapham ... and you spelled my name wrong. There's two ells in Wansell.'

A stroke of divine inspiration fell at Lytton's feet. 'Henry Field,' he blurted out, as Wansell closed on him. 'He's your man. I've been trying to remember. He wrote that story about you when I was at lunch. The first I knew about it was when I saw it in the paper. He's a devious chap is old Henry. I tell you what I'll do. I'll tell him that you're upset, shall I?'

Billy shook his head. 'You're a rotten liar, Lytton,' he said. 'You want to watch out or one of these days some-one's going to do you over.'

'I'll keep my eyes skinned, Billy. Thanks for the warn-ing,' said Lytton, and smiling politely at the receptionist, sidled past the glowering moose and out of the front door.

Lytton wrote his story on Wayne Monroe that afternoon while David Sellier was fiddling his expenses and Dolly was trying to arrange an interview with Michael Caine. Dolly always fancied herself as a glamorous show business writer. As Lytton typed, Wesley gazed over his shoulder waiting for the letters to fall. Wesley was very keen on the politics of Fleet Street.

'Is this guy really gonna buy the *Post*?' he asked.

'Looks like it, Wesley. At the moment he's prowling around the outside of the fence like a hungry dingo trying to panic the management and unions into accepting a tup-penny ha'penny offer.'

'"Like his great-great-grandfather, Monroe has a deft, almost light-fingered touch when it comes to choosing attractive female companions,"' Wesley read.

Putting a finger to his lips Lytton quietly took the copy

41

from the boy and dropped it into his drawer. He had noticed Henry watching. 'Not a word now, okay? Happy Henry will never let this into the paper, so we'll have to wait until it's his night off. Let's hope the Aussie Ogre doesn't join the Ship of Fools before then, eh? Now, what about getting me some coffee?'

At the head of the desk Henry Field returned to discussing the night's page with the mournfully misanthropic Diary sub-editor Norman Allen. By process of natural selection, sub-editors are frequently miserable, jealous and destructive people since it is their job to take the words of the reporter and do all the boring chores of putting them into the paper, checking for mis-spellings, libels and errors along the way, the most thankless task imaginable. But Norman Allen had perfected the state of misanthropy. Once a front page splash sub, and hopeful of high places in Fleet Street, his career had peaked too early and as his rapid decline had accelerated so had his derision for all about him. He was a failure, by his own standards, and resented deeply having been put out to grass on the Diary page when he felt he ought to have been overlording the front. What's more, he also believed himself possessed of a highly-developed news sense, and since the *Daily News* Diary rarely printed any hard news, he found it hard to hide his scorn for the material he was asked to process.

'All good stuff tonight, Norman,' Henry babbled enthusiastically before the blank contempt of Norman's gaze. 'We'll be leading on David Frost. I thought perhaps a two-column picture showing him and his wife. What d'you think?'

Norman considered Henry with acute contempt. 'David Frost? Do you honestly think there's anyone left alive who wants to read any more about David Frost?'

'What d'you mean? It's a perfectly good lead.'

Norman scanned through the first few lines, shaking

his head balefully. 'Do you think so? Do you really think so?' he asked.

Before a row could develop, Beryl, the editor's secretary, interrupted with a message. 'Just to say that conference will be at six tonight. The editor's been called away to a management meeting,' she bleated. Years of working for a tyrant had robbed her of any recognizable self-confidence.

'Which will give him more time to anticipate the delights of tonight's Diary page, won't it, Henry,' chortled Norman.

Henry ignored him. His eye had fallen again upon Lytton typing earnestly down the table. 'What are you doing, Lytton?' he asked.

'Oh, nothing that you'd be interested in. Nothing at all,' smiled Lytton, and went back to his work.

Henry squinted suspiciously at him: 'You aren't still pursuing your Rabid Dingo, are you? Because we don't want it, you know.'

'Oh, don't you? What a shame,' grinned Lytton loftily, continuing to type.

Giving up, Henry turned to his secretary. 'The first thing I'll do when I become Diary editor is get rid of that arrogant fiction writer,' he hissed.

Jenny looked up from the expenses she was retyping. 'You don't really mean that, do you, Henry? It would be a tragedy if anybody ever split you two up. You'd have no one to bitch about.'

Basil Boater phoned Lytton at just after five. His voice sounded strangely hoarse on the telephone, so that Lytton could scarcely understand what he was saying. Believing him to be ill, Lytton bade him stay where he was and, grabbing his raincoat, hurried down to the Galley Proof. The bar was already filling with magazine writers and evening paper journalists when Lytton arrived. Basil was crouched over the bar in a far corner, quite alone.

'What is it, Basil? Are you all right?' Lytton was worried. Basil looked grey and ill.

Basil turned to him. His eyes were red and wet, his hands were trembling, while the veins in his face were etched bright scarlet against his ashen skin. 'I've been . . .' he started, then stopped. 'They've made me . . .' Again he stopped. The word wouldn't come.

Lytton guessed with sudden dismay what he was trying to say. 'Two more large ones, on my account, please, Deirdre,' he said, waving to the bar girl, and then putting an arm around Basil's shoulders led him across the bar into a vacant alcove.

'It's the old heave-ho, Lytton. After thirty-nine years, they've told me to go.'

'Oh God, I'm sorry, Basil.'

'I've had it coming. I should have known. I've spent more time down here than in the office. There was no job for me there, anyway. It's like the war. You never think it can happen to you.'

'But why now, Basil?'

'I suppose some accountant wanted to tidy his books and chop off the dead wood,' said Basil, blowing into a handkerchief. 'They were very nice about it. Very apologetic. But it's hard, Lytton, it's just so bloody hard.'

Deirdre brought the drinks around and left them on the alcove shelf. Basil hid his face from her. Lytton could see that he was crying. 'Have you told Mae yet?' he asked.

Basil shook his head. 'No, no one in the office either. They've got enough to worry about with Monroe at the gates. I'm sorry, Lytton. I'm sorry to be such a bore.'

'You're not a bore. Look, what are you doing tonight?'

'What I do most nights, I suppose. Getting drunk.'

Lytton considered the evening that he had intended to spend. There was a reception at the Connaught, followed by a small dinner party for British Film Year which he had been invited to, and which he had accepted in the hope that he might be seated next to Joanna Lumley who, he understood, was on the committee. There would be other occasions, he told himself, and putting an arm around Basil, pulled him to his feet. 'Well, don't let's mope around here,' he said. 'If you're going to get drunk I'm going to get drunk with you. Shall we go?'

'Where to?'

'I dunno. You know all the pubs around here. Lead the way. We're going to celebrate.'

'Celebrate what?'

'Your new freedom. Your escape from the imminent clutches of the Rabid Dingo.'

'Haven't you any work to do?'

Lytton shook his head: 'Nothing that can't wait.'

'You know, you're a lunatic, Lytton.'

'I like to think so. Now come on. Let's get at it,' said Lytton, and the two of them, Lytton with his arm around the smaller Basil, made their way from the bar.

The editor was in a worse mood than anybody had ever seen him at the especially arranged late conference that afternoon, and even heads of department with many years' experience in dealing with his scathing laser beam attacks kept silent and hoped he would not notice them. The features editor was not successful. 'You call that a leader page feature,' snapped Cruickshank. 'Even *the Star* would hesitate about putting that on the early page for Aberdeen. Get out there and throw it back at him, laddie. Now, who's next?'

The sports editor coughed and then mumbled something about an interview with a football psychiatrist, but the editor wasn't listening. 'What about the Diary?' he asked, fixing Henry with a savage stare.

Henry swallowed hard. 'David Frost is planning to –'

That did it. The editor exploded. 'God help me, I'm

surrounded by half-wits. David Frost? What are we, a newspaper or a publicity handout?'

No one spoke. No one even looked at him. Those who were not embarrassed for themselves were embarrassed for the editor. It wasn't dignified for a powerful man to be behaving in this way.

Cruickshank stared at the floor. 'If this is all you can offer, newspapers don't deserve to survive. Wayne Monroe, a wild man from the bush, is about to change the face of our industry. Doesn't that mean anything to anyone? You've all seen what effect Murdoch has had on Fleet Street. Well, Monroe's said to be ten times worse. Can you imagine that?' His eyes were zealot bright with emotion.

'It's very sad,' someone murmured.

'Aye it is, very, very sad,' said Cruickshank, and with a wave of his arm dismissed the conference.

'Mr Cruickshank, they want you upstairs again,' said Beryl as the editor and his staff emerged from his office.

Cruickshank shook his head. 'Sometimes I think the incompetence of our staff is only matched by the cupidity and stupidity of our board of directors.'

'Is something going on, Mr Cruickshank?' asked Beryl.

'If it is, Beryl, you can rest assured the editorial floor will be the last to find out,' he barked, and set off back upstairs to continue with the board meeting.

Back at his desk, Henry studied the plan of the Diary page carefully. Even he had to admit that it was not the best page they had ever produced. He had never seen God react so violently to anyone the way he reacted to Wayne Monroe. Perhaps Lytton had been right after all with his Rabid Dingo. He wondered what Lytton had on him. 'Wesley,' he called to the messenger who was in the act of putting on his bomber jacket. 'You don't know where Lytton is, do you? I think we might need him tonight.'

'He called to say that he wouldn't be back,' said Wesley.

'Typical,' snorted Field.

'Okay if I go now?' asked the boy. 'I'm already late for my class.'

Field checked his watch: 'I suppose so,' he said ungraciously.

With an expression that said, 'Don't do me any favours,' Wesley fastened his coat and hurried away to night school. For several minutes Henry Field sat silently at his desk. If only Lytton were there they might have been able to salvage something of the page. What they really needed was a story on Wayne Monroe. That was what the editor obviously wanted to see in the paper. Henry scratched his head, worried and remembered the story Lytton had been writing.

Now normally Henry Field, albeit a pompous little operator who antagonized his colleagues beyond tolerance, was as honest as the next man. But desperate straits called for desperate remedies. Looking cautiously around him, Henry ascertained that he was alone and unobserved. Norman, the only man who would normally have been present at this time of the evening, was out having his regular early evening pint with some cohorts from the news pages. Getting up from his chair, Henry sidled quietly along to Lytton's desk, his eyes continuously scanning the entire office. Guilt smeared a warm coating of perspiration on to his forehead. With one hand held behind him, Henry pulled open Lytton's drawer. The Rabid Dingo copy lay on top of Lytton's address book.

With one swoop Henry had the copy and was back at his desk, pushing new copy paper into his typewriter when Norman returned from the pub.

'Norman, I'm sorry to mess you about, but the editor's not keen on David Frost. We'll be going on a piece about Wayne Monroe instead, just as soon as I've written it.'

For once Norman looked interested. 'Now that sounds more like it. I'll get the pictures down.'

Norman hurried away, and Henry began to type his story, or to be accurate, to retype Lytton's story, changing the order of the words, adding the odd adjective here and there and generally giving the piece his own style while using all Lytton's carefully researched information. The editor was going to be very pleased with him indeed for bringing in a story like this, he decided. It was Lytton's own fault really, he told himself, doing his best to assuage his guilt. If Lytton had briefed him as to the little pearl he was sitting on he would have insisted that they use it immediately. God knew why Lytton should choose to hide it. A story which linked Wayne Monroe with Sabrina Wallis was too good to throw away. They were lucky Dempster or Hickey hadn't got it first.

Henry had finished typing by the time Norman returned with the photographs of Monroe and Sabrina Wallis. 'Tell me, what do you think?' he said, offering him the copy.

Norman quickly looked through the three sheets of paper, a smile broadening on his usually morose cheeks: 'Well, if this doesn't get you a ride in the Rover, nothing will,' he said, and set about redesigning the page, without David Frost and with Wayne Monroe.

At eight Henry went in search of the editor with the remade-up page proof, only to be told by Charles Harrison, the deputy editor, that he was likely to be busy with the board meeting for the rest of the evening. Henry was disappointed. He particularly wanted the editor to see the page before it went to press. 'I suppose the lawyer's seen it?' said Charles as he scanned the Monroe story.

Henry confirmed that he had, but that he wished the editor could give it a brief glance, too.

'Tell you what then, Henry,' said Charles, 'you get off and I'll make sure the editor sees it when he comes down.'

Relieved, Henry returned to his desk, leaving the page

proof on the back bench. 'Fancy a drink?' said Norman, well pleased with his night's work.

'Oh, not tonight, if you don't mind, Norman,' said Henry, and scurried away to an intimate little dinner party which his wife had arranged for a visiting New York gay novelist socialite. He was glad of the excuse. The editor of the Diary could hardly be seen swilling beer like a navvie with a moron like Norman.

Lytton had no such reservations about who he drank with, and by ten-thirty, having traversed through wine bars, printers' pubs and lawyers' snugs, he found himself swaying alongside Basil in a corner of the Cheshire Cheese, a medieval hostelry where generations of boozers had drowned their talents.

Basil looked around through glazed eyes. 'This is Fleet Street as I want to remember it, Lytton, smelling of beer and steak and kidney pies. You can keep all those poncy new wine bars with their sawdust and barrels and girls with tits like press studs. Barmaids should be blonde and well endowed.'

From his alcoholic haze, Lytton suddenly remembered Angela Monroe. 'Speaking of which . . .' he said, and then stopped. He couldn't remember what he had planned to say next.

'Speaking of which what?' asked Basil.

'Oh nothing. I was just thinking you're probably better off out of it, you know. At least you won't have Monroe's men examining your expenses.'

Basil wasn't that drunk. 'I won't be having any expenses,' he said glumly.

'Oh, sorry.'

'It's all right. No expenses. No 11.25 last train from Blackfriars to Bromley South. That was why Mae and I moved to Bromley, you know. The late train. Now I can't imagine living anywhere else.'

Lytton hauled him to his feet. 'Come on, you're becoming maudlin,' he said, and together they toddled out of the Cheshire Cheese and promenaded down Fleet Street.

'I have to admit I've often wondered why they kept me on so long,' said Basil candidly as they walked. 'I've been a drunk for years but they never complained. Not until today, that is.'

'You're not a drunk, Basil. You might like a drink, but you're not a drunk.'

'I suppose they tolerate drunks better in Fleet Street than anywhere else,' continued Basil, conversing with himself. 'I suppose that's it.'

By this time they were passing the loading bay of the *Daily Post*. All along the street, vans were queuing to rush first editions of the paper to the stations to catch the overnight trains for the farthest corners of the British Isles. Lytton stopped and stared into the lighted bay, now restless with anticipation. Somewhere below pavement level a hooter sounded, an indication that the first edition of the paper was coming off the presses.

'D'you fancy a copy of the *Post* for old times?' said Lytton, as the bundles of newsprint began to be thrown from the conveyor belt into the back of the first van.

Basil shook his head: 'To be honest, I never much liked the *Post*,' he said. 'It's far too right wing for my taste.'

'So why did you stay so long?'

Basil shook his head for a moment and smiled. 'I suppose the company was convivial,' he answered simply, and set off down the road with Lytton following.

They said goodbye on the platform at Blackfriars Station after Lytton had helped his old pal into his seat, and bade him take care not to fall asleep and miss his stop. It was, for Lytton, a sorrowful parting. Basil made all kinds of noises about being back to show everyone what a mistake they'd made, but Lytton knew there would be no return. Basil was too old and too far gone ever to come back. He was facing the desert of enforced retirement.

'Give my love to Mae, Basil,' he said from the platform as Basil hung his tired head out of the window.

Basil smiled weakly. 'Thanks, Lytton. Thanks for tonight. You're a good chap.'

'Don't let that get around or you'll ruin my reputation.'

Lytton walked slowly back down the platform after the train had left. Perhaps if Fleet Street had tolerated Basil's early symptoms of alcoholism less kindly he would still have had a job and a future. He picked up a taxi in Ludgate Circus and asked to be taken home.

'Fancy a look at tomorrow's paper,' the cabbie said, cheerily offering him a copy of the *Daily News* which he had just picked up at the late-night café in Fleet Street.

Lytton took the paper without any great enthusiasm. Slowly he leafed through its pages, observing the style, headlines and make-up with the casual eye of the professional. Suddenly he stopped. He had reached the Diary page. Spread right across the top of the six columns ran the headline CITIZEN WAYNE AND THE HAT CHECK GIRL. Underneath were photographs of Monroe and Sabrina Wallis.

'Henry Field, you cheating bastard,' he exploded.

The phone woke him at half past ten. It was years since he had been really merry, let alone thoroughly drunk, and, despite his disappointment, he had slept like the dead. But, with the sunlight shafting in through a gap in his bedroom window curtains and the telephone by his bed drilling holes in his skull, he returned to consciousness, with a splitting headache and a sensation of dried cinder on the roof of his mouth.

'Hello,' he whispered into his telephone. One effect of alcohol seemed to be that it had robbed him of the power of vocal communication.

51

'Is that you, Lytton?' Laura's voice sounded extremely loud, very near and over excited.

'What do you want?' he groaned and pulled the receiver under the sheets with him.

'What?' Laura sounded confused. 'I don't understand. Why aren't you here? Are you ill?'

'No. I don't think so.'

'You ought to be here, you know.'

'Why?'

'You mean, you haven't heard?'

This was becoming very boring. 'Heard what?' demanded Lytton, wishing that she would go away and bother somebody else.

'About Monroe. He's changed his mind. The Rabid Dingo hasn't bought the *Post*. He's bought us. It's just been announced.'

From the depths of his bed Lytton experienced the slow dawning of astonishment followed quickly by the beginnings of a smile. Well, well, well, he thought, poor old Henry. Perhaps there is a God up there after all.

'Lytton, are you still there?' demanded Laura. 'Are you sure you're all right?'

Lytton chuckled. 'I wasn't, but I'm improving all the time. See you in half an hour.'

As Lytton drove into the office, the news of Monroe's apparent sudden change of tack was confirmed by a lengthy news bulletin on London's news radio station LBC. He wasn't sure whether the Rabid Dingo was going to be good for Fleet Street; he suspected not. But he was certain he was going to be bad for Henry, and he could hardly keep himself from smiling as he tried to imagine Henry's expression when he had heard the news.

The radio report did not have too many details, but it illustrated perfectly the precarious nature of the newspaper business at a time when papers were becoming increasingly small parts of huge multi-national conglomerates.

'Monroe's bid for the *Daily News* came apparently after he had met with surprising resistance from the board of Allied Newspapers, the owners of the once preferred *Daily Post*,' read the announcer. 'In conditions of great secrecy he launched an all out campaign for the *Daily News* instead, and early this morning Wayne Monroe got his way and joined fellow Australian Rupert Murdoch as the proprietor of a British national newspaper.

'Ironically the news of Monroe's sudden switch of targets came too late to prevent the *News* from carrying an item linking Monroe with hat check girl Sabrina Wallis in its gossip column. An associate of Monroe said, however, that there would not be any immediate changes ...'

At that point Lytton parked his car on a double yellow line and hurried inside the *Daily News* building, past the usual collection of militant trade unionists holding placards up for the attendant TV cameramen and demanding that fellow workers 'say "no" to Monroe'.

'If you ask me, Bob,' said Lytton to a chap he recognized, 'I think it's a bit late for saying "no". The bugger's already our employer.'

'Just showing solidarity with our brothers in asbestos,' grinned the protestor. 'Besides I quite like being on the telly.'

For once the editor did not shout. He just sat there and stared at some imaginary object way over Henry's head, intoning quietly and thoughtfully. 'I'm sorry, I really am,' he mourned, 'but you must understand Mr Monroe's position. He was very embarrassed by the story.'

Henry tried to interject but there was no way in.

'I must say I was quite surprised myself. There is a tradition, you know. Dog doesn't bite dog. I would have thought you would have known it. It wouldn't be so bad if somebody else had written the piece, but ...' He stopped and stared at Henry's copy.

'I did actually show it to the lawyer. And Charles saw it ...' Henry was hanging on by a thread.

The editor nodded. 'Yes, lamentable oversights. And, of course, it was such a pity that I wasn't here myself. But now you know why. Henry, in the circumstances, I think the best thing would be for you to go on, say, a month's sabbatical and resign while you're away. I'm sure you'll have no trouble in finding something with one of the other papers.'

'But I thought there weren't to be any immediate changes?'

'And nor are there,' smiled Cruickshank. 'But in the circumstances ...'

It was hopeless. Henry could see that. Slowly he pulled himself to his feet and walked out of the editor's office.

On the editorial floor little groups of journalists huddled in knots, gossiping and telling each other how surprised they were.

'I can't imagine why no one changed the page,' Dolly murmured to Lytton as the pallid face of Henry moved towards them. 'The editor was sent the paper at midnight, but he just let it run all night.'

'He must have wanted the piece to go in, but he'll never admit to it,' said David Sellier. 'Now there's perversity for you.'

Lytton watched and said nothing.

No one needed to be told that Henry had been fired. The news was written in bold in his eyes. 'I'm sorry, Henry.' Jenny tried to be consoling.

'If there's anything I can do ...' Dolly stopped. She didn't want to appear too ridiculous. Everyone knew she really despised Henry.

Henry looked at Lytton. 'What do you say, Lytton.'

Lytton shrugged his shoulders philosophically. 'I say it serves you jolly well right, Henry, if you want my honest opinion.'

*

The ride in the Rover proved to be worth the wait. For once God was almost human. 'Of course, we'll be upping your salary by, I thought, seven thousand a year, commensurate with your new responsibilities,' he said as they drove sedately down Fleet Street, every word, no doubt, being committed to memory by the chauffeur. 'And then there'll be the usual perks of a new car, and an improvement in your expenses. How does that sound?'

Lytton gazed out of the window as they sped past the Law Courts. 'It wasn't Henry's fault, you know,' he said.

'Oh come on now. No crocodile tears for Henry, please. The chap's a born survivor. I wouldn't worry about him, if I were you.'

'I'm not worrying. I just thought I ought to tell you,' said Lytton, before adding, 'you haven't met Monroe's wife, have you, by any chance?'

'As a matter of fact I have. She's a friend of yours, I believe.'

'Hardly a friend, but is that why I'm being offered the job?' asked Lytton. They were now waiting at the traffic lights in the Strand.

The smile dissolved from God's features. The granite returned. 'Lytton, let me remind you, I run the *Daily News*, not some get-rich-quick Aussie from the outback. If you don't want the job, just say so.'

Lytton smiled. 'Oh, I want it all right. I want it like mad. I wonder, though, might I make just one suggestion?'

The car had stopped. The Savoy Hotel doorman opened the door for the passengers to alight. 'Ask away, if it doesn't cost anything,' said Cruickshank.

'Well, I thought we ought perhaps to personalize the page more. Readers identify better with a real name than a catch-all title like Diary. Perhaps we could call the page Lytton's Diary.'

Half out of the car the editor stopped. 'You know, laddie,

you might just have something there. Lytton's Diary. Yes, I like it. Come on. You can buy lunch.'

Lytton smiled to himself. He had finally made it. This time there would be no fictions.

Chapter Two

Daddys' Girls

It was one of those days when everything in the world seemed perfect. Lytton lay in the hammock, warm, peaceful and secure, and with a straw hat covering his face, he daydreamed of how things might have been. A few feet across the lawn Catherine stroked the neck of Holly, her docile Labrador, and sipped a glass of lemonade. She was, thought Lytton, the perfect wife.

When lunch had first been suggested Lytton had been rightly suspicious. Why should his estranged wife want him to drive out to the depths of Sussex for lunch on a working day? But he had gone all the same. Catherine clearly wished to discuss something on her own territory when her boyfriend could not be present, and the least Lytton could do was listen. Besides, he wanted to see her.

Catherine had met him at the gate to her cottage, looking devastating, not in the smart style of the women of town, with their silk shirts and cool professionalism, but in the unsophisticated freshness of someone who had accepted herself for what she was and decided that the only way to live comfortably was to avoid trying to compete. It was this quiet contentedness which had attracted Lytton to Catherine when they had first met in Paris all those years ago.

They had had a light lunch of cold salmon on the terrace, but because Lytton had to drive back to town Catherine had refused to allow him even a glass of wine. In some ways she acted more as a mother than a wife. They had been pleased to see each other again, but, because they had both avoided any aspects of conversation which might prove wounding, much was left unsaid.

As he relaxed before his journey back to London, Lytton guessed he was about to discover the reason for the invitation.

'Well, what do you think?' Catherine asked. 'If we started now it could all be over by Christmas. Neat, quick and painless. I mean it's obviously over, so why not draw the line and end the chapter. Neville, are you listening?'

Lytton was listening all right. But he didn't much care for the direction the conversation was heading. 'D'you remember that holiday we had in Corsica?' he asked. 'The time you got stung by a jellyfish and blamed me?'

'I didn't blame you. I just said that you should have told me if you knew it was there. Anyway, what about it?'

Lytton pushed the hat back off his face. 'Nothing, nothing at all. I was just dipping into our joint account of memories and making a quick withdrawal before the statement came, so to speak.' He glanced across at her. 'I don't suppose there's any more lemonade, is there?'

'It isn't as though we haven't had time to think about it, or that we're rushing into it,' Catherine went on as she poured him another glass.

'Out of it, actually, darling,' said Lytton, unnecessarily pedantically.

'So what d'you say?' Catherine was determined not to be interrupted. 'A simple, quick divorce. No acrimony, no rows ...'

'Did you make this yourself?' Lytton was off on a tangent again. 'It's terribly good. Much better than all that awful fizzy bottled stuff.'

'... no more parallel conversations which never manage

58

to meet, because you're avoiding the issue. All we have to do is see a couple of lawyers.'

At last Lytton sat up. Catherine meant business. 'Is that what Tom thinks?' he asked flatly.

Catherine smiled. At last she had his sole attention. 'Well, yes, he'd like me to be free to marry him. I don't think he feels quite proper living with me for so long and never being able to make honourable his intentions.'

It was time for Lytton to be off when Catherine began talking about Tom and honour in the same sentence. Lytton levered himself to his feet, and, taking off the straw hat (no doubt it belonged to Tom), he began putting on his jacket. 'Tom never had an honourable intention in his life,' he rasped irritably. 'He's a wife poacher, a marital pirate, a –'

'How's Laura?' Catherine broke in deftly.

How typical of a woman to change the subject at a crucial moment, thought Lytton. His relationship with Laura was nothing remotely like the one Catherine seemed determined to share with Tom. 'She's fine,' he said crisply, and, crossing the lawn, headed around the side of the cottage towards his car.

'So I can tell Tom it's all arranged?' Catherine was scampering after him.

'Well . . .' Lytton reached for his car keys. He was blowed if he was going to make it easy for them.

'You know I can do it without your consent, anyway, don't you?'

Lytton placed an affectionate kiss on Catherine's forehead. 'Why don't we have lunch sometime and discuss things?'

'Crumbs, Neville, I thought we just had. I really don't get you. Why are you so keen to hang on to something that was finished ages ago?'

Why indeed? thought Lytton. He said: 'D'you think if we'd had children things might have worked out differently?' It was a question he had asked himself occasionally after Catherine had left.

Catherine gave up. There was no way he was going to discuss the divorce seriously. 'Who can tell?' she said. 'You'd probably have turned into a jealous and possessive father. It's probably better this way.'

Lytton climbed into his car. 'I suppose so,' he said. 'Look, I'll give you a call about the other matter. All right?'

Catherine nodded. It was the best she was likely to get. 'Drive carefully, Neville,' she said as he manoeuvred his BMW out of her narrow drive and into the lane. And with an air of resignation she watched as he accelerated rapidly away.

On the drive back to town Lytton considered his marital status carefully. It was indeed true that Catherine could get a divorce any time she wanted, but it did seem to him that the longer they left it the greater were the chances of a reconciliation. When in doubt, do nothing, had always been his motto, and he made a mental note to remind himself to send Catherine a bunch of flowers to thank her for lunch.

It was late afternoon when he arrived back at the office where the rest of the Diary staff were stabbing out their various stories in great humour. While no one could accuse him of being a difficult man to work for, he had noticed that whenever he was absent for a few hours a holiday atmosphere developed around the desk.

'Anyone know what the exact prayers are for casting out devils?' David Sellier was asking.

Norman didn't even bother to look up from the copy he was subbing. 'Shove off, satan, push off, poltergeist and on your bike antichrist?' he said.

David groaned: 'Thanks for nothing.'

'That'll teach you to ask a man who once subbed for the *Daily Mirror*,' said Lytton as he strode past him to

60

the top of the table. 'Sorry I'm late, Jenny. Important business.'

Jenny shrugged. As the Diary secretary she had now worked for three different bosses in as many months. Lytton was by far the politest – over-polite, actually – but she saw no reason why she should care if he was late into the office. 'You've caught the sun, too,' she replied.

'How observant of you,' said Lytton, and turning to his writing staff he demanded to know the state of play for the night's paper.

'Norman's already got the lady and the love child,' reported Dolly. 'Her security alarm salesman's gone to ground, though.' This was a Dolly special, a wonderful example of a titled lady becoming pregnant after a liaison with a door to door salesman. 'Then we had a call from Gilly Hodgson at DDA with a bit about Pia Zadora's bodyguards. Apparently she's terrified of being kidnapped.'

Lytton, who was going through his day's mail as she talked, dropped a handful of uninteresting publicity bumph into his bin. 'Who on earth would want to kidnap Pia Zadora?' he asked. Then turning to David he said. 'What about you? How did last night go?'

'Her name was Sophie and she's already called twice today,' mocked Dolly, jumping in before the young man could answer.

The previous evening David had been sent to cover a very smart ball for the latest crop of debutantes. Screwing up a piece of copy paper David chucked it at her. 'Actually, there was a bit of a row,' he said. 'Jake Cutler got very nasty when the girl he was pursuing was whisked away at midnight by her father's driver. I thought he was going to clobber him. The pictures are on your desk.'

Lytton leafed through the collection of eight by ten black and white shots of London's youngest, richest and smartest: the usual collection of pretty, lookalike long-haired girls in their first ball gowns and boys in cast off black tie, most of whom bore familiar surnames. Lytton had no doubt that he was looking at the people he would be writing about in ten and fifteen years time as their careers hiccuped and their marriages tumbled.

There were several pictures of Jake Cutler and a very pretty girl of about seventeen. Jake was older than most of the other men at the party, being all of thirty, and possessed a diabolically attractive air. Alongside so many fresh-faced young men he looked like a worldly-wise cavalier. But then he was from a very different background. A self-made millionaire at the age of twenty-two, he owned a recording company, a Porsche and a flat in Holland Park which was not much smaller than a Dutch barn.

'This is a bit of an upmarket do for old Jake, isn't it?' commented Lytton. 'I bet some of these girls' mothers are thinking Mick Jagger's hobnobbing with the toffs in the Sixties has a lot to answer for. Who's the Cinderella?'

'Guy Phillips's daughter, Belinda,' said David.

'Really?' Lytton was suitably surprised. 'Old money and new ... and too much of both.'

'Lytton.' Jenny put down her telephone. 'Pandora Mortimer's on her way up to see you. Remember?'

Lytton nodded. Since the departure of the last Diary editor, closely followed by Henry Field, the Diary had been badly understaffed, and he had let it be known that there was a job available for the right kind of journalist. So far only the wrong kind had applied. 'Show her into the television room,' he said as his phone rang. 'Hello, Neville Lytton.'

There was a short silence, before a squeaky upper class girl's voice asked for David.

'David, it's someone called Sophie, for you. I hope you haven't done anything you'll regret,' he said, and, passing him the telephone, he headed off towards the television room.

David almost blushed. Obviously he had. He took the phone wearily. 'Look, Sophie, I don't want to be rude, but I really do have a lot of work to do . . .'

Lytton smiled to himself. David was going to have to learn the art of sexual discrimination if he was to be allowed out among the fleshpots of young London.

When an attractive female stranger enters a newspaper editorial office she is guaranteed to disrupt production. So it was with Pandora Mortimer. Not only was she pretty, young, dazzling and fashionable, she also looked very, very rich. And as she was led by Jenny, past the rows of ogling sub-editors and hairy-backed reporters, to the tiny cubby hole known as the TV room, she was aware of a general air of appraisal. Over on the features desk Laura Grey, who had been examining an advance copy of her first book, *Work As An Erogenous Zone*, and wondering whether she had chosen the right picture of herself for the dust jacket, raised her eyes to examine further this potential rival, while on the Diary desk Wesley put down his copy of *Smash Hits* and David hung up on Sophie.

'She looks like another of daddy's little darlings to me,' scoffed Dolly, immediately hating the girl's style.

'Not bad, though,' said David. 'What d'you think, Wesley?'

'Nice,' confirmed Wesley.

'I think she looks rather sweet,' said David.

'Which is exactly what we don't need on a gossip column, someone who is rather sweet,' rasped Dolly.

A similar thought was at that moment occurring to Lytton as he began his interview. 'St. Mary's, Wantage, Queen's Gate sixth form, *Harpers and Queen*, *Tatler* . . .' he read from the brief resumé of her education and career which Pandora had sent him. 'Tell me, Pandora, why on earth do you want to work on Lytton's Diary?'

Pandora took a deep breath. 'Because I want to be a real journalist,' she said.

'Well, yes, but without putting too fine a point on it, if you don't mind my saying you have had a rather rarified upbringing. We aren't ministering angels here, you know. How d'you think you'd feel about betraying your friends' trust? How will you take it when you're accused of working in the gutter, being a snoop, a destroyer of careers, a wrecker of marriages, a yellow journalist, a mischief maker, a social parasite?'

There was a very long silence. Even Lytton wondered whether he had not overdone it just a little bit. 'How do you?' asked Pandora at last.

Touché, thought Lytton. At least the girl's got a sense of humour. And she was very, very pretty. His first thought was to joke his way into an answer, but pomposity got the better of him. 'Well, I suppose I tell myself it may be true, but it doesn't matter. Because sometimes, not often, but sometimes we bag a big one who's gone wrong. And then, you know, everything seems worthwhile. In the meantime I just grow an extra layer of skin and pretend I don't care.' He smiled at her, aware that he was showing off in front of a pretty girl but unable to prevent himself. 'D'you think you could do that?' he asked.

'I'd like to give it a try,' Pandora replied.

So it was agreed that Pandora should be given a two-week trial, starting that minute. Lytton was not at all sure that she had what it took to be a gossip writer in terms of ruthlessness, but her background and social contacts, particularly with the younger people of London, could be very useful. The rest of the staff reacted predictably to their new colleague. David and Wesley quickly made room for her, while Dolly sulked.

'You wouldn't happen to know someone called Belinda Phillips,' said Lytton as soon as Pandora had been found a place to sit. He had been examining the photographs of Jake Cutler again. On a thin night such as this, one of them would make a marginally interesting down-the-page filler if it had a suitable caption.

'As a matter of fact, I do. She's a friend of my sister.' Pandora was delighted to be useful so soon.

'Jolly good. Look, while I'm squaring things with God about how much we're going to pay you, why don't you do a couple of hundred words about her and Jake Cutler. David will tell you anything you need to know, and Wesley will get you anything you want. All right, Wesley?'

'Nice,' said Wesley.

By eight o'clock the Galley Proof wine bar was full and noisy, as reporters called for a quick drink on their way home, and sub-editors popped out to have a liquid supper before returning for the serious second half of their evening shifts. The pubs, and more recently the wine bars, of Fleet Street are more than simply the energy refuelling spars of EC4. They are small clubs, visited at least twice daily by men and women of a like profession in search of companionship and stimulation. They are the social cornerstones of the newspaper industry: forums for debate, concourse areas for relaxation. They are also places to get drunk.

It was in the Galley Proof that Lytton met Laura after their day's work, standing by the bar scanning a copy of her book which he also had been sent.

As she approached him he began to read: '"Quite the most potent of all the workplace erogeneous zones is the chairman's outer office, where the scent of power intoxicates both executives and those who work ..."' he paused suggestively, '"under them." Oh hello, Laura, I didn't see you there.'

Laura snatched the book from him and put it down on the bar. 'We'll discuss this tomorrow night. How's your new girl getting on? She's very pretty, isn't she.'

'Is she?' asked Lytton wickedly before adding, 'It's too

early to say, really. She's just spent three hours writing a three-inch filler. She must have telephoned half London. No stone unturned. Every fact checked, cross-checked and then re-checked. It was a remarkable performance.'

'Come on, we all do that when we start. Well, most of us. In a few weeks' time you'll be pleading with her to check her facts.'

'Perhaps. If she lasts three weeks. Pretty little toffees aren't particularly renowned for their resilience.'

'Unlike obsequious little lizards ...'

'Sorry?'

Laura was looking over Lytton's shoulder. A familiar figure was approaching. 'Don't look now, but your former comrade in filth is slithering towards us.'

Lytton grimaced: 'Not the one with the webbed feet?'

'The very same ...'

'Oh dear,' said Lytton, and turned with massive insincerity to greet Henry Field. 'Henry, what a lovely surprise. I hear you're clawing your way to great heights over the road. Still doing your Ides of March act, are you?'

Henry laughed, quite unruffled by the welcome. Since his ignominious departure from the *Daily News* at the hands of the Rabid Dingo, he had, in fact, done rather well for himself, having walked straight into the number two job on the *Daily Post* diary page. This was a not uncommon occurrence in Fleet Street, and one which his former editor might well have predicted when he disposed of his services. From being a rival to Lytton inside the paper, Henry had metamorphosed into a rival on a competitive paper. 'What about a double celebration, eh?' he asked, putting a bottle of champagne and three glasses down on the bar and picking up Laura's book. '*Work As An Erogeneous Zone*, indeed. They tell me it's very provocative, Laura. What's this? "Computers – Sex and the Floppy Disc." Isn't that rather vulgar? If you

66

worked for a decent paper we might have serialized it for you.'

Laura took back the book. 'I seem to remember it isn't so very long since you despised the *Post*, Henry.'

'Oh yes, but that was before they had me writing for them,' Henry replied, now pouring three glasses of champagne.

'You said it was a double celebration? Is there something else we don't know?' she inquired.

Henry tasted his champagne and then giggled, very satisfied with himself. 'Larry Allen gave in his notice this afternoon,' he said.

'Dear God,' Lytton interjected. 'Don't say they've given you the Diary editorship, Henry. Tell me they aren't all complete fools at the *Daily Post*.'

'Cheers, Lytton,' said Henry, and downed his glass.

'They are,' said Laura, and shook her head woefully.

'We're rivals again, Lytton, and I'm going to walk all over you this time. It shouldn't be difficult. You always did write like a doormat.'

Lytton raised a glass. 'Bless you, Henry. May your scales never rust.'

Lytton was secretly pleased for Henry's success. Although he had enjoyed much satisfaction from the way Henry's piece of sharp practice had come unstuck when Wayne Monroe had bought the *News*, he bore him no real ill will. Besides it would have been churlish to be still angry with Henry when everything was going so well. Now three months into the new Monroe-style *Daily News*, the editorial staff could not honestly claim to have been affected by the change of ownership in any way other than the improvement in toilet facilities on the editorial floor; while Lytton's Diary, with its heavy personal promotion, was quickly becoming the most provocative gossip column in Fleet Street. Of course there were still the usual aggravations which any Diary editor had to contend with, the writs for libel (usually issued to prevent further revelations being made, rarely because a serious libel had been published) and the complaints to the editor. But for a journalist of Lytton's experience these were minor irritants.

It was not, however, a minor irritant who rang him at home shortly before nine the following morning. It was Guy Phillips, chairman of Phillips Bank and a man of great wealth and considerable influence. 'In view of your column today, Mr Lytton, I wondered whether you could possibly have lunch with me at the bank.'

Lytton, who at that moment was in the act of opening a carton of orange juice in his kitchen, looked down at the newspaper which was spread across the cluttered kitchen table. His eye fell on to the picture of Belinda Phillips and Jake Cutler. 'Today?' asked Lytton, so surprised by the call that he did not even wonder how Phillips had managed to get hold of his private number so early in the day. 'I'm sorry, I already have a –'

Phillips was a man not familiar with being refused anything. 'I'm sure you do, and normally, of course, one would hesitate to press matters, but in view of the serious nature ...'

Lytton was intrigued. He looked again at Pandora's piece. It was totally innocuous. 'Well ...' he began.

Guy Phillips's chauffeur picked him up from the *Daily News* lobby at ten to one, and delivered him, via a brand new Mercedes, to the marbled hall of Phillips Bank, a discreet, private place, at exactly one minute to the hour. Guy Phillips was, the chauffeur said, 'punctilious about punctuality.'

He was also, Lytton quickly discovered as the two men sat down in the panelled dining-room, of a disturbingly possessive and suspicious nature. 'It isn't easy bringing up children these days,' he said, as they ate lunch, 'particularly not a seventeen-year-old daughter without a mother to help and guide her, or to understand how she feels.' He paused for effect. 'You know, of course, that my wife, Antonia ...'

Lytton nodded. Although he had never met Phillips before he remembered that his wife, reputed to be the most beautiful woman of her set, had died suddenly at their country home in the early seventies.

'It was particularly hard on Belinda,' went on Phillips. 'She was only three at the time. I think we've had a normal, healthy relationship as father and daughter, but you know what these teenage years can become – rebellious, difficult ...'

'I don't suppose any of us can really understand what it feels like to be young today,' said Lytton. 'Things change so quickly.'

Phillips topped up their glasses. He was a handsome, powerful looking man of about fifty, with thick grey hair and a beautifully cut navy blue herringbone suit. Lytton noticed things like that. Another thing he noticed was that the servant who served lunch, bringing it course by course from some private kitchen at the back of the bank, kept his eyes down in polite, deaf subservience, enabling Phillips to talk as though he were not there. 'Precisely my point,' Phillips said. 'But parents bear a heavy responsibility. We have to protect our children from themselves, and from all the unsavoury characters roaming London these days. I've always felt I owe Antonia at least that.'

Lytton had absolutely no idea what Phillips was driving at, and was beginning to wonder if indeed he was not a little bit unhinged.

At length Phillips worked his way round to the point of the meeting. 'Yesterday your reporter seemed to get the wrong end of the stick in an article about my daughter,' he said, selecting his words carefully. 'At least that is the charitable view I am choosing to take.'

At that moment he took a photostat of the offending

69

article from his pocket and put on his glasses. Lytton did not reply. He was quite used to being accused of making mistakes.

'Your reporter describes this individual Jake Cutler as a "close friend" of my daughter. She goes on to say that Belinda seems very smitten with the "dashing, romantic, pop millionaire."' He read the quotations with vehemence. 'Those are hardly adjectives which I would have chosen to use about a man like Cutler.'

'Well, you know how these girls are,' said Lytton equably. 'They see things rather differently from us.'

Phillips ignored the interruption. 'And lastly my daughter is quoted as saying: "No one understands Jake. He isn't at all like his public image. He's been helping me with my music. I sometimes go round to his studio after school. I don't know whether I'd say he's a boyfriend, but he's a friend and he's a man and we get on well together."'

Phillips stopped reading and tossed the photocopy down on to the table. Lytton took another sip of wine and wiped his mouth with his napkin. He hadn't the foggiest idea what Phillips could possibly be complaining about. 'Well, all that seems pretty innocent to me,' he said lightly.

Guy Phillips met his levity with a steely derision. 'To associate my daughter with a cheap thug, a dope-peddling layabout who makes his money by exploiting other young people is hardly innocent. Particularly when –'

Lytton could not take any more of this nonsense. 'Don't you think you're rather over-reacting?' he asked.

Phillips again ignored him: 'Particularly when she said none of those things. You see, Mr Lytton, they're made-up quotes. Every one of them.'

There are made-up quotes and made-up quotes, considered Lytton as he strolled down Ludgate Hill back to the office that afternoon. He had declined the offer of the car. It had been such an unpleasant lunch he wanted to be rid of everything to do with Guy Phillips as quickly as possible. Ever since reporters had been writing down what people said they had been 'helping' their stories by changing the inarticulacies of everyday speech into what they believed to be newspaper English. When writers were accused of making up quotes by outraged stars, politicians or union leaders, it usually transpired that the complaint was about the way the quotes for the interview had been selected to suit the angle the reporter was after, or the way in which he had condensed a meeting of possibly several hours to just a few paragraphs. But it wasn't often that anyone accused a reporter, certainly not on the *Daily News*, of completely fabricating a story. If Guy Phillips were right, Lytton would have to do something about Pandora Mortimer, which would be a pity. Lytton knew better than most what disastrous consequences that could have for her career.

He found Pandora sifting through cuttings in the library, with Wesley at her side. They had already struck up a firm friendship, which probably compensated for Dolly's coldness to her new colleague. 'Pandora, I've just been having a chat with Guy Phillips about your story yesterday. He says you made up his daughter's quotes,' said Lytton as delicately as he knew how. After all, it was only the girl's second day.

Pandora went scarlet. 'But I didn't. That was what she said. I've got a shorthand note,' she said, suddenly producing a brand new reporter's note book. Lytton was both surprised and impressed. He had no idea they taught shorthand at any of the places where Pandora had been educated.

He was also very puzzled: 'Now why on earth would Guy Phillips say such a thing then? Why make a mountain out of a molehill?'

Pandora shook her head. 'There is one thing,' she said. 'Yesterday when I was trying to find out why Belinda

Phillips had to have a driver take her home, three different people mentioned her mother. I kept getting these strange vibes about her.'

'That's very understandable. She was very popular. Very beautiful. It was a great shock to all that set when she died.'

'Noddy White thinks there was something a bit rum about it.'

'Who?'

'Noddy White. He used to drive the Phillipses around. He works for my uncle now. I asked him. He said Guy and Antonia Phillips were mixing with some very dicey company just before she died.'

'What does he mean, "dicey company"?' Lytton asked. The nearest he could imagine Guy Phillips getting to dicey company was the Chancellor of the Exchequer.

'He wouldn't say exactly, but he did suggest I talk to Harvey Sobell. Trouble is I haven't exactly traced him yet.'

All these names were too much for Lytton so soon after lunch. Pandora read his expression.

'Guy and Antonia's best man. Godfather to Belinda. He was a deb's delight in the early sixties. I thought you'd probably know him. He dropped out of sight in the seventies.'

Lytton looked towards Wesley who was smiling widely. 'Well I don't know what you're looking for, but I like the way you're looking,' he said, backing away towards the door, half afraid she was about to come up with another name from the past. 'Let me know if you find anything. All right?' And with that he left the library.

Common sense told him not to waste any more time wondering why Guy Phillips should be so protective of his daughter, but Phillips's paranoia had now taken control.

'More complaints, I'm afraid,' said Jenny as Lytton arrived back at his desk. 'Jake Cutler was on while you were out, screaming blue murder about some threatening phone call he'd had from Belinda Phillips's father.'

'Curiouser and curiouser,' mused Lytton. 'He really has got a screw loose over this daughter of his.'

'I thought the only thing bankers ever cared about was money,' said Jenny.

'You might just have something there. Get on to City office, will you? Let's see if we can't flush something useful out of Charlie Adams for once, repulsive and lecherous though he is.'

Jenny did a theatrical cringe as though slimy fingers were fondling the back of her neck. 'Just so long as we don't have to have the disgusting creature in this office,' she retorted, and began to dial the cell from which Charlie operated in Throgmorton Street.

Charlie Adams was indeed repulsive. Grossly fat, with pink, shiny cheeks, tiny eyes, and a handshake which betrayed his over-active sebaceous glands, he had two major interests in life: money and the furtive sexual encounters he constantly dreamed about.

Lytton met him for a drink just after six in a pub near St Paul's, a place chosen by Adams because it boasted, according to him, the best typists in the City.

'What I like, Lytton, are bottoms. Curvaceous ones, semi-spheres of delight, half moons balanced on the edges of seats, rocking backwards and forwards like those little toy birds who have to keep dipping their heads in that saucer of water. D'you know what I mean?'

Lytton knew exactly what he meant. As he talked Adams never took his eyes from a couple of dolly secretaries perched on high stools at the bar, girls less than half Adam's age who would surely have sent for a policeman had they had any idea just what was going through the mind of the fat man in the corner. 'About Guy Phillips ...' Lytton had work to do. 'He isn't a friend of yours, by any chance, is he?'

73

Adams shook his head, his eyes never leaving those perfect semi-spheres. 'No way. He'd freeze your blood at twenty paces, that one.' Suddenly he stopped, and his lips formed into a tight pucker. 'Did you see that? *Gluteus maximus in excelsis.*'

Lytton had seen it. One of the girls had dropped a beer mat and had bent down to pick it up, displaying amply those curves which Adams found so captivating. 'Well, this may be nothing at all, but if you know of anything strange or unusual about him or his business dealings, anything you can think of, I'd be intrigued to hear it,' said Lytton.

Adams sniffed and shook his head. 'If you're looking for a financial scandal I think you're on the wrong track. Phillips Bank had a shaky period about fifteen years ago, but they're as sound as a bell now.'

'What exact area is Phillips Bank in?' asked Lytton.

Almost disdainfully Adams shook his head. 'Very small. Traditionally they were involved with trade to India and Pakistan. They're mainly advisers. Perhaps the occasional seed money for development.'

'And what happened during the 'shaky period' you mentioned?' wondered Lytton. But it was to no avail. Adams's memory had gone. 'Perhaps,' said Lytton, 'you could give me a call if it becomes operative again.'

'Of course I will,' said Adams. Then dropping his voice he put a sweat-stained hand across his mouth. 'Now, Lytton, what's all this about Andrew Lloyd Webber and his jacuzzi parties?' he asked. 'Wall to wall crumpet, I hear.'

'Well –'

'The question is, can you get me into one?'

Laura cooked dinner for Lytton that night. It was an evening intended as a private little celebration for the imminent publication of her book, but, not for the first

74

time, Lytton was unable to cast off the questions which were forming in his mind about Guy Phillips. He had not liked the man, but he recognized in him a similar loneliness to the one he inhabited himself. Was there a mystery about the death of Antonia Phillips, he half-wondered. It was unlikely in the extreme, but, confused by Phillips's attitude, he had asked Harry Drury on the crime desk to make a few discreet inquiries before leaving the office that evening.

As he sat and played with his food before the flickering candelabra of Laura's dinner table he felt an empathy with the lonely, worrying banker.

'Well, are you going to tell me about it or shall we have a game of guess the gossip?' asked Laura at last, turning off the romantic Spanish guitar playing she had laced into the evening.

'I'm sorry, you'd think I was being silly.'

'I already think you're being silly. Here we are supposed to be celebrating my elevation to hardcovers, earnesly discussing my thesis on labour as an erotic occupation and you sit there like a custard on a kipper. If you're going to be worried let's talk about it so that we can both enjoy it.'

'I'm not worried, Laura, I'm thoughtful.'

For once Laura betrayed her own insecurities. 'If you're thinking about Pandora Mortimer, let me tell you now, Lytton, you're too old for her.'

Lytton was irritated by this. Laura ought to have known better. 'Don't be silly. It's Guy Phillips. There's something spooky about that chap. His obsession isn't normal.'

'You can hardly blame him for not liking the look of Jake Cutler, can you?'

'This is true,' said Lytton, and went silent again. Glumly Laura cleared away the dinner dishes. She lived in a smart mews house in Notting Hill Gate, a pastel-coloured former working man's cottage behind an Italian restaurant, whose chef had, in fact, provided dinner tonight. As a working girl she had never mastered the art of cooking, and if her home was spotless it was because she was very rarely in it.

'You didn't tell me, how was Catherine?' she asked, as she served figs for pudding.

'Oh blooming. She looks wonderful,' said Lytton, absently.

Laura frowned slightly. 'That must be nice for her,' she said. 'What exactly was the purpose of the meeting?'

'She thinks we should get divorced.'

'Well, that isn't unreasonable after all this time.'

Lytton picked up a fig. 'I suppose not.'

'You suppose not. I despair of you sometimes, I really do.'

Lytton put the fig back on to his plate. The evening was now filled with all kinds of divergent tensions. 'You don't understand,' he said. 'You and me, we're friends. Good friends. *Very* good friends. But there are no ties on either side. That's the way we both want it.'

'Well yes, of course,' said Laura. This may have been true but it was exactly what she did not want to hear Lytton say on an evening when they should have been celebrating. It was something she liked to tell herself, not have Lytton tell her.

'But I was married to Catherine for years,' Lytton continued. 'We were more than friends. More than lovers. We were lifers. And even though I know it's over, and am glad it's over in some ways, I don't want to admit that we failed together.'

Laura could feel herself about to erupt with anger. Sometimes Lytton could be the most insensitive man in the world. 'Hell's bells, Lytton, for the celebrated happiest bachelor boy in London you're in a funny mood tonight.'

'Am I? Oh sorry,' said Lytton, then remembering the reason for the evening he reached out and took a copy

76

of Laura's book off the sideboard. 'Anyway, tell me,' he said, trying to lighten the conversation, 'how are your erogenous zones getting on?'

Laura glared at him. 'No thanks, not tonight,' she murmured icily. 'I'll get the coffee.'

Pandora Mortimer's invitation into the rigours of national newspaper reporting was proving just as exciting as she had anticipated. There had been no real reason to phone anyone other than Belinda Phillips about the caption story, but she had been anxious to impress with her list of contacts. If Noddy White were right and things were a bit rum then Harvey Sobell should be found, she decided, and after several more telephone calls she had his place of work, if not his home address. 'Harvey may not wish to talk to you,' she had been told, but dismissed the idea. She was not over-confident, but she had the unpunctured belief in herself which all girls born rich and beautiful share. No one ever did not wish to see them.

She found Harvey Sobell as she had been instructed, in the rose garden in Holland Park. A boy roller-skater, who looked as though his entire life were spent practising on the smooth surface of the car park, pointed him out to her. Sobell was spraying the bushes for greenfly. From a distance he looked like any other gardener, but on leaving her car and treading across the lawn she saw that he was wearing a paisley cravat tucked into the collar of his shirt. In his late forties, he was thin and hollow-eyed, his weatherbeaten skin stretched across prominent cheek bones. It was hard to believe that he had once been a debs' delight.

'Mr Sobell ... Harvey Sobell?' she asked.

He started nervously as she approached him, then, seeing that she was alone, smiled in relief. 'Hello, you're early. Nice surprise.' He put down his can of spray, and taking off his gloves moved across the lawn towards her.

'I wasn't sure ...' began Pandora, not at all certain

what was a nice surprise, or why he should have been expecting her.

'It's all right. You're new, aren't you? Deliver by car now, do you?' As he had been speaking his hand had gone to his back pocket. Withdrawing it he pushed a bundle of notes into Pandora's hand.

'I'm sorry, I . . .' Pandora stared at the money.

'It's all right,' he said, looking around him as if to confirm that they were not being overlooked. 'It's all there. There's no problem.'

'I'm sorry. There's some kind of mistake. I'm from the *Daily News*. I'm a reporter,' she got out at last.

Harvey Sobell froze. 'What?' He snatched the money back from her still open hand. 'You mean, you haven't –' He stopped.

'I wanted to talk to you about Antonia Phillips.'

Harvey Sobell looked around again, his face now contorted with anxiety. 'Who've you got with you? Why did you trick me?' he gasped.

'There's nobody else. You were a friend of her's, weren't you?'

But Sobell was not listening. Turning, he moved towards his can, gloves and wheelbarrow. 'I'm sorry. There's been a mistake. I thought you were bringing me something.' Even in distress he spoke precisely.

'But you are Belinda's godfather, aren't you?'

'Please, look, I'm very busy. I think it's going to rain.' Sobell was becoming increasingly agitated. 'I can't tell you anything about Antonia. It was a long time ago.'

Across the lawn a motorcycle courier had driven into the rose garden and was watching Sobell and Pandora. Suddenly Sobell began to hurry towards him. Uncertain of what to do Pandora followed. For a moment the motorcyclist peered at the two of them, then wheeling his cycle around he accelerated across the grass, out of the gate and into the road.

'No,' Sobell shouted hopelessly after the retreating motorcyclist.

Pandora joined him. 'Who was ...?' she began, but Sobell wasn't listening.

'Please. I have to make some telephone calls. I have to go. You called at a bad time. You frightened him away,' he said, and without further explanation he hurried away.

Upset by what she had seen, Pandora went back to her car. The roller-skater was still there. 'Now see what you've done,' he taunted, obviously highly entertained by the episode. 'You've frightened the man away. There's gonna be no henry for Harvey today.'

At last she understood.

Unlike his newest reporter, Lytton wasn't looking for any leads on Guy and Belinda Phillips. He didn't actually think there was even a story there, so when he found his arm grabbed by Harry Drury, ex-policeman and now crime reporter, as he entered the Galley Proof for lunch he was more than surprised.

'You were right last night about Antonia Phillips, Lytton,' said Harry. At six feet four he was the largest reporter Lytton had ever seen. 'There might just be something unusual about her death after all. Apparently she was buried without an inquest.'

'And how unusual is that?' asked Lytton.

'When an apparently healthy young woman of thirty is involved, and when the ambulance wasn't called until four hours after her death it's, let's say, very surprising.'

'Who signed the death certificate?'

'A family doctor in the country. He's dead now. I checked for you,' said Harry.

'There wasn't any reason to suspect any kind of foul play was there?' asked Lytton.

'None that we know of. Guy Phillips was in a terrible

79

state. They say he never really got over it. She was with some pal of theirs when she died, and Guy blamed him ... or so the rumours went.'

'And who was that?'

Harry reached for an envelope in his inside pocket and peered at it. 'Someone called Sobers ... Sorry, Sobell.'

'Harvey Sobell?'

'That's the man. Well, anyway, that's all I know. There's a retired copper down in Cheltenham and a stringer in Cirencester looking forward to receiving brown paper envelopes from Lytton's Diary, I'll let Jenny have their addresses if I may.'

'Of course you may, Harry. Many many thanks. This may not add up to a row of beans, but ...'

'... as the rich farmer said "What price are beans?" I'll see you later.' And with that Harry Drury rejoined his friends at the bar, happy to know that his contacts would be receiving small cash payments for their contributions.

Thoughtfully, Lytton pressed on through the crowd to the corner he and his staff regarded as Diary territory, and where Pandora was being consoled by David. 'Pandy, your friend Harvey Sobell ...' began Lytton.

The girl turned, near to tears. 'It's no good. There's no story. He's a heroin addict. I've been chasing phantoms. I'm sorry.'

Lytton shook his head kindly. 'Now come on, don't tell me you're giving up just when we might be getting somewhere.'

Where they were getting Lytton was not exactly sure, but piece by piece a pattern was emerging to Phillips's overreaction. It still wasn't a story, but it was intriguing enough for him to put in a call to the repulsive Charlie Adams as soon as he got back to the office, just in case Charlie had overlooked to call him back. He had. The person he should speak to was Arthur Frobisher, said

Charlie. He knew all there was to know about Guy Phillips. If there were any skeletons buried anywhere Frobisher would know their whereabouts. So, having promised Adams the name and address of an excellent blue video supplier, Lytton gave Frobisher a call and then set off to meet him in a tea shop behind the Barbican.

He knew immediately that he would not take to Frobisher. He was a thin, moithering man of late middle age, a lifelong non-drinker, and, Lytton guessed, a pillar of some ultra strict, to-the-letter-of-the-Bible, nonconformist religious sect. He probably doesn't even give blood, Lytton thought, as he stirred a cup of weak tea, and tried not to gaze at the man's rodent-like moustache.

'You said you left working at Phillips Bank because you were worried,' Lytton said. 'I wonder why?'

Frobisher bit into a rock cake, and nibbled it as he talked. He wore false teeth and they were loose. 'Phillips had a very bad run of luck in the late sixties, Mr Lytton,' he said. He spoke in a whining voice, which did not quite camouflage the south London accent with which he had started life. 'They invested heavily in the wrong commodities, took the wrong advice and then found themselves with a liquidity problem. Mr Phillips became involved in some very sensitive negotiations.'

'What exactly does "sensitive" mean?' asked Lytton.

'Secret? Yes, secret will do,' said Frobisher. 'The board became very anxious and began to put pressure on Mr Phillips. He never encouraged too much participation from them usually, but it was all he could do to keep them at bay that time.'

Frobisher chewed some more rock cake, while Lytton waited for him to carry on. 'Then suddenly one day the liquidity problem disappeared. Almost overnight, you might say. And the problems were over.'

'How?'

Frobisher shrugged his shoulders. 'I understand there were hurrahs from the board at the next AGM.'

The longer Lytton spent with this man the more he disliked him. 'Forgive me for being so dense, but what exactly are you implying?' he asked. 'Financial hanky panky?'

Frobisher was enjoying himself. 'Business has been very good for Guy Phillips ever since,' he said.

'But surely it can't be possible to rig the books at a bank like Phillips?'

Frobisher pasted what he believed to be his enigmatic expression on to his face. 'No one questions good news too closely when they were expecting bad,' he said. 'It isn't easy, but it isn't impossible either.'

'And how do you suppose the liquidity problems were solved?' asked Lytton.

'Perhaps Mrs Phillips would have been the best person to tell you that,' came the gnomic reply.

'But she died years ago.' Lytton was thoroughly fed up.

'Yes, that was a great pity.'

That was also enough for Lytton. He had more to do than spend his day playing silly asses with a man who believed his mission was to bring mystery to the world. Getting up, Lytton thanked Frobisher for his time, and paid the bill.

'If the cheque could be made payable to the Rugged Cross Church, Beckenham,' said Frobisher.

'You wouldn't happen to know an old friend of Phillips called Harvey Sobell, would you?' asked Lytton as he scribbled down the name of the church.

Frobisher grinned so that his top set of teeth wobbled. Then turning to the lady behind the counter he said: 'I think I'll have another rock cake, if that's all right.'

Lytton said down again.

★

Harvey Sobell had just finished weeding his roses when Lytton found him. 'Do I know you?' he asked, as Lytton watched him nip a tiny new sucker from the roots of a bush.

'I think we may have one or two mutual friends. If you've got a few minutes I'll make it worth your while.'

Lytton could see Sobell weighing him up. He had dressed particularly well for the meeting. He wanted Sobell to know he was a man of means.

'What do you want?' Sobell asked.

Got him, thought Lytton, and telling him who he was he made him his offer. A hundred pounds for information about the death of Antonia Phillips. Sobell stopped. 'I should have known. Sorry. You've got the wrong man.'

'Look I know you're a heroin addict. I'm not asking you to betray anyone. I just want to know what happened,' said Lytton. 'I also know it wasn't a simple heart attack. There was something else. I might even go to two hundred if I knew what it was.'

'I can't. I know what you want me to tell you, but there's no way. Believe me, there's nothing for you people in this. We can't bring Antonia back.'

'Tell me, Harvey, why does Guy Phillips still send you a monthly allowance?' Lytton asked.

Sobell was thrown: 'How d'you know that?' he asked.

'Is it hush money?'

'Don't be crazy. Guy's an old friend. He knows I'm going through bad times. He's fond of me.'

'He hates you. He blames you for his wife's death. Yet still he sends you an allowance. Why?'

Sobell tried to get away. 'I can't tell you. Really. It's better you don't ask.'

'Better for who?'

'I've got to get back to work.'

Lytton stood directly in front of him, blocking his

escape. 'How did you get in this state, Harvey? You were a bright man. The future was brilliant. What happened?'

'Please.' Sobell was breaking up in front of him.

'It's a long time now, isn't it?' went on Lytton. 'Do you ever think about your golden days ... the balls, the parties.'

'For God's sake. When you get like this you never think of anything apart from today. Anyway, what does it have to do with you? Why are you so keen to know? You're only a reporter.'

Lytton shook his head. 'Well, not quite. You see, Harvey, I was once close to Antonia, too. She didn't ever tell you?'

Tears now ran down Sobell's face. 'No, I had ...'

'As you say, Harvey, it was a long time ago.'

'It wasn't an affair. I wanted it to be. But she wouldn't. We were just friends,' sobbed Sobell.

Lytton nodded. 'She *was* wonderful, wasn't she? I've always wondered ... the night she died. You were there ...'

Sobell was shivering violently, his hands were gripped tight closed.

'Yes, I was there. In a manner of speaking,' he said.

Lytton put an arm round him. 'Why don't you tell me all about it.'

Above the editor's desk a polished mahogany station clock ticked loudly. Ian Cruickshank had brought it south with him as a memento of his childhood in Perthshire where his father had once been a station master and had it installed in his office. It was both a permanent reminder of his origins and of the fact that to a national newspaper the times of trains are paramount. No matter how good the story it is worse than useless if the edition misses the train and cannot be distributed.

It was this clock that Lytton found himself examining vacantly as Cruickshank and the lawyer, a double-breasted, striped-shirted young man from Finchley called Colin Griffin, read and re-read his copy on Guy Phillips. In all his days as a newspaperman Lytton doubted if he had ever seen a lawyer quite so worried.

Cruickshank, however, was jubilant. 'This is incredible,' he said at last. 'What does Phillips say?'

'Nothing yet. He's promised us a statement through his lawyer later,' replied Lytton.

Griffin sucked on his teeth. As the newspaper's lawyer he could see all kinds of problems. 'Legally this is very dangerous,' he said. 'The police will obviously have to be briefed –'

'After we've broken the story, though,' interjected Lytton quickly. He didn't want this ending up in a rival paper first because of some chatterboxing PC.

'Lytton's right,' Cruickshank agreed. 'We'll have to find some way of phrasing it.'

'If you don't mind my saying, there isn't any way of accusing a semi-eminent banker of getting out of financial trouble by funding a series of massive heroin deals which won't see us all in the dock at the Old Bailey on a charge of gross criminal libel.'

The lawyer's comments were aimed directly at Lytton. He would never have dared speak so forcefully to the editor. Even so his demeanour was jokey, almost as though trying to hide his real concern behind a screen of levity. Lytton knew what he was doing. He was trying to raise enough doubts to kill the story. He didn't blame him. It would be his neck if Lytton got it wrong. But he hadn't, and he said as much.

'Don't worry, we won't throw this away even if we have to put every reporter in the building on to standing it up. It's wonderful,' Cruickshank reassured his Diary editor.

The lawyer shook his head: 'The repercussions are end-less. If I've read this correctly you're saying that the recent prosperity of Phillips Bank was built on funding massive heroin deals in Pakistan in the late sixties.'

Lytton nodded: 'Ironically we were actually chasing the wrong story. Antonia Phillips did die of a heart attack. She was with Harvey Sobell at the time she became ill, but he was too far gone to summon help quickly enough. He'd originally been Guy Phillips's route into heroin. Any hope Harvey might have had of getting off the stuff went out of the window that night. He's spent fifteen years hating himself since.'

'I'm not quite sure where the daughter and Jake Cutler fit into all of this,' said the editor.

'They don't really,' said Lytton. 'It was just that Phillips didn't like the look of Jake. He's terrified of anything happening to that girl. He'd seen the way Sobell went and, like a lot of people, he believes that everyone in the rock business is a drug-taking freak.'

'There are going to be some pretty sick expressions in the City when this comes out,' said Cruickshank gleefully. He loved to see the rich and pompous discomfited.

'Not to mention on the board of Phillips Bank?' chimed in the lawyer, still unhappy.

'Most of the members from that time have retired,' said Lytton. 'They're completely legitimate now.'

'Amazing, amazing,' murmured the editor as he began to read the story again.

The lawyer was troubled. 'There's one thing I don't understand. How on earth did you get Harvey Sobell to tell you so much?' he asked.

For a moment Lytton looked almost bashful. 'Oh, I just told him about Antonia and me in the good old days, and of how much he and I had in common ... in love with the same woman, all that stuff.'

'Really? I didn't know you knew her,' said the lawyer.

Lytton smiled: 'I didn't. I lied,' he said, and left the room.

★

He found the rest of the Diary team squandering their evening away in their regular corner at the Galley Proof, where David was explaining how he had finally managed to cool the ardour of the persistently telephoning Sophie. 'So I finally said to her,' he was saying as Lytton entered the bar, 'I said "Sophie I find you wonderfully, incredibly sexy and romantic and I'd love you to move in with me, but I'm afraid my boyfriend gets very violent when he's jealous."'

'And did she believe it?' asked Dolly.

'Well, she hung up,' said David. With the exception of Pandora everyone laughed. She looked pale and tired. Lytton suspected she had been crying.

'I did warn you it's never easy to betray one's friends,' he said.

'I just don't understand why it was so necessary,' Pandora said finally. 'It all happened years ago. Surely he's paid enough with what happened to him. What more can you possibly want? All he was trying to do was to protect his daughter, and now ...'

'Isn't it a pity he never felt so protective towards anybody else's daughters.' Lytton did not enjoy being lectured on journalistic ethics.

'But he stopped being involved ages ago.'

'I know,' said Lytton, trying to steer Pandora away from where a group of *Daily Express* printers were listening. 'But his chain didn't stop. Guy Phillips had the opportunity to make amends for what happened to his wife and Harvey by admitting it fifteen years ago, by naming names and smashing the chain. But he didn't. He just took his profits; paid Harvey enough to keep him quiet and carried on playing the bereaved but responsible businessman. Feel sorry for Belinda, if you want. But don't bleat to me about Guy Phillips. He might have worried about his own little daddy's girl, but he didn't give a damn about anybody else's.'

As Lytton had been speaking his voice had increased in volume, until the chamber of silence around him had stretched right across the bar. In embarrassment one of the *Express* printers sneezed, and his friends guffawed.

'Er, Lytton, can I get you anything?' asked David.

'No thank you. Good night,' said Lytton and strode back out of the bar.

David, Jenny and Dolly looked at Pandora. She was trembling. Even Dolly felt sorry for her. 'Don't worry,' she said. 'He's usually quite nice. Just wait till you get to know him.'

'I'm not sure that I want to get to know him,' sniffed Pandora.

'Of course, you do,' said David. 'You're going to make a great reporter.' She was, after all, very, very pretty. The Diary could not afford to lose anyone like Pandora Mortimer.

It took several days for the *Daily News* financial and crime reporters to work out, to the lawyer's satisfaction, all of the different elements in the Guy Phillips story; days in which Pandora became reconciled to having been the original investigative force in what was likely to be the eventual imprisonment of Guy Phillips, and the alienation from him of his daughter. It was a tough way to learn the power the press has in dislocating people's lives. But, though some friends she shared with Belinda were later to cut her socially for what they considered a breach of their social etiquette, she quickly acquired the journalists' skill (or is it a self delusion?) of telling herself that whatever had happened was for the greater good, and that her responsibility from now on was to her readers and not her social circle. Lytton, for his part, duly reported to the editor that Pandora Mortimer was rapidly becoming a competent reporter and took her on to his staff on a permanent basis, despite the usual rumblings of discontent from the National Union of Journalists who considered her experience insufficient.

There was, however, one interesting postscript to the Phillips affair. A few months later Jake Cutler was arrested and charged with being in possession of a quantity of drugs. Actually a small mountain of dope would have been a more accurate description. Guy Phillips had been right about the millionaire pop producer all along.

Chapter Three

The Lady in the Mask

Lytton was late into the office that Friday, which suited his staff admirably. They were all younger than he was and less wedded to his work ethics and relentless ambitions. It was a lazy day and they felt lazy, too.

'Anyone seen this about the one-legged rapist in Budleigh Salterton?' asked Dolly as she examined a story in *The Sun*. No one answered. '"The Court accepted that the balance of his mind was disturbed",' she read.

Jenny looked up from Black's Medical Dictionary, which she had borrowed from the medical correspondent to try to diagnose a personal problem. 'Only his mind?' she asked.

'He got five years, anyway. That should settle his equilibrium,' said Dolly and dropped the paper into the bin. She had read everything of interest in just forty-five seconds, which she thought might be a record, even for *The Sun*.

'Anybody else want any coffee?' Lytton had entered unnoticed by the back stairs. Wesley was already waiting for further orders. David asked for a tea with milk, Pandora a lemon tea and Dolly a black coffee. Wesley glowered at them all.

'All right, Jenny, what have you got for me?' asked Lytton as Wesley went for the drinks.

Jenny passed him his mail, a large collection of invitations to films, gallery and restaurant openings, photographs of the semi-famous and half a dozen private letters.

Casually he rifled through it all. 'By the way, God wants you,' added Jenny.

Lytton didn't even look up. 'What d'you think, a big one or a little one?' he asked.

'It may not even be a writ.' Jenny was the persistent optimist.

Lytton looked sceptical. 'Lytton's law says that when God wants Lytton it's a writ; when Lytton wants God he's out to lunch.' Suddenly he stopped. 'Hello, what's this?'

Now it was Jenny's turn not to look surprised. She sneaked a look at David, who was watching Lytton carefully.

'Not bad, eh?' said David.

'No message, no name, just a naked lady,' said Jenny, as Lytton stared at a large black and white photograph of a woman in an elaborate face mask performing what looked like some kind of striptease routine.

'Postmark?' asked Lytton.

'Ah', said Jenny, 'I never thought,' and delving down in the bin she pulled out the large manilla envelope in which the picture had arrived. 'West Eight. That's Kensington,' she said.

'Don't worry, it came under plain wrapper just like all your other porno stuff. It's probably just a stage you're going through,' said David.

Lytton ignored him and looked again at the nude. She certainly had a very attractive body.

'Lytton!' Beryl, the editor's secretary, was approaching. He dropped the photograph into a tray.

'Just coming,' he said, and, like a schoolboy being taken to see the headmaster, trotted obediently after her.

He knew it was going to be trouble, but he was surprised when the source of the problem was identified. Lucky Jim Diamond.

'Colin says he can take us for anything up to ten

thousand if we can't stand it up,' said the editor. He was sitting with his feet up on his sofa, which meant that those he was in discussion with had for once the slight advantage of being rather higher than he was.

'As much as that?' said Lytton casually.

'If it isn't one hundred per cent. Your sources are reliable, aren't they?'

'Oh completely,' lied Lytton. In this case he wouldn't have staked a shilling on their reliability.

'Ah good. Because the suggestion that a chap might have been known to welch on a gambling debt, should it be proved untrue, doesn't actually endear a newspaper to a judge when he's assessing damages.'

'He's bluffing, of course,' said Lytton, bluffing madly himself. 'He was always good at that.'

'Very likely, but let's see if we can't put some flesh on our story just in case things go awry. Get someone to delve around in the bowels of his past, okay.'

'Fine,' said Lytton, and got up to leave. He had just reached the door when the full draught of disapproval hit him. 'Otherwise, everything all right? Quite happy with the column, are you?'

Lytton turned. 'Well, yes. Aren't you?'

Cruickshank reached for a bunch of the grapes which he had taken to eating at all times of the day, and which he kept in a bowl on his desk. 'Tepid', he said, 'that's the word that springs to mind. It's been a bit on the tepid side recently. I don't feel as if I want to plunge in first thing in the morning. Do you know what I mean?'

Lytton knew exactly what he meant. He was gingering him up because Lucky Jim Diamond had decided to issue a writ over what had sounded like a silly little piece of gambling gossip.

Heading out for lunch he bumped into Dolly in the corridor, and told her the bad news. Lucky Jim had been her story originally.

'He's only trying it on,' said Dolly, in much the same voice of appeasement Lytton had used to the editor.

Lytton wasn't happy. 'I know that, and you know that, but God in there is being very difficult. So can we please have names, dates, amounts and any other filth you can get on the little monkey? Give Luigi a call at the Monaco. He's indiscreet and owes us a favour.' And with that he sloped off for a quick lunchtime drink with Laura in the Galley Proof.

Laura was amused. Since she had had a rollicking from the editor a week earlier it was good to see somebody else on the end of his needling. 'Tepid,' she said relishing the word.

'That man would freeze a volcano.'

'I wouldn't take it too seriously if I were you,' she said. 'He's just keeping you on your toes.'

'On my toes? I've been on my bloody points for months now.'

'What you need is a good old-fashioned sex and society exclusive. A Lambton or Profumo. Something he could boast about at the Garrick. He loves all that.'

'Hello, Lytton, good page today, I thought.' For once Lytton hardly even bothered to look up as Henry Field forced his unwelcome self on them. 'I was surprised to see you falling for that Britt Ekland nonsense, though. We had it last week but spiked it. It's all a stunt, you know. She doesn't mean a word of it.'

Lytton stared morosely at his drink. He could well do without Henry and his banter. 'How are your piles, Henry?' he asked. 'I hear they've been giving you a bad time again.'

Henry coloured and drew himself up to his full height, which was, in fact, only five feet eight and a half inches. 'That's a malicious and distasteful rumour, Lytton, which, as you well know, is completely untrue,' he said.

'Is it, old boy? I'm sorry. It must have been one of

your chaps who told me. We never can trust the *Post* to get anything right these days, can we?'

Embarrassed in front of Laura, Henry's appetite for the daily sparring left him, and huffing a little bit he pushed his way back through the lunchtime crowd. 'If I ever get my hands on the bastard who started that ...' he threatened as he went.

Invigorated by his effort Lytton grinned and emptied his glass.

'Was it you? Did you start that rumour?' asked Laura.

'Would I stoop so low?' Lytton was smiling.

'Who said anything about having to stoop,' replied Laura.

'Such wit. How's your friend Gregory and his collection of Krugerrands?' Lytton turned the tables. Laura had recently become very friendly with a rich South African who had taken to giving her gifts of Krugerrands, obviously as part of a campaign to get her into bed (if he hadn't already).

'He's in New York this week speculating in optical fibres,' she replied. 'I'll give him your love when he calls.'

'Yes, do that, and add that I hope he buys enough to hang himself from the nearest skyscraper. Now, what about another bottle?'

A bottle was exactly what Dolly felt she could have done with as her taxi drove her through the streets of Mayfair. Lytton had looked so cross about everything she had cancelled what had been planned as a nice boozy lunch with a couple of old schoolfriends, and, after a couple of hours sifting through the cuttings in the library, had set off on a tour of London's casinos, starting at the Monaco. She discovered quickly that she hated casinos. It wasn't just that she was scornful of anyone foolish enough to risk hard earned wealth on the throw of a dice. She felt intimidated by the tonnage of crumpet assembled in these places. London was full of beautiful, long-legged, good time girls, and nowhere was more thick with them in the afternoons than the Monaco.

'We aren't hiring,' said a gibbon in an evening suit as she entered. He didn't intend it, but Dolly found that quite flattering. 'I'm not *for* hiring,' she said. 'I'm looking for Luigi.'

With an exaggeratedly casual Latin wave of his head the gibbon indicated that Dolly venture into the gloom of the perpetual night. 'He's in there,' he said, gesturing to where a display of girls in evening dress were lounging around a television at the back of the club.

Intrepid adventurer Dolly ventured into the gloom of the grotto, aware of a dozen pairs of scornful, lovely eyes dismissing what, until now, she had always considered a rather smart little suit and some not unattractive calf-skin boots. Clothes never looked quite right on her.

Luigi was sitting in front of the television, holding a remote control in one hand and fiddling with a calculator in the other, as he worked out the form for the afternoon's racing. He was handsome all right, about thirty, Sicilian dark with spaniel eyes and the beginnings of a small pot belly. He looked Dolly over with a professional's eye for women as she moved towards him. 'Didn't the man tell you, no more girls? Already we got a glut of girls. What d'you think this is, a finishing school or something?' he said, his eyes darting between her and the start of the next race.

'Lytton sent me, Luigi,' said Dolly. 'He wondered if you knew anything about Lucky Jim Diamond?'

'Lucky Jim, eh?' He was suddenly interested. Then turning off his television he dismissed the girls: 'Hey, you guys, why don't you go take a skinny dip in the jacuzzi? I'll join you later.'

Silently the girls melted away.

'We hear he's in financial trouble,' said Dolly, feeling easier now that the audience had left.

'Show me a gambler who doesn't have his little liquidity problem from time to time,' said Luigi.

'Big liquidity problems.'

'Well, maybe,' he admitted, and then changed the subject. 'Hey, how would you like a little revitalization in the sauna? Normally members only, but you can be my personal guest. See these muscles. I give the best massage in London. Ask anyone. Vibrotic massage. Out of this world.'

'No thank you, I'm revitalized enough, I think,' said Dolly, wondering what her partner in life on *The Guardian* would think if he knew that such suggestions were being made to her.

'Okay, suit yourself.'

'Do you know where we can find him?'

'Hey what do you take me for?' Luigi affected offence.

'A friend.'

'A friend, maybe. A canary never. I'll see you,' he said, and, getting up, he threw back his buffalo shoulders and strutted across to a couple of very large American-looking gentlemen who had just entered the casino. 'Hey, Michael, how's your father?' he said, throwing his arms around the younger of the two and giving him a hug and a kiss.

Helping herself to a handful of salted peanuts, Dolly got up and began to make her way towards the door. One of the girls who had been sent for a skinny dip approached. 'If you're looking for Lucky Jim, you should look here,' she said, slipping Dolly an address scribbled on a piece of toilet paper. 'And if you see him tell him Toni says thanks for all the good times.'

'What?' said Dolly.

'Just tell him, okay.'

'Why don't you tell him yourself?'

The girl shook her head. 'It's too late now. Besides, I don't want to get involved,' she said, and she slipped away in the direction of the Golden Nugget room.

Outside in the street Dolly examined the piece of paper. The name of a block of service flats near Marble Arch (incorrectly spelled) was scrawled on it.

She had never reported on this aspect of London life before and it excited her. What she yearned to be was a show business interviewer with her photograph at the top of the page, but in the meantime gamblers, gangsters and hookers had glamour, too.

The porter in the apartment block where Lucky Jim lived was pleased to have someone to talk to. It was a lonely job, he said, but it was the only one he could get at his age. He confirmed that a Mr Diamond lived there, adding that he kept to himself, but was always very polite. 'He's only been here for a couple of weeks and has his mail forwarded from several other addresses,' he said. 'Most evenings he goes out for a few hours, and he has a regular cab at nine-thirty every morning to take him to see someone at the London Clinic.'

'That's odd, isn't it?' said Dolly.

'Is it? I thought he must have an invalid wife or relative,' said the porter. 'I visited my Eileen every day for three years before she went. That was in Purley, though, of course.'

Dolly waited as the old man remembered other times. 'Is there anything else you can think of?' she asked at length.

'Only that you're the second person this week who's asked about him. A good looking young man, American he was, and big, was in yesterday. I told him I'd never heard of anyone called Jim Diamond, that he didn't live here.'

Dolly was puzzled: 'Why did you do that?'

The porter wrinkled up his nose. 'He had a smell about him,' he said. 'A smell of violence. You know some people are just no good. You get an instinct for folk in this job.'

'And what does your instinct tell you about Mr Diamond?'

'He's a rogue,' he said, 'but he's all right. I wish him well.'

Norman, the Diary sub-editor, was being difficult. Lytton had returned from lunch with the editor's needlings about the tepidity of his page forgotten, but within moments of his arrival for the afternoon shift Norman had revived his worries.

'We'll be going on a story about ex-King Constantine –' Lytton had begun to say before Norman's expression stopped him.

'Ex-King Constantine? If it's royal, print it, I suppose,' said Norman. Lytton could feel a knot of anger forming inside him.

'Yes, something like that,' said Lytton despite himself. He certainly didn't mean it.

'Even bubble royalty?'

'He's Greek, for heaven's sake. Almost in the family, Norman.'

Norman snorted and looked at the copy. 'This isn't a lead,' he grumbled.

'Well, it's the best one we've got,' came back Lytton, and stalked back to his desk.

At that moment his telephone rang. Jenny took the call on her extension. 'Lytton,' she said, after a moment, and putting her hand over the receiver, 'that picture of the naked woman ... there's some nutter here wants to talk about it.'

Lytton shook his head irritably. He wasn't in the mood for nutters today. Norman and the editor were bad enough.

'I think you should listen to him,' Jenny persisted.

With as bad a grace as possible Lytton took the phone from her. The caller was a man, obviously disguising his voice, and referring to the lady in the picture as La Belle de Soir. This annoyed Lytton even more, but, with his free hand, he picked the photograph out of his tray and examined it further. 'Who is Belle de Soir?' he asked. 'And if it comes to it, who are you?' At that point the caller hung up. 'Great,' groaned Lytton, 'first an anonymous nude and now an anonymous caller.' He raised his voice to address the rest of the table. 'Has anyone heard of a London socialite who calls herself Belle de Soir?'

Blank faces met him. '*Belle de Jour* was Deneuve and Clementi, wasn't it,' said Pandora. 'I've never heard of Belle de Soir, though.'

'Wasn't that the Bunuel film where she plays the perfect housewife who works in a brothel during the day?' asked David.

'And dreams about being degraded at night,' said Pandora nodding enthusiastically.

'Sexist filth really,' sniffed Jenny.

Lytton was astonished by the irrelevance of the exchange. He turned to Wesley who was sitting in Dolly's place reading a copy of the *International Herald Tribune*. 'Wesley, help me. Why do people wear masks?'

'So that they won't be recognized,' the boy replied, laying down his newspaper and coming over to look at the photograph Lytton was holding in his hand. 'Cor, look at the state of that,' he added.

Lytton took the photograph from him. 'Thank you, Wesley,' he said pointedly. 'Now listen, everyone, it's probably a PR stunt but we might all keep our ears skinned for La Belle de Soir, whoever she is. It's time the great British public were able to enjoy another of its periodic fits of morality. It does them good and it might heat up our tepid little column a bit, too.'

Lytton got back to his novel the next day. If the editor was getting bored with him, he decided, he ought perhaps to develop his second career. The trouble with writing novels, however, was that he didn't much enjoy the act of writing. He found it lonely and not a little boring.

Occasionally (very occasionally) he might become excited by some new strand of thought, description or the structure of a sentence, but for much of the time it was all he could do to keep himself at his desk. On this day, however, he worked well, and was beginning to wonder if indeed he might not have a future in fiction, when the telephone rang and brought him back to earth.

It was Pandora. She was having lunch with some chums in Peter Jones and had news about Belle de Soir. 'I don't actually know who she is yet,' she admitted, 'but everyone says she's supposed to be terribly grand.'

'And who's everyone?' asked Lytton, suspiciously.

'Jane Fox ... well, actually her brother, Richard ...'

'You don't mean Porky Fox who was caught nargling in the bicycle sheds at Heathfield?' asked Lytton. Porky Fox had been a notorious ne'er do well ever since he had been expelled from Eton after having been discovered sniffing bicycle seats at the local girls' school.

'The very one,' said Pandora. 'According to Jane, old Porky hired Belle de Soir the other night for a stag party for Charlie Harrington, you know, that wet little underwriter. She was definitely toffee-nosed, Jane says, and insisted her fee be made payable to some children's charity. You should hear who the rumours are suggesting she is.'

'Tell me,' demanded Lytton. She did. Lytton didn't believe it. Belle de Soir's body, excellent though it was, was that of a woman in her late thirties, not a young mum in her early twenties. Thanking her for the information, Lytton told her to enjoy her lunch and hung up.

He had thought he recognized the voice of the anonymous caller. Now he knew; it had to be Porky Fox.

He met Porky for a drink at the Goodtimes Bar, an over-expensive Knightsbridge club, where sharks from the music and advertising world liked to meet models and starlets. Porky loved the place. He was a rotund, jovial fellow, who made his living mainly by keeping in with those of his station who were doing better in life. In the time that Lytton had known him, which was less than four years, he had dabbled in several professions, from property to advertising and even restaurant owning, but his success was always limited by his dislike of proper work and his inability to turn down the chance of a quick buck.

'Five hundred quid for all I know,' he said as Lytton sat down beside him.

Lytton laughed. 'What do you know that's worth five hundred quid?'

'Give me the money and I'll tell you.'

'Ah, Mr Lytton, Marx's secret weapon,' said the barman as Lytton ordered a Sancerre and soda and another Scotch for Porky. Then, taking the fat man by the padded shoulder of his jacket, Lytton led Porky out of anyone's ear shot and made his deal. 'Two fifty it it's a page lead.'

'Done,' said Porky, rather too quickly. Lytton wished then that he had only offered one hundred.

'It was you on the phone yesterday, wasn't it?' said Lytton. 'Why couldn't you just come out with it then instead of the silly voice. As for getting your sister to set up Pandora. You're very tiresome, you know.'

Porky laughed. 'I had to drum up interest. When a reporter gets a story too easily he never appreciates it. If I'd come to you and said there's a mystery lady taking them off for a gang of toffs you'd never have come across with three hundred quid.'

'Two fifty,' corrected Lytton. 'Where did you find her anyway?'

Porky pulled a copy of the *Tatler* from his raincoat pocket. 'Surprised you missed this,' he gloated. 'The parish magazine.'

Circled in the Personal column at the back of the latest issue was a three line advertisement. "Belle de Soir," read Lytton. "Specialist one woman after-dinner cabaret for gentlemen's soirées. Box 592." Who is she then?' he asked.

Porky shook his head. 'That I honestly don't know. She's very careful. Hardly speaks to anyone and never shows herself without the mask. But she does wear a wedding ring.'

'She sounds a bit loopy to me,' said Lytton, feigning disinterest.

'Could be. Want me to give it to Henry Field?' asked Porky.

Lytton didn't want that at all. 'Well, an anonymous nude at a crummy stag night doesn't sound much for two fifty quid.'

'I don't know, Lytton. You're a hard man to convince. Tell you what. How about a ringside seat for her next performance for an extra hundred? It's tonight, but you must promise not to leave my side.'

Lytton considered how he had intended spending that evening. Laura was away for a weekend with her mother in Hampshire, and he had planned to concentrate on his novel. This sounded like more fun. 'Well, at least it won't be tepid,' he said.

Belle de Soir had chosen an out of town venue for her next performance, a handsome Georgian house in the Buckinghamshire countryside which was being used that weekend for an EEC seminar on something known as 'the third force'.

'Just remember, keep talking Common Market,' said Porky as he and Lytton, both now dressed in black tie, slipped through a side door to mingle with the forty middle-aged Eurocrats. Terrified of being exposed as a Peeping Tom, Lytton said nothing. He could scarcely believe that Belle de Soir was about to do her act in this dry and funeral setting.

All around him earnest voices talked about superdollars and devaluations. He didn't understand a word of it. Porky, however, quite familiar with the role of imposter, was handling it all with great skill. When asked by an observant French delegate why they hadn't been there earlier in the day, Porky shrugged magnificently and explained how he and Lytton had been battened up in town working on the new budget. Fortunately he was not asked which budget, and Lytton turned and examined a painting when the man looked in his direction for further conversation.

At last the surprise cabaret began. After what seemed to Lytton like an eternity in which they were certain to be discovered, an elderly Englishman with a very large nose, protruding eyebrows and a shiny bald head (he looked, thought Lytton, like a bald eagle) clapped his hands to draw attention. 'Well, gentlemen, I know we've had a very long and stimulating day but tonight to celebrate our little seminar we on the UK committee thought that perhaps a little stimulation of another kind might not be unappreciated. So without further debate, may I introduce to you ... La Belle de Soir,' and swinging open a door, he dimmed the lights and stood well back among the now confused delegates.

Into the room danced a woman in a long dark cloak and a large lace face mask, accompanied by torchy, vampish music which, Lytton noticed, was coming from a portable tape recorder she set on a table by the door. A chuckle of astonishment ran around the assembled delegates. The UK committee was providing an unusual entertainment, to say the least. Moving forward into the midst of the men, Belle de Soir let slide the cloak from her shoulder and stepped out of it. Underneath she was wearing black camiknickers with red lace trim, and black fishnet stockings. From the back of the room, close to the French windows, Lytton peered at her. Then, as the music increased in tempo, Belle de Soir began to perform her striptease, with an amateur's enthusiasm, first the garters, tossed into the crowd of now slightly embarrassed men, then one stocking followed by the other. It was, Lytton had to admit, an outrageously provocative performance, startling in its lack of subtlety, touching in its self-consciousness. As the bits and pieces of garment became fewer, and the audience began to get over its initial embarrassment and to enjoy the show, Lytton stared hard at Belle de Soir's mask. Was this anyone he knew? he wondered. Suddenly the climax of the show had been reached. Belle stood naked before the applauding delegates. Then, reaching down, she grabbed her clothes from the floor, and, picking up her tape recorder, fled the room. While the audience chanted for more, Lytton quietly opened the French windows and, unseen by anyone, particularly Porky who was bellowing loudest of all, slipped into the garden.

Quickly Lytton made his way around the side of the house towards the car park. Before entering he had noted which cars had already been parked there. Now there was another, a Renault 5.

Moments later the front door of the house opened and Belle de Soir, again wearing her cloak, hurried across the drive to the Renault.

Lytton watched the car go. 'LGO 495Y,' he mused and then, in case he should forget, wrote it on a book of matches.

Walking back towards the house he was met by Porky Fox. 'Lytton, you really are a duplicitous bastard.' Porky was pink with indignation. 'You promised me.'

Lytton shook his head apologetically. 'Sorry, Porky, a treacherous nature is a prerequisite for this job . . . you'd be a natural.'

Dolly told Lytton everything she had discovered about Lucky Jim Diamond the following Monday morning. It wasn't very much. What puzzled Lytton most was why Diamond should be paying visits to the London Clinic every day. 'What's the betting he's found some rich old widow to milk,' he said suspiciously. 'Keep after him, anyway. Anyone who threatens to sue over something so petty has to have something to hide.

'Being accused of not paying your debts isn't necessarily petty,' said Dolly. She was beginning to like the idea of Lucky Jim.

Lytton was unimpressed. 'When you've made a lifetime's habit of sponging off those at the top table it's hardly crippling to the soul either,' he said. Dismissing her, he picked up his telephone and asked Bill Withy, a pal on the news desk, if he wouldn't mind bribing an operator on the Swansea car licensing computer. That was always the quickest way to pairing a number with a name. Fifteen minutes later Withy came back to him with a name and address: Lady Isabelle de Montfort of Victoria Road, London W8 was the registered owner of vehicle number LGO 495Y. Lytton's eyebrows arched. Isabelle de Montfort and Belle de Soir, one and the same person? Lytton had never met the de Montforts but quickly found them in *Burke's Peerage*. They were an English family who stretched right back to the Norman Conquest, and whose male members, in the marked absence of brains, had always taken up careers in the armed forces. The present generation was no exception. Lord William de Montfort, husband of the Lady Isabelle, was attached to NATO in Brussels.

'Wesley, could you go to the library and get cuttings and pictures on William and Isabelle de Montfort, please,' Lytton asked, passing the boy a note of the name.

'What's this? Another toff been putting it about a bit?' asked Wesley.

'Better than that,' said Lytton, 'far better than that.'

There was surprisingly little in the de Montfort cuttings to give Lytton much insight into their lifestyle. Isabelle was the only daughter of a retired diplomat, while

William had had a straightforward career up the military ranks from cadet corps at Wellington, to Sandhurst, the Royal Welsh Fusiliers, some action in Aden and Cyprus followed quickly by backseat jobs in Hanover, Washington and now Brussels. Lytton realized instantly he was in the most perfect position to be blackmailed.

Normally Lytton would have made a quick telephone call to the Lady Isabelle and told her that he believed her to be the owner of LGO 495Y and almost certainly Belle de Soir, but this was a story of worldwide implications. It would be unpleasant, but he had to face her. Taking a taxi across town he approached the pretty white stucco house in the fashionable Kensington road with some misgivings. He did not enjoy the foot in the door aspect of a gossip column.

A Filipino maid answered the door.

'Hello, I've called to see the Lady Isabelle,' said Lytton, turning to her and affecting a wide smile. He had been looking at the Renault 5 parked outside. It's number was LGO 495Y.

'Is she expecting you?'

'Oh yes.'

'And what name shall I say?'

Lytton paused. 'Neville,' he said slyly.

'If you wouldn't mind waiting,' said the maid, holding the door open, and showing him into a sitting-room, 'she's with the little ones at the moment.' With that she left the room.

Lytton looked around. It was a large square Victorian room, with a small rear balcony which looked out on to a pretty, well kept garden. Crossing to the window Lytton looked down. In the middle of the lawn Isabelle de Montfort sat surrounded by a group of very small children. 'The ladies on the bus go chatter, chatter, chatter,' she sang, flapping her fingers and thumbs together to suggest rapid talking. Lytton stared down at her. Could this be

Belle de Soir, the woman he had seen performing a strip-tease only two nights earlier. For a moment he wanted to forget what he had seen and leave her with the children. But just as quickly he dismissed the thought. Below him the maid stepped from the basement on to the lawn, announcing his arrival.

Moving away from the window, Lytton considered the room. He had been in many such sitting-rooms. 'Trad-itional' would have been the word he would have used to describe it in his column. There were heavy comfortable sofas, a large marble fireplace, long velvet curtains, pic-tures and small plants everywhere and, on the mantelpiece, various photographs of the family, together with a couple of invitations to social functions. On a sideboard was a picture of Isabelle and William de Montfort at what looked like a Buckingham Palace garden party.

The sound of footsteps in the hall announced the arrival of the Lady Isabelle. The children's songs had finished. Lytton turned to the door. The woman who entered was about thirty five, neat, and girlishly attractive.

'Hello, I'm told I was expecting you,' she said, looking curiously at Lytton. 'But I don't think ... do we know each other?'

Lytton smiled. 'Only by sight. My name is Neville Lytton. I was lucky enough to –'

'You mean Neville Lytton from Lytton's Diary?' She suddenly looked uneasy.

'Yes. As I was saying, I was lucky enough to see your performance at Mallory the other night. And I thought ...'

'What performance?' She stared him straight in the eye. 'I'm sorry, I don't think I know what you're talking about.'

'As Belle de Soir.'

'Sorry? Who was that?'

'She's a striptease artist of a sort. But of course you already know that.'

Isabelle laughed, slightly theatrically, and turned to look down into her garden. 'Are you trying to say you've come here to tell me you think I've taken up stripping? You're absolutely crazy.'

'I don't think so.'

'Look, if this is some sort of joke . . .' She was becoming increasingly agitated. She turned towards the door. 'This conversation has gone on long enough.'

Lytton ignored her invitation for him to leave. 'You mean you're saying you aren't the lady in the mask, and that isn't your car parked outside, and that I don't recognize you from the other night.'

Hopelessly Isabelle tried the grand manner. 'I've absolutely no idea what you're talking about, and I don't like your manner. I want you to leave.'

'At least let's talk.'

'We've nothing to talk about.'

'Not even why you're endangering your husband's career.'

'Please, I asked you to go.'

Lytton took his card from his wallet and put it down on the table. 'If you should happen to change your mind, perhaps we could have lunch sometime. It's been so good to meet you . . . properly. Goodbye.' Then he added: 'Don't bother, I'll show myself out.'

As a hardened old tabloid pro, this was the sort of story Laura relished. 'Well, it sounds to me like you've found the story that's going to get the editor off your back for ever,' she said when Lytton told her of his morning's work over a lunchtime drink. 'If you run this there'll be investigations at NATO, questions in the House, dismay in Washington. The repercussions are endless.'

'I like to think so,' said Lytton, before groaning as Henry Field made his daily sortie towards him.

'I hear you were involved in a spot of gate-crashing

the other night, Lytton. I was disappointed not to read it in today's paper.' He had obviously been talking to Porky.

'Come on, Henry, you can't believe everything that great oaf of a fox tells you.'

'Some kind of tatty little strip show, I hear.' Henry had obviously only been told half the story.

Lytton attacked back. 'It's very painful to sit down, I'm told. And to do other things.'

Henry's crowing ceased. If he had piles, and there was no evidence to suggest that he had, they were a subject of great embarrassment and distress to him. 'One of these days, Lytton, you're going to go too far.'

'But in the meantime, Henry, you're never going to go far enough. Now push off, will you, there's a good chap.'

For once Henry did indeed push off. 'Porky Fox talks too much,' said Lytton as soon as he was out of earshot. 'Lucky he didn't know who Belle de Soir was or he'd have sold her to the *News of the Screws* for fifty thousand. He'll be livid when he finds out.'

Laura wagged her head in dismay. 'Your contacts really are the pits, Lytton. They'd sell their own daughters for a fiver.'

'Oh, they've been known to fetch far less than that,' said Lytton.

Without an admittance that Isabelle de Montfort was Belle de Soir, Lytton still had some way to go in standing up his story. Traditionally a newspaper which knows something but cannot prove it will employ a teasing technique of running increasingly provocative hints until its quarry can no longer stand the strain and shows his hand. And with this in mind, Lytton, that afternoon, typed a short, enigmatic paragraph which he gave to Norman for prominent display. It read: 'Smart London society has an intriguing new mystery. What is the identity of the beautiful striptease artiste known as Belle de Soir who performs regularly among gilded circles at stag nights, old boys' meetings and even economic conventions? Rumours chasing around town suggest scurrilously that she is a titled lady and the wife of someone deeply concerned with the defence of the realm. But, for the moment, discretion seals my lips. Watch this space for further details.'

The ruse worked more quickly than he expected. Isabelle de Montfort called him at home the following morning, and at Lytton's suggestion, they met for lunch at Monsieur Thompson's in North Kensington, a place well away from his usual Fleet Street haunts. Isabelle arrived first and was nervous and already drinking when Lytton joined her. 'How much do you want?' she asked.

Now it was Lytton's turn to appear bemused. 'Sorry?'

'How much. I'll pay you to lay off.' Lytton ordered a drink, while Isabelle prepared to deliver what he knew would be a planned speech. 'Look, I know you're determined to ruin my husband and me. So let's settle this thing as painlessly as possible. Just tell me your price.'

'If you don't mind my saying, you know no such thing. In fact, were I to take a more cynical view, I might assume something very different – that it is you who have embarked upon a course of self-destruction, which will quite probably wreck your husband's life along with your own.'

'If that's what you think, why don't you print it? Why don't you tell the world that William de Montfort is married to a tart.' Her voice had risen to the brink of hysteria.

Lytton looked around him. Heads at other tables raised momentarily. 'Because I'm not sure that I want to become part of any game you might think you're playing until I know exactly what's involved,' he said quietly.

Isabelle was now wringing her napkin. 'I don't know what you mean. What game?'

'That was rather what I hoped you would tell me.'

Suddenly Isabelle de Montfort began to cry, blubbing great tears down her nose and on to the tablecloth of this fashionable bistro. 'It isn't a game, Mr Lytton. It isn't any kind of game.'

Ever the gentleman, Lytton passed her a freshly-starched handkerchief. 'Those children I saw you with, was it some kind of playgroup? They didn't look much like the children of the well heeled rich to me.'

'They're local. They come to me three days a week. The playgroup had to close down because of lack of funds so I began one in the basement. I haven't got any children of my own ...' She fought the tears away.

'Look, why don't you just tell me all about it?' said Lytton. He had enough experience to know that he was about to be told everything he wished to know if he could keep up his kind uncle act. Emotionally disturbed people will talk to anyone, even reporters, if prompted with kindness.

'Can I trust you?' asked Isabelle, blowing her nose.

Lytton considered for less than a moment. 'No, I'm afraid not,' he said. There was no advantage in lying. 'But seeing how much I know already you really don't have many options left, do you? And now while we're talking, why don't we have something to eat?' And putting up his hand he summoned Monsieur Thompson and began ordering lunch.

In Lytton's experience there was little to beat a good bottle of wine or two and a compassionate listening manner when it came to worming out secrets, and long before they had finished their pudding Isabelle was chattering compulsively.

'You must think I'm a right trollop. Isn't that right?' she asked. 'You should, anyway. Because that's what I am. A real scarlet trollop.' She giggled nervously. She had confided earlier that following the story in that day's

Lytton's Diary she had been unable to eat breakfast and now the wine was going straight to her head.

'How did it start? You didn't say?' prompted Lytton.

Isabelle pushed her dish away from her. 'I don't know. Who can tell? I suppose it was some kind of dare I made with myself. When I was younger I always admired those girls who didn't care ... you know, the vampy sort. Men always seemed to like them best ... to admire them. I suppose I wanted to be admired. It's terrifically exciting, you know, to behave like that ... to be tempting and alluring, just like people in films. Everyone knows me as good old straight, boring Isabelle who wouldn't know a romantic opportunity if I tripped over it. But they don't know the other Isabelle, the one I've kept locked up for the past fifteen years. Can you understand that? No. Why should you. Why should I tell you all these things, anyway? I can't trust you. I couldn't trust the girls at school either. Nor William. Nobody. Just me, behind my mask, watching you all ...'

Lytton poured them both some more wine. The restaurant had emptied and Isabelle was talking increasingly loudly. A waitress listened from behind a low screen. 'It's sometimes better to talk about these things, though, isn't it?' said Lytton. 'We all live some kind of secret fantasy life, I think. I know I do.'

'We're none of us just one person.' Isabelle was talking now, oblivious to who was listening. 'When I was at school I used to go on the roof, dress up as a nun and drink gin and smoke Gauloises. It was only play acting, but there was always the thrill and fear of being caught. You can do anything when you're in disguise. Anything at all. In my mask I become someone quite different. Someone men desire. It's exciting.'

'What about your husband?' broke in Lytton. The restaurant would soon be closing and he had to get his information before they were turfed out.

'My husband wouldn't notice if I ran stark naked all along Park Lane. He thinks of nothing apart from his missiles and tanks and Sarah Boswell.'

'I'm sorry?'

'His secretary, Sarah. She's very pretty and sexy and they have candlelight dinners in Brussels.'

Lytton broke in: 'Are you sure you aren't just imagining that. Lots of husbands have attractive secretaries, but that doesn't mean to say –'

'It's common knowledge,' came back Isabelle. 'He hardly even bothers to hide it. Are you married?'

'Well, yes and no,' said Lytton, uncomfortable at suddenly finding himself the interrogated. 'I'm separated.'

'You mean you found something younger and prettier?'

Lytton thought of Catherine and her snivelling little consort Tom. 'Well, no. She did. I mean she found somebody else,' he said.

'And how did you feel?'

'Well, at the time it was very upsetting,' said Lytton, choosing his words carefully. 'Sometimes it still hurts a little when I think about it. But I suppose life provides other compensations.'

'Are there children?'

'No. Happily for them,' said Lytton.

'Unhappily for me. Perhaps life would have been different if William and I had been able to have a family. He won't adopt. He wants his own. A family might have kept him at home. All those grand army men want to have sons to follow the family tradition. I was a big disappointment to him over that.'

'You know,' said Lytton, 'it seems to me that you spend far too much time being sorry for yourself.'

Isabelle went silent, perhaps realizing for the first time just how outspoken she had been. 'What are you going to do?' she asked at last. 'Are you going to write about me? Will you unmask Belle de Soir?'

The closeness which had been building between the two of them had dissolved. 'That's what I'm paid to do,' said Lytton. 'And I think in a perverse way that's what you expect me to do. Isn't that right?' He was beginning to feel very sorry for her. He needed time to think how he should handle this story. He couldn't ignore it. That would be unprofessional.

At that moment the waitress who had been listening to the conversation interrupted. There was a telephone call for Lytton. As always before leaving the office at lunchtime, he had left a number with Jenny where he might be contacted. The message was short. He listened, thanked Jenny for calling and then returned slowly to Isabelle. 'I'm sorry, something's come up. I have to go,' he said.

'But you didn't tell me what you're going to write.'

'I'll write what I think is best ... for everyone,' he said.

Dolly was waiting for him outside Lucky Jim's flat, standing a little adjacent to the crowd of police and busybodies who surrounded the ambulance.

'This is hardly the place for a flipperty-gibbet of a Diary reporter like you, Dolly,' said Lytton, putting on an expression considerably more casual than the way he was feeling. 'How did it happen?'

Dolly turned to him, her face drawn, her eyes heavy. 'He shot himself,' she said. And immediately turned away.

Moving through the small crowd Lytton edged towards a burly, double-breasted detective he knew. He didn't need to ask any questions. 'There was a note,' he was told. 'Said he was broke, that the Nassau mafia were after him and that he was being hounded by the press. I suppose he beat the mafia to the draw. He also had stomach cancer.'

Lytton's expression never changed. Behind him Dolly listened with increasing self-revulsion.

'Thanks, Alan,' said Lytton as two ambulancemen came out of the block of flats carrying a stretcher.

Dolly stared at the sheet which covered the face and body of Lucky Jim Diamond. 'He meant us, Lytton,' she said. 'We were hounding him and he was already dying.'

Lytton watched as the body was slipped into the back of the ambulance, the doors were closed and the remains of Lucky Jim Diamond were borne away. 'I wouldn't shed too many tears for him if I were you,' he said. 'Lucky Jim had been making enemies for thirty years. We just happened to be the last in the queue. Come on, let's go and give him a good send off. At least he won't be able to slap in any more writs now.'

'I never knew you could be so callous,' said Dolly.

Lytton looked at her. 'Didn't you?'

For once Norman was interested and had splashed the Lucky Jim Diamond story across the entire Diary page under the headline THE DAY LUCK RAN OUT FOR JIM DIAMOND, while under separate headings Lytton and the Diary team had provided background information appropriate for the sub-headings of Girls, Glamour and Gold. It was a pretty impressive page by anyone's standards and even the editor was pleased.

'Marvellous page, Neville,' he congratulated as, carrying a page proof, he sortied from his office. 'What a rum bit of work he was.'

'Litigious bit of work, too,' reminded Lytton, before adding, 'Dolly did most of it. She'd been assembling a dossier on him for some days just in case he wasn't bluffing about the writ.'

Casting a compliment in the vague direction of Dolly the editor moved on to praise or castigate other members of his staff.

'Who's a clever little louse, then?' asked Laura, examining the page.

'If you've nothing better to do you can buy me a drink,' said Lytton. It had been a difficult day.

Laura looked awkward. 'Perhaps I'll see you down there. I'm waiting for a phone call from New York.'

'From your King Kong of cable?' Lytton tried not to sound either suspicious or jealous but managed to do both. He turned to Dolly. 'What about you? Shall we go and assuage our guilt together?'

Dolly frowned. She had come back to the office and helped with the story, but purely from professionalism. 'I won't if you don't mind,' she said, pulling on her coat. 'I think I'd like to go home now and have a good bath. Goodnight.'

Lytton watched her go. He knew exactly how she felt. But he was the Diary page editor. It wasn't for him to show sentiments of guilt. Chucking the page proof into the waste bin he picked up his raincoat and made his way alone to the Galley Proof.

'Mine's a large one, Neville,' someone shouted as he entered. It was Bill Withy from the news desk, wanting a reward for being so helpful in matching Belle de Soir's car number with Isabelle de Montfort. The Lucky Jim Diamond suicide had quite driven her out of Lytton's mind.

'Of course, Bill,' said Lytton and moved across to join the group of reporters with whom Withy was drinking.

'Any joy with your Lady Isabelle and the Renault 5?' asked Withy as the clarets were served.

Lytton swallowed slowly. 'Right car, right lady ... but wrong story, I'm afraid,' he said at last. 'Just another hysterical wife trying to get her husband to notice her. It happens all the time.'

'What happens all the time?' The voice was Laura's. Lytton was surprised to see her so soon.

'I was just explaining to Bill why we won't be running the Belle de Soir story.'

'What? I thought you said it could be dynamite,' protested Laura.

Lytton frowned, uneasily. 'Did I? Well that was before …' He stopped. 'Belle de Soir is just an elaborate cry for help from an emotionally disturbed woman. She's a mass of self-destructive urges. Most women in her situation take to shoplifting. She takes her knickers off. She needs to see a psychiatrist, not be exposed by the yellow press just because a chap's column has been a bit tepid recently.'

Bill Withy watched all this with bemusement. 'What?'

'Oh it's nothing, Bill,' said Lytton. 'It's just that one suicide's enough for one day.' Then turning to Laura he said: 'Weren't you waiting for a phone call from Gregory?'

Laura shrugged. 'I changed my mind. I thought you might like me to make you some dinner.'

'I'd like that very much,' said Lytton, and, seeing Withy had already turned back to his friends, he finished his wine and led Laura out of the bar.

As they left the Galley Proof Lytton nearly bumped into Henry Field coming in. Alongside him was Porky Fox. On seeing Lytton Porky looked almost embarrassed.

'Hello, what's this,' crowed Henry. '"Diarist and beautiful hackette scurrying away for secret assignation."'

Lytton looked at the fat man. 'I must warn you about the low life you're keeping, Porky. Henry Field is definitely not a chap to be seen around with.'

'Sticks and stones,' said Henry as he led Porky into the bar.

'Now I wonder what those two little termites are plotting?' Lytton said to Laura when they were alone again.

Laura pushed her hand into his trouser pocket: 'I'm prepared to bet it's got nothing on what I'm plotting,' she said.

On this occasion she was probably wrong. The following morning, leaving Lytton snoring in between her Laura Ashley sheets, she went downstairs to pick up her morning letters and newspapers. She always had four delivered, but usually opened the *News* first followed by the *Post*. As she climbed back up the stairs she checked her own page in the *News* (she had an article on 'Women and celibacy: the eighties way to success'), glanced at Lytton's page on Lucky Jim Diamond and then unfolded the *Post*. 'Crumbs,' she murmured, and going back into her bedroom began to shake Lytton.

'Oh, don't wake me,' he complained. 'I was dreaming I was back at school and matron was just about to –'

'That little reptile Henry Field's done well today,' said Laura spreading the *Daily Post* out on the bed.

Lytton opened his eyes and sat up. The name of Henry Field could waken him from the deepest sleep. The front page of the *Daily Post* contained only one story. 'LADY IN MASK REVELATIONS SHOCKS TOP TORIES,' read Lytton. 'By Henry Field. Exclusive.'

Further down the page were other headlines: 'Playgroup leader who strips for society men', 'Lord William says "I didn't know".' Lytton lay back on the pillows. Porky had found out the identity of Belle de Soir and made himself a little killing. And Henry Field had scooped Lytton.

'You know, Laura, I sometimes think I'm too nice for this job,' he said.

Chapter Four

Tricks of the Trade

There is probably nothing enjoyed quite so much in Fleet Street as a good funeral. So it was when Toady Oswald died suddenly of a surfeit of claret one night in the arms of a Metropolitan policeman on the pavement outside El Vino. They came from far and wide that day to say good-bye to Toady, although more than a few had been on the receiving end of his pen, on many an occasion.

Toady was an institution in and around Fleet Street. While *Private Eye* might have been the magazine to make satire popular with the commuter belt, it was *Cyclops* that, for years, had waged relentless war upon the mandarins and narcissists of the British establishment. Some might have complained that *Cyclops* was understood only by those working in newspapers and television, but Toady never claimed to be in it for anything other than the fun. Then the poor chap died, and his friends and enemies, and many who were both and some who were neither but simply wished to be there, went to his funeral at St Paul's Covent Garden, the actor's church, as it is known, which was appropriate because Toady had always had a theatrical style.

Everyone turned up. Absolutely every one of those who considered themselves belonging to the sophisticated Press of Fleet Street, or the worthy inner rim of self-congratulatories who produce and present the country's most prestigious television programmes. Ian Jack brought half a dozen or more from the *Sunday Times*, Peter Hillmore led a contingent from *The Observer*, Dempster was there,

McKay, on leave from Washington, went, even Max Hastings from *The Standard* turned up along with Maureen Cleave who remembered Toady from the sixties. They came, too, from ITN, and the music and arts department of the BBC, and Melvyn Bragg wore a black tie and popped over from London Weekend Television carrying a book to read in the taxi. If it hadn't been such a sad occasion, it would have been a jolly good reunion, but that's usually the way with funerals. There were four editors, five women's editors (women always liked Toady) and an odd assortment of assistants, deputies and associate editors. There was also Neville Lytton.

Four rows from the front, Lytton listened with some sadness as a foppish, aristocratic man of about thirty-five, in an old corduroy suit with a large yellow handkerchief in his breast pocket which clashed violently with his pink and peach-coloured shirt, stood by the coffin of the former editor of *Cyclops* and orated lustily. He was Tim Beauchamp, Toady's deputy at *Cyclops*, and a man for whom Lytton had never had much affection. If Toady had one failing it had been in his choice of staff.

'Toady Oswald is dead and London is so much the poorer for it,' mourned Beauchamp. 'Because Toady was a natural born satirist and gossip. For twenty years he was the scourge of Westminster and Fleet Street, as he and all of us at *Cyclops* endeavoured to reduce the level of pomposity in the land with ridicule and humour. But just because Toady is dead let no one think that *Cyclops* will die with him. We, who worked with Toady, owe it to him to keep *Cyclops* alive.'

With that Beauchamp dramatically hung his head and walked back to his pew so that prayers might be offered and the service concluded.

'Very nice oration, Tim,' Lytton told him as, the funeral over, the congregation gathered on the steps of the church. 'You should take it up professionally.'

Beauchamp turned his recently bereaved but still terribly social expression on Lytton and thanked him for coming. 'Toady would have been pleased to see you all here today,' he said with admirable insincerity.

'I doubt it,' snapped Henry Field, who was also leaving the church. 'He'd have scoffed at all the crocodile tears. And he'd have been right. When I go they can just bolt me down and chuck me in the ground. I don't want any of this.'

'Don't worry, Henry, I shouldn't think you'll get any of this,' replied Lytton, surprised to see Henry looking quite puffy under the eyes.

Laura joined Lytton on the steps. She was wearing a pretty little canary-coloured summer suit. 'What's got into Henry?' she asked as he walked briskly away.

'Poor Henry,' said Lytton. 'He's upset and he's too embarrassed to show it. Despite what he says, he always liked Toady, did Henry.'

'And here was I thinking that all reptiles were cold-blooded animals.'

'It's good to hear that *Cyclops* is to survive,' Lytton told Beauchamp as they strolled through the church courtyard back towards the street. 'Any word on who the next editor might be?'

Beauchamp twitched his nose in pretend embarrassment. 'I rather thought I might have a go at editing it myself, actually. Working with Toady all these years, well ... I learned quite a lot. We all did, didn't we, Jacko?'

Beauchamp's pal, a little man of similar age, who looked as though he might once have been the school skunk, had joined them. He was wearing a customary idiot smile. Lytton looked from Beauchamp to Jacko and back. '*You* as editor of *Cyclops*?' he said, a shade less than flatteringly.

'You sound surprised,' said Jacko.

'Oh no, not at all ... er, congratulations, Tim,' Lytton muttered. 'I'll look forward to seeing your first edition.'

'And we'll do our best to keep up the Toady tradition,' smiled Beauchamp, not at all put out by Lytton's obvious surprise. And bidding them goodbye he turned to discuss an outbreak of spanking among secretaries at the *New Statesman*.

'You didn't sound very enthusiastic,' said Laura, as she and Lytton approached the street together.

Lytton shook his head miserably. 'Tim Beauchamp may possess some excellent qualities – I don't think he does, but he may – but one thing I'm sure of is that he's quite the most unsuitable person to become editor of *Cyclops*.'

'And why's that?'

'Because,' replied Lytton, 'he's one of the few people I've ever met to have been born without a single shred of morality. As for that grinning ape Jacko . . .' He broke off. An elderly woman, tall and thin and upright as a broom, was weeping silently into a handkerchief as she passed him. 'I'm very sorry, Kathleen.' He murmured his consolations.

Without looking up the woman sniffed her reply. 'He was too young to die. Heaven knows what'll happen to us now. The vandals have claimed the crown,' she mourned, and scurried away.

'Who was that?' asked Laura.

'Her name's Kathleen. She was Toady's right hand, left hand and most of the bits in between. She's been the engine behind *Cyclops* for years. She knows everything.' Suddenly Lytton realized what had been bothering him about Laura. It was the custard-coloured suit she was wearing. 'Aren't you a bit overdressed for a funeral?' he asked.

'Oh, didn't I tell you? I'm on my way to Brazil. That's my taxi waiting to take me to the airport.'

'Come off it.'

'No, honestly. And I've got a present for you, too, because I'm going to miss your birthday.' She pulled a package out of her bag and pressed it into his hand. 'I hate surprises so I'll tell you what it is. It's a micro-recorder to dictate your novel into. It even has a remote microphone. All the rubbishy novelists use them nowadays, so it'll be perfect for what you're writing. Gosh, is that the time? I'll miss my plane.' She reached up to kiss him.

'But what are you going to Brazil for?' All this was too much for Lytton. Laura always seemed to be going away these days.

'To write a piece on worker priests and revolution. God's wife suddenly thinks they're fascinating. I'll send you a postcard.'

'You know, if you spend any more time in the air you'll begin to grow feathers,' said Lytton peevishly. He would have rather liked a trip to Brazil himself.

Laura opened the door to her taxi. 'For heaven's sake, Lytton, I dunno what's got into you today. You're really grumpy. I don't think funerals agree with you. Bye.'

And with that she slammed the taxi door and was driven away down the street.

At just about the moment that Laura was boarding the Varig jumbo jet to take her to São Paulo, a meeting was being concluded in a Central London hotel suite. Two men sat in silence facing each other. One was dark, handsome and Arabic. He was Hamil. The other was English, elegant in a good suit, but suffering the dis-advantage of having a receding chin. He was Tom Westaway, a Conservative Member of Parliament, and aspirant international wheeler dealer. They had just reached an impasse in their negotiations. Hamil stood up and took off his glasses. Spread across the glass coffee table in front of them were lists of figures and sheafs of diagrams. 'You're a hard man to do business with, Mr Westaway,' sighed Hamil. He spoke with the impeccable English of someone who had received an extremely expensive education. 'Might I suggest a couple of days adjournment while I ask for new instructions?'

Westaway smirked and getting up began to pack his briefcase. 'Take as long as you want,' he said. 'There's no hurry.'

A frown crossed Hamil's forehead: 'Not for you perhaps.'

Westaway smiled: 'So you'll be in touch when you can make a better offer.'

Hamil nodded. They shook hands and Westaway left the room. Five minutes later, just long enough to have considered the implications of the meeting, Hamil tried to make a long-distance telephone call to Sybia. Sybia was the Middle Eastern state where he had been born and which he now represented. As so often happened since the fundamentalists had taken over, all the lines were blocked and there was a three-hour delay on calls from London.

Hamil needed a change of scenery. Leaving his room he went downstairs into the lobby where he bought a selection of the day's newspapers and made his way to the coffee shop. He had arrived late the night before, slept on and been unable to examine the newspapers before Westaway had called for their meeting. He always enjoyed the English newspapers, particularly the tabloids. They were so appalling. Over a cup of coffee he glanced firstly through the *Daily Mail*, then the *Express* and finally the *Daily News*. He had almost finished it when something caught his eye. Turning back a page he stared at the photograph at the top of the Diary page.

In the *Daily News* editorial office Wesley was being a complete pest. While Lytton tried to read the latest edition of *Private Eye*, Wesley did his best to prevent him. 'Lytton,' he said. 'Can I ask you something?'

'Can I stop you?' Lytton looked miserably at the boy.

'This lecturer geezer on my day release course was talking about you the other day,' he said. 'He reckons that all gossip columns are pernicious, irresponsible and supportive of the divisive class system in this country.'

Lytton looked bored. 'Oh yes?'

'Yes. He says they're an illusion by which the masses are fed a diet of trivia to keep their minds off the really important issues like revolution.'

'Really!'

Jenny and Pandora were now watching Wesley affectionately. 'Right,' he said, 'so I was wondering how you would defend that damning indictment of your livelihood?'

Lytton looked from Pandora to Jenny. 'Well, I wouldn't, would I? I think that's about broadly right, don't you?'

Wesley's brow puckered. 'So why d'you do it then?' he asked.

Lytton smiled. 'Ah, why indeed? Why does the piranha eat flesh? Why does the vampire suck blood? Because they like it, Wesley. And so do I. I love gossip. D'you understand? So you can tell your teacher that so far as I'm concerned he can shove his revolution. Now why don't you run along and annoy somebody else?'

Wesley stared at Lytton. But whatever he intended to say in reply was frozen when a telephone rang on Lytton's desk. Darting forward he reached it just before Jenny. 'Hello,' he said, 'last bastion of capitalism.'

At the other end of the desk Dolly burst into laughter and applauded while Jenny grabbed the phone from him. 'Diary,' she said, as Lytton threw a handful of press handouts at the boy, then added, 'Just a minute.' To Lytton she said, 'It's someone saying he's an old friend from "way back in the outback". Are you in?'

It was a thin day. Lytton would have been in to anyone. Taking the telephone from her he recognized the voice of the caller immediately. Only one person he knew spoke so perfectly. It was his old comrade from the cell block.

Hamil and Lytton had dinner in Hamil's hotel suite that night, a quiet room-service dinner, heavy in wine and memories.

'I still can't believe that an ex-con like you is now a celebrated journalist,' laughed Hamil, as they both plunged down the hill of happy drunkenness.

'Hardly an ex-con,' protested Lytton. 'It was only one night. Drunk and disorderly I think they called it at the time.'

Hamil laughed. 'We were carefree and careless in those days. Life was better then.'

Lytton wasn't sure about that. He had met Hamil during his sojourn in Australia, a place he had considered to be marvellous for children but in which no fully adult human being should ever consider spending more than half an hour. 'D'you think so?' he asked. 'You were poor and homeless. Now you're rich and influential.'

Hamil shrugged slightly. 'Perhaps,' he said sadly.

Drink had already got the better of Lytton. 'Oh come on,' he enthused. 'You're an important chap back in Sybia. You must be or they wouldn't let you out.' Lytton didn't know too much about world politics but he did know that Sybia, a close ally of Libya, had recently become an extreme Islamic republic, where the hands of pickpockets were docked and rapists considered themselves lucky to be given a straightforward death sentence. Anyone who could fly in and out of Sybia must indeed be a very important individual.

'Sybia isn't the place I was born into,' said Hamil. 'Everything is changing and not much for the better. You know that. We have as bad a reputation as almost anywhere. Your papers are full of us.'

Politics was the last conversation Lytton wanted to be

drawn into at a reunion of cell mates. 'Well, yes,' he said, 'but I've always rather taken the view that you can't believe what you read in the newspapers. Anyway, you and I shouldn't be discussing politics.'

'Unfortunately politics are my life now,' said Hamil, pouring them both extremely large cognacs.

'Oh really? Are you attached to the embassy?'

Hamil was shocked at the suggestion. 'Heavens no,' he said. 'They're all religious zealots, which is another reason why we're eating room service tonight. They don't approve of the high life. It wouldn't do for me to be seen around town with a reprobate like you.'

'So what d'you do?' asked Lytton.

Hamil became coy. 'Mainly I work outside the system,' he said, 'finding funds for famine relief, irrigation, new crops, that sort of thing.'

'That all sounds very –' Lytton stopped himself, but he was too late.

'Worthy?' asked Hamil. 'I suppose you still think of me as the rogue who tried to con a Rolls-Royce off you in Sydney, don't you?'

Lytton laughed at the memory. That was exactly how he thought of Hamil. They had met after a cricket match when Lytton, too drunk even to speak, had been hurled into a cell alongside this handsome brown man whose only crime, Lytton was to discover later, seemed to have been in allowing the girlfriend of the chief of police to seduce him. At least that was how Hamil had put it. On release the following day they had become firm friends, a friendship which had survived many a scrape, not least Hamil's bungled attempt to become the owner of a Rolls-Royce motor car which officially belonged to Lytton's employers.

'You can't drink in Sybia any more,' said Hamil, enjoying his brandy. 'Whenever any of us goes out of the country for a couple of days he comes back with a blinding hangover he knows which has to last him for the next couple of years.'

Lytton helped himself to another drink. 'Well, one thing's certain. They'll never be able to make a religious zealot out of you.'

It was only later, when Lytton was bidding goodnight to Hamil as they stood by the hotel lifts, both as drunk as they had been in a very long time, that Hamil began to confide in Lytton. 'You know, I said I was here to attend a conference on famine relief,' he said, as they leant heavily against the wall waiting for the lift to arrive. 'Well, that's only half the reason. I'm also supposed to be helping in a deal with a chap called Westaway.'

Lytton was never too drunk not to recognize a story when it came his way. 'You mean Fixit Westaway, the MP?' he asked. 'He's some sort of catalyst, isn't he?'

'He's a crook,' said Hamil bluntly.

Lytton hesitated. 'If you're doing a deal with him are you sure you should be telling me this?'

Hamil nodded his head vigorously. 'I don't like to do business with crooks,' he said. 'Don't worry. I'm not drunk. What I'm going to tell you is the absolute truth. But you must confirm it yourself. All right?'

Lytton was not at all sure that it was all right. Some of the fundamentalist Middle Eastern countries were known to have singularly brutal ways of dealing with those subjects who did not see things quite like their governments. But Hamil was unafraid. He said: 'When you work for fanatics you sometimes wish that fate would take a hand and torpedo your efforts. Do you understand me?'

A lift arrived and then left. 'You mean you want to scuttle your own deal?' asked Lytton.

Hamil nodded: 'Something like that. But whatever happens, no one must ever know that I'm your source. All right?'

Lytton grinned. 'All right,' he said. 'What's Fixit Westaway been up to this time?'

Lytton put the Diary staff on to the Westaway story first thing the following morning, although his head was spinning from dehydration. First David tried to call Westaway, and then Pandora rang him. But he was unavailable. Finally Dolly found someone in a Hampshire arms factory who was almost prepared to admit that he was not prepared to talk to the press. It was the usual case of beating one's head against an unopening door.

'Let's go through it from the top, shall we?' Lytton suggested, after a couple of days of fruitless research.

David began. 'Tom Westaway, well connected MP, looks up an old pal from Cambridge while on a fact-finding trip to Sybia. The pal introduces him to –'

Dolly took up the story: '– the minister in charge of the environment who immediately hires him as a consultant in a big desert reclamation scheme –'

It was Pandora's turn: '– and pays £50,000 into his Swiss bank account –'

'– for which Westaway pretends to be a consultant on something he knows absolutely nothing about –' said Lytton.

At the far end of the desk Norman looked up from the page he was subbing. 'Like some of our specialist reporters,' he said. 'They get expenses as well, though.'

Lytton ignored him. '– while really running an elaborate scheme for getting export licenses for new generators for Sybia's British-built nuclear reactors.'

Pandora raised her head. She was the only person who dared admit that she could not quite follow the scheme of things. 'Forgive me if I'm being particularly dense,' she apologized (Dolly smiled and nodded to herself), 'but why can't the Sybians buy their generators through the front door like everybody else?'

'Good question,' said Lytton, immediately sitting on Dolly's arrogance. 'Apparently the present government there is on a Whitehall blacklist. We used to like them. Now we don't.'

'And they're stuck with a nuclear plant needing new parts which our lot won't sell,' explained Dolly, illustrating neatly the advantages of living with a man on *The Guardian*.

'This £50,000 ...?' began David. Money fascinated him.

'Untaxed, unacknowledged, straight into a numbered account in Zurich,' said Lytton. 'What d'you think, Norman? This good enough for you?'

Norman shook his head. 'Not really. It's all very Deep Throatish, if you ask me. Insight stuff. The lawyer'll never wear it.'

He was right. While Cruickshank licked his lips and savoured every nuance of the story (although the *Daily News* was a Tory newspaper, that didn't stop him from enjoying any whiff of scandal which might attach itself to the thoroughly unpleasant brigade of smooth-talking spivs whom he saw to be prospering under Margaret Thatcher's brand of Conservatism), the lawyer bade extreme caution. 'It seems to me you've based the entire story on the evidence of some shadowy figure,' he warned.

'He isn't shadowy to me, and anyway we've done a lot of checking on Westaway,' said Lytton. 'We've also tried to talk to him eight times this week, but he's refusing to see us.'

'Are you sure you aren't getting mixed up in a personal vendetta, Lytton?' the lawyer asked.

'Absolutely certain,' said Lytton. He trusted Hamil completely.

'Well, I don't think the story's anywhere near firm enough yet,' said the lawyer, to which the editor agreed. It was, he thought, however, interesting enough for the

Diary to continue their pursuance of Westaway. 'Let's see if we can't smoke him out, eh, Lytton?' he winked. 'Push him until he comes out into the open and talks to us. Run a few hints now, and then a bit more later in the week. Drip, drip, drip ... what d'you think?'

So it went for the rest of that week and into the next, first one tiny piece of information and then another. It was a campaign of attrition. Westaway was doorstepped when he left his house and when he got to Westminster, while every company remotely connected with the sales of nuclear reactors was pestered repeatedly by members of the Diary. Lytton was pleased, and he assumed Hamil must be happy, too, although they had not spoken since their initial meeting.

Meanwhile the first edition of *Cyclops* under the new editorship was published. It was vicious stuff. 'Toady must be spinning in his grave,' chuckled David at the misfortune of those selected as Beauchamp's first targets.

'I'm afraid whatever Tim Beauchamp absorbed at Toady's knee, it was neither the milk of human kindness nor lessons in the art of moderation. He's a real, one hundred per cent *laissez-faire* swine,' said Lytton.

'Quite funny, though.' David showed Lytton a page. 'They describe Henry Field here as quality control officer at the *Daily Post* sewage plant.'

'Poor Henry. He went to the wrong type of school. Those snobs at *Cyclops* will never forgive him for that.'

But later when he ran into Henry in the Galley Proof he could not resist the temptation to tease him about it.

'I suppose you're enjoying all this *Cyclops* stuff, aren't you, Lytton?' Henry was mortified by the teasing he had had to suffer at the hands of his colleagues on the *Daily Post*.

'It does have a certain comic vulgarity.'

'We'll see,' said Henry. 'Anyway, what's all this nonsense about Westaway you're pushing? It's a bit heavy for your gang of layabouts, isn't it?'

'Is it?' asked Lytton, and smiled.

The next day a warning shot was fired at Lytton by a partnership of solicitors in Chancery Lane who were acting for Tom Westaway. Colin Griffin, the lawyer, read it out to Lytton. Their main complaint was that the continued press campaign against their client by Lytton's Diary amounted to press harrassment, and they let it be known that unless a retraction of the smear against him was published forthwith they would have no alternative but to start legal proceedings.

The Diary obviously had Westaway rattled, but were still short of hard facts. If Westaway was a crook they had yet to prove it.

Reluctantly Lytton phoned Hamil. He needed more help, he explained. For some reason Hamil did not now seem so keen on pursuing his Deep Throat role, even claiming that it was dangerous to be seen in public or even to speak by hotel telephone to Lytton. ('Sybian spies are everywhere,' he whispered.) To Lytton, however, it was too late to back out of the story. If he were to let the case drop now Cruickshank would string him up by his ears, he explained, and Westaway's lawyers would have a treat. He then added that if Hamil were unhappy about being seen with him he knew the best rendezvous for them in London: somewhere none of Hamil's fundamentalist Islamic brethren would ever dream of going.

They met in the pew nearest the altar in St Paul's, Covent Garden. Toady, thought Lytton affectionately, would have approved of a campaign against Westaway being planned from such a place.

To Lytton's surprise Hamil was, however, no longer the gossipy, suave pal he had met for dinner the previous week. He looked worried and nervous and did his level best to persuade Lytton to drop the whole story before it became an embarrassment. 'Perhaps you're digging too deep,' he worried. 'You can't tell where it's going to lead you. I'd no idea you were so dedicated. I only intended that there should be a little warning so that Westaway ...' He stopped.

'Yes?' asked Lytton.

'Oh nothing,' said Hamil.

Lytton, seeing that their conversation had reached a dead end, and irritated by the change in Hamil's attitude, got up to go. 'By the way, what are you doing tomorrow night?' he asked.

'Oh, a business dinner.' Hamil quickly found an excuse. 'Why?'

'Nothing really. My girlfriend's away in Brazil and it's my birthday. I thought we might kill a few bottles together. Anyway, it's just as well. You'd only have led me into more mischief.'

With that they went their separate ways, Hamil to worry, and Lytton to work further on the Westaway affair. Like all such stories it had now developed a momentum of its own. With or without Hamil's help, Lytton was determined to get to the bottom of it.

Lytton had spent better birthdays, there was no doubting that. Sitting over his typewriter at nine in the evening was not his idea of a big celebration. He had hoped to find someone with whom he might have spent a couple of hours, but no one was free. And in the absence of Laura, who had called earlier to wish him happy birthday and say that she had done her piece on the revolutionary priests and was off to Rio de Janeiro to investigate beach culture, he resigned himself to a lonely evening with his novel.

He had been working enthusiastically for nearly an hour when the telephone rang. 'Hello?' he said, glad of the interruption.

A young woman's voice greeted him. 'Er, is that 727 4239?'

Lytton said that it was. He didn't recognize the voice.

'I'm terribly sorry to bother you but I've just got home and found this number on my Ansaphone. But unfortunately it doesn't say who I'm supposed to be calling.'

Lytton was both puzzled and amused by the call. The young woman's hesitant manner was almost attractive. 'Well, my name's Neville Lytton,' he said. 'Who are you?'

There was a slight gasp of surprise. 'Oh no, I feel such a fool. I mean, well, I read you every day. I'm a great admirer. Oh gosh, I'm so embarrassed. I'm afraid a trick's been played on me. I'm sorry to have troubled you.'

'It's no trouble.' Lytton was now thoroughly intrigued. 'What sort of trick do you mean?'

'Well, I told a friend that I'd really like to meet you. I once did, actually, at a party, but I don't think you'd remember me. Obviously she's tried to do me a favour.'

'You say we met once?' Lytton was enjoying this.

'A couple of years ago. I was working as a model and you came to a reception at the Dorchester. I'm sure you didn't notice me. I'm terribly sorry to have interrupted your evening.'

Interested already, Lytton's ears pricked up at the news that his mystery caller had worked as a model. Glamour still had charm. 'Oh, it's no interruption at all,' he said, turning off his electric typewriter with his free hand. 'Look, if you're still interested in meeting me, and you've nothing better to do, why don't we have a drink sometime? Tonight even?'

'Oh no, I couldn't.'

'Come on, it's my birthday. I insist.' She hadn't refused him. He knew she wouldn't now.

She didn't. They met at a corner table in the Goodtimes Bar. She was prettier than he had dared expect, fair, well dressed, demure, even a little shy at first, which seemed odd in such a good-looking woman. She was aged about thirty and said her name was Stella.

134

'Well, Stella, you've saved me from a dismal night chained to a typewriter,' he told her.

'You shouldn't have been working on your birthday. What were you doing?'

'Trying to write my first novel, I'm afraid,' Lytton admitted. 'Every journalist's fantasy is to write a bestseller and spend his days idling around the Caribbean, drinking too much rum punch and complaining about how hard life is as a tax exile.'

'You mean you want to be like one of the people you write about?'

'I suppose that's the pipe dream.'

'And then you'd have people like Neville Lytton charting your every move.'

Lytton smiled. He relished the idea. 'Or Henry Field.'

'This really is a treat for me,' said Stella a little later as she enjoyed her second Sundowner.

Lytton was flattered. All around men and women were indulging in extremely heavy chatting. It made him feel young and carefree. 'It's a jolly nice surprise for me, too, to be honest. You said you used to be a model. What d'you do now?'

Stella shook her head. 'Not enough. I was married. Now I'm not.'

'And is that how you wanted it?'

Stella's lips turned down at the corners. 'It can be a little lonely at times. What about you?'

'Oh yes, I get lonely too.'

'I meant are you happy with your life?'

Lytton chose to be oblique. 'Happiness is putting the page to bed,' he said. Then, sensing her confusion, he explained. 'It's a newspaper phrase. When you put your page to bed it means that you've finished everything for the night, the print has been set and put in place and you can leave the office safe in the knowledge that there's nothing more to be done.'

Stella stirred her drink slowly. 'And when you've put the paper to bed . . . ?' she asked.

They left the bar at around twelve. Lytton had intended dropping her off at her flat in Leinster Square, but he needed little encouragement to go inside for another drink when she suggested it. After all, it was his birthday.

'You didn't tell me what your novel's about,' remarked Stella as she poured them both more drinks from a well stocked bar. It was a small but very attractive flat, modern in dressing, with varnished floorboards, rugs, brightly coloured impressionist prints and low angular furniture. She had obviously got a good settlement when she and her husband divorced, thought Lytton.

'Well, Fleet Street, I suppose,' he said, answering her question. 'I'm trying to write one of those big fat American paperbacks. It's all about a chap who writes a gossip column on a popular morning newspaper. Of course, I'm having to jazz up the locations a bit and give him a bit more style.'

'It sounds marvellous.'

'It's rubbish, actually,' corrected Lytton, with a laugh. 'I only hope it's rubbishy enough for me to make a couple of million out of it. I keep wondering whether Robert Redford would like to play the part in the film.'

'Wouldn't his American accent be a problem?' asked Stella. She was now sitting quite close to him. She seemed much more relaxed than she had done in the bar.

'Don't spoil my fantasies.'

'And what about women? How does your hero handle them?' she asked, adding before Lytton could reply: 'All those big paperbacks have men of indefatigable appetites.'

'Well, yes, my man's a bit of a lad, too. Of course it's never his fault. It's all these sexy ladies he keeps running into who insist upon falling head over heels in lust with him.'

'And this character, is he based upon anybody we might recognize?'

'Well, I dare say he does share one or two characteristics with someone not entirely unknown in the Street of Shame.'

A long silence followed. At last Stella said: 'I'm really glad I finally met you. Really glad.'

'Yes, it does seem to have been one of the more happy coincidences of recent days,' he replied.

Stella put her drink down and looked at Lytton firmly, as though suddenly having reached an important decision. 'When I got divorced my husband gave me one little piece of advice. "Take your opportunities, Stella," he said, "because if you don't you will miss out on the stuff of life." Do you know what I mean?'

Lytton thought he knew exactly what she meant. They finished their drinks. 'Happy birthday,' Stella said, and kissed him.

The following few days dragged as Lytton continued to pursue the elusive Westaway connection with Sybia. A couple of times he considered calling Stella, but while he had enjoyed his first encounter with her he did not think it advisable to become more deeply involved. So he kept his head down and worked very hard, even though Laura called to say that she had decided to stay in Brazil for a third week to do some additional research.

Whatever Lytton might have imagined that further research to be was, however, quite driven from his mind with the publication of the latest *Cyclops*, Tim Beauchamp's second edition as editor. David Sellier saw it first and brought it to Lytton while he was lunching in the Galley Proof with Pandora. 'I think you ought to see this,' David said, trying hard to keep a straight face, and dropped the magazine on to the table.

'What's that –?' Lytton broke off from the joke he was telling Pandora to look at the magazine. The joke was never to be continued. Lytton's face froze as he looked at the front cover. It contained a full sized picture of himself: the headline ran TOP GOSSIP HACK IN SECRET LOVE NEST. The story was printed across the middle pages, and accompanied by a picture of Stella and another headline: HE TOLD ME HE WAS GOING TO BE A FAMOUS NOVELIST: I WAS FLATTERED . . .

While David did his best not to giggle, Lytton read the piece. As he did a familiar figure appeared at the bar, also carrying a copy of the new *Cyclops*. It was Henry Field.

Without saying a word to his rival, but standing close enough for Lytton to hear, and having equipped himself with a drink and an audience of chums from the *Daily Post*, Henry began to read the *Cyclops* story in a loud and fruity voice. It was his moment of glee.

'"Colleagues of top Fleet Street gossip hack Neville Lytton will be interested to discover that the aging Adonis has, in the absence of his sometime paramour Laura Grey, taken to visiting a lady of questionable virtue at her Bayswater boudoir,"' he read. Guffaws rang round the bar. Lytton turned his head away. Henry continued. '"Lytton, whose characteristics include an occasional holier-than-thou righteousness, is, it seems, not averse to taking consolation for his loneliness in the bed of a highly paid courtesan.

'"Now former 'model' Stella Clover, 30, is regaling other ladies of the night with stories of how Lytton told her he was soon to become a famous novelist. Fortunately for her La Clover anticipated the dirty diarist's denials and, she claims, had the presence of mind to photograph the lonely Lothario – pictures *Cyclops* is eagerly awaiting. Read next week's *Cyclops* when all may be revealed."'

'Of course, it's completely untrue,' blushed Lytton to David and Pandora, who was now looking at the magazine.

'Oh completely.' Pandora was also having difficulty not to laugh.

138

'Well, virtually. I mean I did meet some woman at the Goodtimes ... I thought she might be a good contact, but ...'

Virtually simultaneously Pandora and David began to giggle.

'Oh, come on, both of you, grow up. It isn't funny,' snapped Lytton.

'Sorry, Lytton, but actually it's very funny indeed,' said David.

'But nothing happened and there are certainly no pictures.'

'Well if it isn't Fleet Street's own little ladies' man.' Henry Field had joined them and was crowing over Lytton. 'Well done, Lytton. I always knew you'd be a star.'

'Get stuffed, Henry.'

But Henry had not finished. 'It's terribly good for your image, you know. Some of the girls in our office thought you might be getting a bit past it, but –'

'You're not funny. You know as well as I do that it's a put up job.'

Henry enjoyed this even more. 'Of course it is. She trapped you, didn't she? I bet you put up a hell of a fight defending your virtue. That must have been an epic struggle. It's very flattering really. No one has ever tried to lure me into a house of ill repute.'

'It was an ordinary flat.' Lytton was becoming careless in his annoyance.

Henry leapt on the admission. 'Oh, so you *did* go back with her. Well, well, well ...' Then turning to his pals Henry said in a very loud voice. 'I think Lytton's trying to tell us he was seduced by a wanton harlot driven mad by desire for his body. Poor chap.'

And amid the general hilarity Henry returned to the bar to show again the story of Lytton's seduction.

One person did not consider the story on the front page of *Cyclops* to be amusing – at least, if he did, he chose not to show it. Ian Cruickshank, as editor of the *Daily News*, had a deeply puritanical streak running through him, most certainly when it came to the behaviour of his staff, although he would absolutely have denied such a charge; and he wasted no time in summoning Lytton to his office after the magazine had been brought to his attention during lunch that day at the Garrick Club. 'So you think you were purposely lured into a situation which could have compromised you, do you, Neville?' he mused.

'Had there been anything to compromise me over, that would appear to be the only explanation.'

'And you've no idea who might want to do that?'

'None at all. It doesn't seem to make any sense. Of course it's all highly libellous. The lawyer's already –'

Cruickshank broke in. He didn't want to know what the lawyer had to say. 'Personally I've always felt it demeaning when journalists sue each other,' he said. 'It doesn't always work either. Look at laddie down the road at the *Daily Express*. It cost him a fortune. Can you afford that kind of money?'

'Well, I had thought perhaps the paper might . . .'

The editor shook his head firmly. The paper would obviously not be bearing any costs in a libel action. 'And you say nothing happened with this young lady?' he pressed, interested now in the steamy details.

'Well, of course not.'

'I see, because while in the normal course of events a man's personal life is obviously of no concern to his employers, our proprietor has already made it clear to me that he doesn't like the idea of one of our star names being seen to be consorting with common prostitutes.'

Lytton was astounded: 'He said that? Wayne Monroe had the cheek to say that?'

'Or words to that effect,' Cruickshank went on.

'That must be the most hypocritical thing I've ever heard,' said Lytton. 'Only a few months ago he was having it off right, left and centre with Sabrina Wallis and God knows who else.'

Cruickshank's expression hardened. 'Proprietors have a franchise on hypocrisy, you should know that by now. His feelings, and I must say I agree with him, are that since you're writing for a family newspaper he'd be very pleased to see the whole matter cleared up pretty pronto.'

'Even though I didn't –' began Lytton.

'The truth of the matter is immaterial. The only thing worrying us is the good name of the *Daily News*. Look at it from our point of view, Neville. And anyway, who would want to frame you?'

'I haven't the foggiest idea but I mean to find out,' said Lytton getting to his feet.

'And hopefully before the next edition of *Cyclops* is printed. We don't want our diarist in a delicate position all over the front of this sordid little magazine, do we?'

Lytton stopped by the door. 'You can tell Mr Monroe that if there's one thing I've never done in my life it's have my picture taken in the nude,' he said firmly. 'It isn't my style.'

The editor looked at him over the glasses he had put on to read some proofs. 'I'm sure he'll be very pleased to hear it,' he said.

Lytton was more angry than he could remember. Striding across the editorial office he ignored the Diary desk, where he could see Jenny giggling with Dolly over a copy of *Cyclops*, and headed straight down the stairs and out of the building. The *Cyclops* office was only a short taxi ride away in a rent-controlled building in Neal Street. Without waiting to be announced by the switchboard girl who sat at the door and also acted as part-time typist, he marched into the small back room where Tim Beauchamp now edited.

'All right, what the hell are you playing at?' stormed Lytton, as Beauchamp looked calmly up at him.

'Hello, Lytton. Just in time for tea. Kathleen, tea time, love,' Beauchamp called to the bean pole lady who sat in an adjacent office. Jacko, sitting at an artist's desk and drawing a caricature of Richard Ingrams, grinned a welcome.

'Never mind the bloody tea. You've just made me the laughing stock of London, you snivelling little creep.'

Beauchamp shook his head. 'Yes, sorry about that, Lytton. There wasn't anything we could do, was there, Jacko?'

'What d'you mean, "nothing you could do"?' Lytton was aghast at the arrogance of the man.

'Well, you read it old boy,' said Beauchamp casually. 'It was too good to throw away, wasn't it?'

'It's a wonderful story,' agreed Jacko, still grinning.

'But you didn't even check it with me,' said Lytton.

'Of course not. You'd have denied it. We checked it with her.'

'She was more than helpful,' Jacko came in.

Lytton looked at the pair of them: two cowboys of satire and smut. 'Who set me up, Tim?' he asked.

Beauchamp shook his head happily. 'I dunno.'

'But where did the story come from?' Lytton was now speaking in a very loud voice.

'Anonymous letter. The usual form. Someone thought we might be interested. They were right, we were fascinated.'

'Doesn't it concern you that the piece was grossly libellous ...?'

'Not really,' smiled Beauchamp. 'The publicity would be very useful if you sued.'

'... or that someone is using you to smear me?'

Beauchamp leant back in his chair and folded his arms. 'Should it? We print gossip, Lytton. You may look upon your work as having some higher social value, just like poor old Toady. But you're wrong. Both of you. The readers don't give a monkey's for ideals. They just want to know who's screwing who.'

'That's right: who's screwing who,' chorused Jacko.

'And that's what we give them – us in our way, you in yours. And you don't like it because you've been caught with your pants down. Well, hard luck.'

Jacko nodded. 'Tough bun, Nev.'

'Toady would never have –' Lytton began, but was not allowed to finish.

'But Toady's dead, Lytton. It's just us merry pranksters here now. And we don't give a damn. Right, Jacko?'

Kathleen appeared at the door with three cups of tea. 'How civilized,' said Beauchamp. 'Tea and tantrums.'

Lytton did not feel like tea. He actually felt like breaking Beauchamp's neck. 'I don't want to disappoint you,' he snapped, 'but you might as well know there are no pictures of me. Whoever sent you the letter was having you on.' And with a curt nod to Kathleen he walked out, but not before there was a burble of laughter from Jacko.

'Poor old Lytton,' he heard him say, 'he can give it but he can't take it.'

Lytton was thoughtful that afternoon. But then he had a great deal to think about. Why on earth should anyone wish to set him up? he asked himself. It was all so elaborate. The telephone call, the flirting in the Goodtimes Bar. Had it happened to anyone else he would have been able to see the funny side of it. But it had happened to him. He had been taken advantage of by – what was it *Cyclops* had called her? – 'a highly paid courtesan ... a lady of the night.' But why?

'Is everything all right, Lytton? You're very quiet,' said Jenny as Lytton pondered the situation, a task not made easier by the constant backslapping of reporters and sub-editors who, having passed *Cyclops* between them, were anxious to exploit Lytton's embarrassment to the full.

'Everything's absolutely perfect, thank you,' replied Lytton stuffily, trying not to be seen to be upset in front of her, and failing completely. Thank God Laura was not there, he told himself, and then realized that had she been the incident with Stella would never have happened.

'Present for you, Lytton.' Wesley loped across the office and dropped a large manilla reinforced envelope on to his desk. Lytton pushed it to one side towards Jenny.

'It's marked "personal",' noticed Jenny. 'D'you want me to open it?'

Nine times out of ten Lytton would have told her to go ahead. On this occasion his guardian angel was alert to the danger. Taking it back from her, Lytton slipped a paper knife under the seal and cut open the envelope. He glanced inside. There was a contact sheet of photographs. Suddenly he looked closer. Slipping the sheet out he looked at the top row of pictures. His heart froze.

'Anything interesting?' asked Jenny.

Hastily Lytton pushed the sheet back into the envelope. He was trembling. 'No,' he lied. In the envelope was a whole sheet of photographs showing him and Stella naked and making love. He hadn't known it but he had had his picture taken in the nude. 'I think I'll get myself a coffee,' he muttered, and hurried across the floor, clutching the envelope tightly. Jenny and Wesley watched him with astonishment. Lytton never got his own drinks.

Lytton didn't stop by the coffee machine but continued up the back stairs to a remote landing. He needed time to be alone and to think. Assuring himself that he was not about to be interrupted he again withdrew the sheet of contacts from the envelope and studied them. They had been taken over a period of a couple of hours while he and Stella had been in her bedroom. An infra-red camera must have been used by someone watching from a peephole, the angle of which suggested that it had been somewhere above the foot of the bed. Quite apart from

144

the fact that he had been set up, Lytton also now felt a chill of fear as he realized that he and Stella had not been alone in the flat. Then he noticed something else in the envelope. It was a small white card, no bigger than a calling card. It bore no name or address, simply a typed message. 'Lay off Westaway or *Cyclops* gets these,' he read. For the first time the affair began to make sense.

He met Hamil in the church again. He needed to talk to someone he could trust. That Westaway should be trying to blackmail him to stop his inquiries would have been unthinkable were it not happening.

'It's all right, I'm a Muslim not a Catholic. I don't want to hear your confession,' said Hamil as Lytton briefly explained the evening with Stella. He was still embarrassed by it, not least that he had at first lied about what had happened. Hamil looked at the card, but did not seem very interested in the pictures, glancing casually at them and handing them back to Lytton, for which Lytton was grateful. Hamil was a tactful friend.

'If *Cyclops* get their hands on these I'll be the laughing stock of Fleet Street,' fretted Lytton. 'They wouldn't be able to resist them. I wouldn't be surprised if the Rabid Dingo didn't find some excuse to sack me ... not the sort of chap he wants writing in his paper.'

'You couldn't appeal to *Cyclops*?' asked Hamil.

'What d'you mean? Rat to rat? No hope. They think I'm a reactionary-old-pussy-footer-in-the-door and they're the brave new assault troops of gossip.'

Hamil went silent for a moment. Then he put a friendly hand on Lytton's arm. 'There's only one thing you can do. You've got to drop the Westaway campaign. It's my fault for ever having mentioned it.'

Lytton was completely astounded. 'I can't do that. I can't give in to blackmail.' The thought had never even occurred to him.

'And you can't let *Cyclops* get these photographs. You'd be finished. Take my advice. Leave it alone. It's not worth it.'

Lytton was hardly listening. This wasn't the kind of advice he needed at all. 'I just can't imagine who would have gone to all this trouble,' he worried.

'You've been upsetting a great many people recently,' said Hamil. 'Do yourself a favour. Forget about the whole Westaway affair. I don't want to see you made a fool of. Do it for me.'

Lytton smiled at his old friend. It was good to see that Hamil cared so much for him after all these years. But he shook his head: 'I can't.'

He caught up with Westaway late that afternoon in the Dolphin Square pool, a private exercising ground for many Members of Parliament who had homes in the Pimlico area of London. Westaway was swimming backwards and forwards along the length of the pool, wearing a white cap to keep his hair dry and tiny goggles.

'I want to talk to you, Mr Westaway.' Lytton stared down at the MP as he reached for the steps to climb out of the water.

'What? Who the hell d'you think you are?' demanded Westaway, with all the bumptiousness of the over-confident.

'I'm the chap you're trying to blackmail,' replied Lytton.

'You're out of your mind.'

Lytton bent down at the side of the pool, blocking Westaway's escape from the water. 'If you think you can frighten me, you're wrong. I know everything there is about your crooked export licence deals, and I'm going to write it.'

Westaway looked at him. He was less arrogant now, more bewildered. 'You're Lytton, aren't you? You're mad.'

Lytton nodded. 'I'll say I'm mad. I'm mad with being made a fool of. Now will you get out of the water before I pull you out?'

They talked while Westaway dressed, the MP in the changing cubicle, Lytton outside the door. Westaway would have preferred more privacy but Lytton was damned if he was going to let the little weasel out of his sight. At first Westaway was nervous and confused, but bit by bit Lytton became aware that Westaway was gaining the upper hand, and very quickly the gloating confidence returned.

'You're making a big mistake, you know,' Westaway said. 'Even if I thought blackmail would work I wouldn't use it against someone like you. It leaves too many traces. You may not believe me but I honestly know nothing about any of this.'

'But your associates ... they must be involved ...'

Westaway cut him off. 'None of them would have the imagination to have dreamed up this. I must say I'd love to meet my benefactor. He's terribly clever. Perhaps you'll leave me alone now.' Suddenly he laughed. 'You know, I'd say it's rather a case of the biter being bitten, wouldn't you, Mr Lytton?'

Lytton left the pool in despair. There was no doubt that Westaway, for all his deviousness in his work for Sybia, was telling the truth about the photographs.

Lytton spent the evening alone in his flat. Complaining of a bad cold he had left a message with Jenny that he was not to be disturbed, and retired away from the bantering jokes with which he would most certainly be greeted had he gone to either of the parties to which he had been invited. Most of all he needed time to think. If Westaway hadn't set him up, who had? No answers came to him. He looked again at the contact sheet. Stella was a very pretty girl. Too pretty for what she did for a living. And he wondered how a girl like that could become involved in prostitution. He put the pictures away again with an inward shudder. Henry would have a field day if *Cyclops* ever published those, he thought.

He went back to the Goodtimes Bar at just before midnight. He had not intended to brazen it out with Stella in a public place, but after getting no answer at her home he had no real alternative. Every minute counted if he was to prevent the negatives of their evening together going to *Cyclops*.

He found her standing by the piano player in the corner of the bar complaining about the price she had had to pay to have her car serviced. He had noticed in the earlier conversation that money and the cost of things played a large part in her consciousness. 'Hello, it was a Sundowner, wasn't it?' he asked, coming up behind her. Then, not waiting for her to answer, he turned to the bar girl: 'That's a Sundowner for my friend, and a Scotch on the rocks for me.'

Stella tried to wriggle past him, but the space between the back of the piano and the bar was too small. 'Sorry. I'm late. I've got to go. Could you let me . . . ?'

'No, I couldn't,' said Lytton. 'You aren't going anywhere.' And putting an arm out he led her firmly towards an empty corner of the bar. The pianist, a middle aged man with a toupée, smiled a welcome and went back to his piano playing. He had obviously not read *Cyclops*. 'Now. I know it wasn't Westaway, so who was it?' Lytton asked, keeping one hand firmly gripped on her forearm.

'What?'

'Who paid for my birthday present and who took the pictures?' asked Lytton.

Stella smiled: 'Oh come on. I'm a tart, I couldn't tell you that. Tricks of the trade. It would be unprofessional.'

'If you don't tell me I'm liable to start being unprofessional with you.'

Stella smiled again. 'I don't think so. You're a gentleman. I knew that the minute I saw you.'

'Well, if you don't mind my saying, you're hardly a lady.' He had released her arm. She rubbed it gently.

'Sorry, but a girl can't afford to turn down work. It's been a very thin summer. I should have gone to Menton with my friend.'

'The one who gave you my phone number?'

Stella laughed: 'What? Oh no, I just said that to make you interested. I could hardly have rung up and said I wanted to meet you. I gave a good performance, didn't I? My mother always wanted me to be an actress.'

'How did you know I'd fall for it?'

'What? A man like you? With your girlfriend away in Brazil and sitting there all by yourself on your birthday? You were a certainty, Neville.'

She didn't even realize the slip she had made. 'How did you know it was my birthday?' asked Lytton.

Stella was still smiling. 'You told me. Don't you remember?'

'I told you after you telephoned me.'

Quickly Stella tried to recover her ground. 'Well, I must have read it somewhere ...' she began. Then quickly she darted past him. 'I've got to go ...' she said, and before he could stop her she had slipped through a door at the back of the bar. Lytton began to follow, but the bar girl blocked the way.

'Would you like another one, or is it going to be an early night?' she asked.

It turned out to be a very late night. At four o'clock he finally got through to Laura in Brazil. He had been calling since midnight. 'Can you hear me, Laura?' he shouted: he could hear someone else in the room.

'Oh yes.' Laura sounded surprised. 'I'm sorry, I was just ... just doing something. How are you?'

'Is there someone with you? I thought ...' Lytton still felt he did not have Laura's undivided attention.

'Oh no. Just the maid. She was turning down the bed.'

Lytton was satisfied. 'Look, Laura, try to think hard, will you? Did you tell anyone about my birthday?'

'What?'

'Just think. Perhaps you let it slip in the office or the Galley Proof. You didn't tell Henry, did you?'

Laura giggled. 'No, of course not. You're always so funny about your birthday, afraid that people will discover how old you really are.'

Lytton ignored her levity. 'Are you really sure?'

'Of course I'm sure. What is this?' demanded Laura, but Lytton's mind was racing ahead.

'Have a lovely time. Bye,' he said and put down the phone. Then, for the first time in many hours, he smiled.

Neville Lytton was the last person Kathleen would have expected to see so early in the morning outside the *Cyclops* offices, particularly after the way Beauchamp and Jacko had behaved to him on his last visit. She had always liked Lytton. He'd been a great favourite of Toady, God bless his soul.

'I'm sorry, Mr Lytton, Mr Beauchamp doesn't get in so early in the day,' she apologized as she discovered him loitering on the steps and holding an envelope just before nine.

Lytton was also carrying the milk. 'Kathleen, you know that scurrilous story about me ...'

Kathleen was embarrassed: 'I'm sorry about that. I did my best. But Mr Beauchamp was adamant. Of course, I didn't believe a word of it,' she gabbled as she led the way up the stairs.

'Well, unhappily ...' They had reached the landing. Slowly Lytton drew the sheet of contacts out of the envelope and showed it to her.

Kathleen's eyes widened as she stared at the thirty-six separate frames showing Lytton and Stella.

'Oh, Mr Lytton,' she murmured.

Lytton rested one hand on hers. 'Kathleen,' he asked, speaking quietly, 'I wonder, could you do me a very great personal favour?'

Kathleen looked again at the photographs and then the hand. 'Oh, Mr Lytton,' she repeated, and opened the door to let him into the office.

After that things began to move more quickly. While the rest of the Diary staff concentrated upon pursuing the daily trivia, Lytton threw himself into the Westaway affair, and by the following Tuesday had the basis of a very good story. 'MP breaks Middle East export embargo,' he dictated to Norman giving him six folios of copy. 'Sit on this, will you, until you hear from me. With any luck I'll be on to you in a couple of hours with a lot more. If we're unlucky we can go on the usual old rubbish. David and Dolly have got lots of that, I'm sure.'

Norman nodded. He was not at all sure what Lytton was up to, but he wished him well. The man deserved a break after being lampooned so cruelly in *Cyclops*.

On the way out of the office, accompanied by a photographer, Lytton bumped into the editor who asked if he had managed to scotch the *Cyclops* rumours. Lytton said he was working on it.

'Well, don't take too long, will you? Mr Monroe's very worried about it and *Cyclops* is due out tomorrow. I don't think our proprietor could stand the shock of another exclusive.'

'Hypocritical old bastards,' thought Lytton to himself as he hurried down the stairs.

He met Kathleen as they had arranged by the National Film Theatre. She was sitting on an outside bench watching the traffic on the river when Lytton reached her.

Alongside her was a very large carefully sealed envelope. Lytton sat beside her.

Kathleen was reminiscing. 'Toady always said he'd had the fun years. I'm glad he died when he did. He didn't like the look of the future at all. "Too brash," he used to say, "the world has become vulgar and brash and *Cyclops* will be dragged down with everything else."'

Lytton had to interrupt. 'The favour I wanted ... there was no problem, was there?'

Kathleen handed him the envelope. 'No. I did as you asked. Everything's here.'

'You've been very kind,' said Lytton, taking it from her.

'Let's just say I did it for Toady. I can't imagine how it will help you, but I think he would have approved.'

'I'm sure he would,' said Lytton, and, peeping inside, smiled in relief at the contents.

After that it took just one telephone call to bring the whole matter to a head. The call was to Hamil. They met just a few yards further along the South Bank in the terrace bar of the National Theatre. 'Nice view, isn't it?' said Lytton, with exaggerated calm.

Hamil looked furtively around him. 'I'm not at all sure that we should be seen together,' he fretted.

'Oh I wouldn't worry about that any more if I were you, Hamil,' Lytton chuckled, and pulled up a chair for his old friend to sit on.

'Neville, I'm very busy,' Hamil protested as he sat down.

'Really? What are you doing? Packing, are you, perhaps?'

'Well, as a matter of fact I *was* thinking of going home tomorrow.'

'Oh, that's nice. Back to the fanatics. Weather warm in Sybia at this time of the year, is it?'

Hamil was perplexed by Lytton's attitude. 'Well, yes, of course. It's always warm.'

'Oh, good, perhaps I'll be able to come too and spend some time with you,' said Lytton. 'I'd like to meet the wife and all the little Hamils.'

'What?' Hamil was completely lost.

Lytton looked at him sourly, and then passed him a rolled up magazine. 'I lost my job,' he said. The magazine uncurled. It was *Cyclops*. On the front cover was a photograph of Lytton and Stella taken in the bedroom. The headline read: CAUGHT: THE KING OF GOSSIP.

Hamil gazed at the magazine in shock. 'Oh my God,' he gasped.

Lytton waited for him to turn to the centre spread where there was another selection of photographs from Lytton's private birthday party. 'What I don't understand is why, Hamil? I thought we were friends,' said Lytton at last.

Hamil began to stammer. He was bewildered. 'But Neville ... I didn't ... I don't understand ...'

'Oh come on. Don't tell me lies. Not after all these years. You set me up with that girl, didn't you?'

'Well, yes, but I promise you, Neville, I didn't give these pictures to *Cyclops*. It must have been the girl.' Hamil looked again at the magazine as though still scarcely able to believe what he was seeing. 'I'm sorry. I really am, Neville. I never wanted this.'

'But what exactly did you want?' asked Lytton, leaning forward slightly in his chair.

'Just to warn you off. To get you to stop your inquiries into Westaway. The whole deal was being threatened because of you.'

Now it was Lytton's turn to be confused. 'But I wouldn't have known anything about Westaway if you hadn't leaked his activites to me in the first place.'

'Yes, but it was never supposed to become so serious. It's only money, for God's sake. Westaway was dragging his feet and asking for too much. He needed a little bit of encouragement to make him get a move on. So

I put you on to him. But you never knew when to stop.
I tried to warn you. I asked you. But no. You were like
a man possessed. Woodward and Bernstein had nothing
on you. I thought you were supposed to be a trivial little
gossip writer. Then I met Stella.'

At last Lytton was beginning to understand the pattern.
'Go on,' he prompted.

'What else is there? It was your birthday. I couldn't
see you myself but I thought I'd do you a favour, cheer
you up and at the same time put you off the scent. It
was only a joke, Neville. You used to enjoy a joke.'

Lytton looked at the magazine. 'I'm sorry. I don't think
this is very funny.'

Hamil was shaking with emotion. 'I don't know what
to say. I can't believe that they can print this sort of
thing in England these days. Not photographs.'

'Times have changed,' said Lytton. 'What about Westaway. Is he still dragging his feet?'

Hamil shook his head. 'No, he's signed. The deal's gone
through. He's another fifty thousand pounds better off.'

'He's a lucky man. What I never understood was how
he got around those export licence embargoes.'

'You're naïve, Neville. You know what these chaps are
like. They have connections everywhere. London is a maze
of networks. All you have to do is become connected to
the right one. He did a double deal and got one of the
South American countries to order spares for similar reactors which had been built there. Then he had them re-
directed to us.'

Lytton leaned back in his chair. 'I see. So instead of
selling to military dictators in the west, we're really supply-
ing the new religious dictators in the east. Oh well, I
suppose it balances.'

Hamil pushed his hands through his hair. 'If only you
hadn't become so professional, Neville.'

Lytton smiled sadly. 'I think we all have to grow up

sometime. I suppose everything you told me about being involved in famine relief was also a little white lie.'

Hamil nodded. 'I didn't want you to think too badly of me.'

'So what do you really do?' asked Lytton.

'Whatever deals are necessary.'

'Oh well, I suppose that shows some kind of patriotism,' said Lytton philosophically.

'Not really,' came the reply. 'I do it for the money. Westaway's pay comes out of mine. That was why I wanted to keep his fee down.'

Bit by bit Lytton was beginning to see the funny side of the situation. He could, he was relieved to discover, still see a joke.

'If I said I was sorry ...'

'I wouldn't believe you. Go away and leave me alone. And next time you decide to pressurize one of your crooked pals into some dodgy deal give someone else a call, will you?'

Mortified by his deceit, Hamil stood up and walked away from Lytton. 'Yes, well, I see ... goodbye then.'

Lytton watched him go, a smile spreading slowly across his cheeks. Then very carefully he withdrew Laura's birthday present from his pocket, the microrecorder. Turning it off he felt under the arm of the chair he had pulled up for Hamil to sit in and detached its magnetized remote microphone. 'Tricks of the trade, Hamil, old boy,' he murmured to himself, standing up and peering across the bar to one of the upper windows of the National Theatre.

At the window a photographer gave a thumbs up sign and grinned. Taking one last look at the dummy magazine, Lytton slowly and deliberately took it apart and tore it up into tiny pieces, which he then dropped into the nearest wastebasket. Then going into the theatre foyer he looked around for the nearest telephone. He had his story, he had a tape of the conversation and he had pictures as evidence. The tables had been turned.

Hamil left for London airport early the next day. From midnight, when the *Daily News* was published, his life had become chaotic. Every paper in Fleet Street had laid siege to him in an attempt to get confirmation of the front page lead that Lytton had written about the activities of Westaway and Hamil, a story which came adorned with a picture of Hamil in the act of confessing all to Lytton. By breakfast the Department of Trade had acted to block all the illegal exports to Sybia, and Westaway's activities were under investigation by Scotland Yard.

It was perhaps as well that Hamil did not have time to stop at the newspaper kiosk at Heathrow or he might just have seen the latest copy of *Cyclops*, published that day. On the front was a picture of Margaret Thatcher. There was not a single picture or mention of Lytton in the whole magazine.

Laura arrived back from Brazil that evening. Lytton picked her up at the airport and drove her back to his place.

'Did you miss me?' she asked as he mixed them both a drink.

'Desperately,' said Lytton. Laura had come back with a tan the colour of a conker.

'I don't believe you. How was your birthday?' she asked.

'Oh, you know, pretty uneventful,' lied Lytton.

'*Cyclops* said . . .' began Laura, but Lytton stopped her. Someone had obviously been doing some transatlantic gossiping.

'It wasn't true,' he said. 'Not one word. *Cyclops* are malevolent mischief-makers and one of these days I'm going to get even with them.'

Laura raised an eyebrow. 'Not true? Are you sure?'

'Not one syllable.'

'Cross your heart and hope to die?'

Lytton crossed his heart. 'Promise,' he lied.

'I knew I could trust you, darling,' said Laura.

'As I know I can always trust you. Cheers.' They sipped their drinks. Then a cloud fell across Lytton's eyes. 'Laura, you remember when I phoned you the other night. I could have sworn I heard a man's voice in your room. You said it was the maid turning down your bed.'

'Oh yes, she had a very deep voice.'

'Oh, I see,' said Lytton, 'because I had the most peculiar call last night. It was from a chap called Sammy Hill. He's a steward with British Caledonian and he does the Rio de Janeiro run. Nice chap. He gives me all kinds of tit bits, mainly about Ronnie Biggs, whom he sees from time to time on the beach there.' Laura's self-confidence was beginning to dissolve as Lytton spoke. 'Well, you know, Sammy's eyesight must be going a bit because according to him someone answering to your description was seen cavorting desperately in the Copacabana surf with some lithesome Brazilian beach boy just the other day.'

Laura looked at him coolly. 'Lytton, do you really think that after all this time I would lie to you any more than you would lie to me?' she asked.

'Welcome home,' said Lytton.

Chapter Five

The Silly Season

August is no time to be working in a newspaper office. With Parliament in recess and half the nation on holiday, it is a month when nothing in the country gets done, and when consequently there is nothing to put in the newspapers. But, although newspapers are traditionally thin at that time of the year (advertisers being less keen to take space when they know no one is in the mood for buying) they still have to come out, and those journalists who find themselves working in August become grateful for stories which in October or March they would not even consider covering. August has, therefore, for many years been known in newspapers as the silly season, or the time when, in the absence of anything worthwhile, the most absurd and pointless stories find their way into even the most serious papers. (There are some who would claim that since Rupert Murdoch took control of *The Sun*, and began the downward spiral of taste that the Fleet Street tabloids have recently displayed, the silly season has become a year long affair.)

Normally Lytton managed a couple of weeks away during August, a guest on a yacht off Rhodes one summer, a cottage in Tuscany another. But this year a planned sojourn to a more remote corner of the Swiss Alps had fallen through at the last moment, and he found himself stranded in a hot and dusty London where tourists apparently outnumbered Londoners, and without a soul in town to write about.

So it was that both he and Dolly turned up for one of the few publishing parties of the month. It took place at a St John's Wood television studio, and was, the invitation claimed, 'one of the few chances to meet one of the all time greats'.

Her name was Margot Shelley, a strikingly handsome, greying, sophisticated woman who was getting on for seventy, but how great she was depended upon how fond you were of British romantic movies between 1935 and 1950. After a decade or more of retirement Margot had written her autobiography, and now, in a tilt for immortality, it was being launched, complete with scores of fans from another day and as much press excitement as her publicist, a fey little American called Curtois, could generate. Not that it was only Margot's story. In the mind of the British public Margot Shelley's name was inseparably linked with that of Hunter Lombard, her husband for many years and her co-star in at least half a dozen great weepies of the past. Hunter had died some years earlier but now Margot was out wooing her public, sitting on a low stage and smiling graciously down at the massed rows of her fan club, as her publisher introduced her and her book to the British press.

'All the world loves a lover,' he said, beaming about him, 'and no one who ever saw any of the great Margot Shelley–Hunter Lombard pictures could fail to have been inspired by their lifelong devotion to each other. So, ladies and gentlemen, it gives me great satisfaction to be able to introduce to you, here in the studios where she made so many of her wonderful films, the very lovely and gracious Margot Shelley, author of *An Immortal Kind of Love*.'

Amidst a collective swoon of delight from her followers, Margot rose to her feet, dabbing her eyes with a pink lace handkerchief. At the back of the studio Lytton grimaced at Curtois, the publicist. He had never been much impressed by show-business over-emotion. 'Didn't you know she got an Oscar nomination for crying?' hissed Curtois. Like all successful publicists he had a bitchy streak.

'*A Girl Who Came To Stay*, 1938,' remembered Dolly.

'I never knew you were a movie buff,' remarked Lytton.

'I checked with cuttings before I came out,' Dolly said. She loved show business and had come to the reception because Curtois had promised her an hour alone with the great lady, which, in such a thin summer, might end up as a by-line feature and set Dolly on her way to her own show business column.

At the front of the studio Margot was wowing them just as she had always done. 'It's good to be back,' she said looking around at the lights as she had seen Gloria Swanson do in *Sunset Boulevard*. 'This place brings back a lot of memories, although in my day they made movies here, not ...' she became dismissive, 'television programmes.' Applause erupted in the hall. Margot shone her smile around at everyone. 'You know, Jack Warner once called me and said, "Margot, if you come to Hollywood I'll make you the biggest star in the world." And I said, "Mr Warner, we'll be on the next boat."' She stopped and dramatically shook her head. '"Not we, Margot," he said, "just you ..."' She again dabbed the handkerchief to her eyes. 'I never told dear Hunter that. It would have broken his heart. But, you know, I never regretted not going ... never for one minute. England was big enough for Hunter and me. And Hunter was all I ever wanted ...' Again the tears flowed.

Curtois looked at Dolly. '*The Sun Place*, 1941. End titles then fade to black. Don't you just love it?'

'Personally I can't stand it,' said Lytton cringing at the hammy mawkishness of it all.

But Margot had not finished talking. She put her hand out on to a pile of autobiographies. 'So now, as I approach

160

the end of my life, I want all the people who have been so loyal to me and the memory of Hunter to have and keep something of us both. That's why I have called my book *An Immortal Kind of Love*. Because that's what Hunter is to me, and that's what he always will be.' Then, dabbing her eyes again, Margot sat down, while the audience stood and gave her the ovation she had been playing for.

'Remind me never to go to the pictures with either of you two cynics,' complained Dolly. 'You should be ashamed of yourselves, especially you Curtois. You're supposed to be her publicist.'

'Margot Shelley doesn't want a publicist. What she needs is a crash barrier to keep you guys out,' exaggerated Curtois. 'You should have seen the stampede when she agreed to be interviewed again.'

'See how lucky you are, Dolly,' said Lytton, beginning to push his way through the crowds. 'You go and talk to her and I'll see you back at the office.'

'Going so soon?' asked a pretty book publicist as he reached the door.

Lytton nodded. 'The trouble with fairytale romances is that they are always incredibly boring,' he said. 'What I like to read are tales of lust, violence, greed, hate, unbridled desire and betrayal.'

'You mean like Lytton's Diary.'

'On a good day,' smiled Lytton, and walked on, well complimented.

At the front of the studio Dolly and Curtois were having difficulty pushing a path through the dewy-eyed adoration of the Margot. 'How come I'm so lucky?' Dolly wanted to know. 'Why is she talking to me when she could have had any other paper in Fleet Street?' She knew that Margot had promised to do one newspaper interview and one interview only.

Curtois grinned: 'She liked your stars.'

'What?' Dolly didn't understand.

'I fed her the star signs for every hack requesting an audience. She chose yours.'

'How did you know what my star sign was?'

Curtois smiled again. 'I didn't. I made it up. I made them all up. It seemed fairer that way. Don't let me down, will you?'

At last Dolly saw her gap and pushed up to the legend herself. She smelled, Dolly was surprised to find, very strongly of Rosewater. 'Hello, I'm Dolly Brown,' she said eagerly, 'the reporter you agreed to do the interview with.'

Margot turned her still beautiful profile to her. 'I expected someone rather older.'

'I've seen all your films.'

Margot was not impressed. 'How clever of you. But you'll have to wait. Today's not the time. You must come down to the house. Curtois will tell you when.' And with that she turned back to the milling elderly ladies.

Curtois led Dolly away: 'As Norma Desmond said in *Sunset Boulevard*, "I'm still big ..."'

'"It's the movies that got smaller."'

'I'm sure you two are going to love each other,' said Curtois.

If it was the silly season for the national press, it was no less difficult for the producers of the nation's radio and television programmes to find suitable subjects, as Lytton discovered upon arriving back at the Galley Proof. Laura and Pandora were drinking with a very sweet looking, eager young girl who looked as though she had not been long out of university. Her name was Michelle, explained Laura, and she was a researcher on 'Clare Copeland Interviews'. 'CCI', as it was known, was BBC Radio 4's prestigious interview programme, where every week celebrities were invited to be interrogated by the fearsome Clare. Although she was renowned for the toughness of

162

her profiles, it was undoubtedly highly flattering to be invited to face her.

'We were wondering if you'd like to be Clare's subject this week?' asked Michelle.

'It's a bit short notice, isn't it?' said Lytton, aware that both Henry Field and Colin Griffin the lawyer had over-heard Michelle's request.

'It's summer, Lytton. They're probably pushed, too. What d'you say, Henry?' laughed the lawyer enviously.

'Whatever would Clare Copeland want to interview Lytton for?' Henry retorted. 'It's laughable.'

Pandora offered immediate advice. 'You'd better watch her, Lytton. Clare Copeland's a piranha in gingham.'

'Nonsense,' came in Laura. 'She's all right. I was at university with her.'

'She's a great admirer of yours,' Michelle pleaded. 'She reads you every day.'

'Really!' Lytton could not have been more flattered. He turned to Henry, enjoying his moment. 'What d'you think? Would you take on the dreaded Clare Copeland in unarmed combat?'

Sensing that there was no profit in inflating Clare Copeland's reputation any further, Henry changed tack. 'Well, of course, if you want to become another media pundit buffoon figure –' he began, before Pandora cut him off with a cry of, 'Sour grapes.'

That settled it for Lytton. He accepted the invitation.

'Well, don't say I didn't warn you,' muttered Henry peevishly.

'Henry, I'm thrilled by your concern,' said Lytton.

Then, finishing his drink, he agreed the time and place with Michelle and hurried away for the afternoon conference, where, in the absence of the editor, who had gone off on his yearly visit to the Western Isles, the deputy editor Charles Harrison was standing in. When Cruick-shank was in the office Charles could be a valuable ally, having a good eye for a story and an occasional loyalty to the journalists who peopled the *Daily News*. But in God's absence Charles was hardly less unpleasant than the regular incumbent of the editor's chair.

'Look, I know it's summer and the silly season and the editor's away,' he told the heads of department that afternoon, 'but that's no reason why we've got to stop trying. Every day it's all the same old tosh. "Topless girls on the beaches" from Fashion; "how to survive in a heat-wave" from Features, and the Diary on some boring old twaddle about who's been left in London during August ...'

Lytton didn't like that. When God criticized him he had no alternative but to accept it. But Charles wasn't God. 'Oh come on! Nothing's happening. We're performing the loaves and the fishes act every day to fill the damned paper.'

'Well, we aren't performing it very well, are we?' snapped back the deputy editor, angry at having his authority questioned. God never had people answering him back. 'So can we all get off our bottoms and come up with something interesting? Circulation are screaming for something to put on the bills, and before he went away the editor specifically asked that we start thinking now about the autumn promotion. There's money available for the right ideas. So let's be having them, shall we?'

A few minutes later the heads of department filed miserably from his office. 'You know, when Charles is acting as editor he becomes a completely different personality,' complained Bill Withy, who was himself standing in for the news editor.

'A proper Little Caesar, isn't he, trying to cover himself in glory while God's away,' Lytton agreed, and walked on to his desk, where Jenny, engulfed in the *ennui* of a long lonely summer, was working her way through the entire list of Virago Modern Classics. 'Jenny, if you should

164

happen to see a one hundred per cent proof, copper-bottomed circulation booster around, do young Charles a favour, will you, and collar it for him.'

Jenny carried on reading: 'What's the creep on about now?'

'He thinks the paper's dull.'

'It is,' chimed in Wesley.

'We *know* that,' explained Lytton, 'and Mark Anthony in there knows that. But unfortunately August is the little weasel's only chance to show what he can do, so can we all keep our eyes and ears skinned.'

David had been waiting for a chance to break in. 'Lytton, do we know that Solveig Lindstrom's writing her memoirs?'

'You're kidding.'

'I'm not. A girl I know who types scripts has just been asked for a quote on a seventy thousand word book on those whom Solveig has loved.'

'Only seventy thousand words?' quipped Pandora cheekily.

'I bet there are going to be a few anxious husbands around when this becomes known,' added Jenny tartly. Solveig Lindstrom's reputation had that effect upon women.

'Oh, I dunno,' Lytton said. 'I think most men would be flattered to be in that not very exclusive club. Anyway, the question is, do we have a number for her?'

Solveig Lindstrom had never been a big time glamour girl of the British cinema, but, since arriving in Britain from Sweden in the early sixties, she had carved for herself a prodigious reputation as a marathon attender of first nights. For years she had been a gossip columnist's dream, flitting from man to man and ever ready with a merry quote or two. Her career as an actress had once looked interesting, and she had indeed done well in the few dramatic roles she had been offered. But her prettiness and her obliging nature had led her to accept too many silly parts. Now, in her early forties and with her looks fading, those parts had all but dried up.

Lytton met her for lunch at Gebler's the following day. She turned up in a pretty summer frock, her hair loose and long around her shoulders. She was, thought Lytton, the best looking forty-odd-year-old he had seen in a very long time, and was gratified by the admiring glances she attracted from men all over the room. He asked her how the writing was going.

She groaned. 'I never realized it was so hard. It's murder.'

'Hemingway said it was like breaking stones,' he replied.

'Oh no, it's much harder than that. Anyway, to what do I owe this little treat?' She had a charming directness which, in the past, had accounted for thousands of saucy headlines.

'Well, two things, actually,' admitted Lytton. 'Firstly, why are you writing your memoirs, and secondly, it's just possible that the *Daily News* might be interested in buying the serial rights.'

Solveig laughed, sensing the tone of disapproval in Lytton's voice. 'A typical newspaperman,' she said. 'You don't like what I'm doing, but please can you buy it? I promise you it won't be cheap.'

'You were never cheap, Solveig. That's why I'm a little surprised.' Lytton had always liked Solveig. The most notorious good time girl in London, she was also renowned for her generosity. In survival terms she might have been considered her own worst enemy.

'You know, you almost sound disappointed,' she replied.

Lytton shook his head. 'No, not that, but you know as well as I do that girls who kiss and tell don't exactly endear themselves to either their former lovers or their readers.'

'You mean I'll become known as a scrubber who couldn't keep her mouth shut.'

'Something like that. Is that what you want?'

'I don't want it, no. But if that's the way it's got to be there's nothing I can do.'

'Is money so important to you?'

'*This* money is.'

'I don't understand. Why?'

Solveig put her hand on his arm. 'Don't ask, Neville. I can't tell you. But thanks for caring. I have to write it. And a little bit of publicity in Lytton's Diary can't do any harm at all in pushing up the price.'

'It's the least I can do,' said Lytton, and, seeing the owner of the restaurant bearing down on them, quickly poured the last of the wine in case he should decide to help himself to it.

'My God, what is this, Lytton?' bellowed Gebler as he approached, drawn like a magnet by Solveig's long blonde hair. 'Crumpet Corner or Nookie Nook?' Solveig had her back to him and he had not recognized her.

Lytton winced slightly, but Solveig turned with a smile: 'Hello Nathan,' she greeted.

Gebler's onward rush was halted in mid-flight. 'Solveig,' he said, the bawling turning into a purr. 'Didn't your mother tell you never to hang around street corners with layabouts like Lytton?'

'Nathan and I are very old friends,' she explained to Lytton. 'Old as bookends.'

That was the way it was with Solveig, Lytton explained to Charles the next day. She was old friends with so many men that her memoirs would look like a *Who's Who* on the London social scene. 'You name him, he'll be there,' said Lytton.

'I love it to death. When can we get a look,' asked Charles.

'Well, she's still writing. But I think we ought to make our pitch now if we're to be in with a chance,' Lytton replied. 'Get our names down early, so to speak.'

'We'd pay a hell of a lot for that, you know.' Lytton had never seen Charles so excited.

Accross the office the lawyer sniffed to himself. 'You don't think it's a bit down-market for us, do you, Charles? Those kiss and tell stories can be very expensive if they go wrong.'

'Of course not,' snapped the deputy editor. 'You keep after her, Lytton. Butter her up. Do whatever's necessary. All right?'

'Okay,' said Lytton, 'but I doubt we'll need the butter.'

Not knowing whether Lytton was making a joke, Charles suddenly guffawed, thus covering himself against the charge that he was a thick plebeian twit who had gone too far in Fleet Street.

'I was telling Charles you're going on "Clare Copeland Interviews" tomorrow,' the lawyer remembered.

'Oh yes. I'd watch out if I were you,' warned the deputy editor. 'She's got a tongue like a laser.'

'Oh I think I can manage Clare Copeland all right, thank you,' said Lytton, and left the room.

The next afternoon he found out exactly how well he could manage Clare Copeland. Using the occasion as an opportunity to meet her old friend from university, Laura accompanied Lytton to Broadcasting House from where the programme went out live every Saturday afternoon. Michelle met them in the lobby and took Lytton straight down to the basement studio where the renowned inter-rogator was waiting. For the duration of the interview it was decided that Laura should sit in the box with Michelle, the producer and the sound engineer.

Lytton was no stranger to broadcasting but Clare Cope-land's reputation was formidable, and he found himself clearing his throat slightly nervously before they went on the air. There was something about Clare Copeland which unnerved her guests. She had a habit of staring them straight in the face at all times, and never giving a moment's respite for the interviewee to recover his or her composure. She was not an unattractive woman, but there was nothing flirtatious about her. Rather she was coldly practical, and extremely experienced at the art of talking on the radio.

At first the interview went well, Clare generously flattering, almost jokey, and Lytton quickly found himself seduced into the odd incautious remark. But he was not anything like as experienced at radio as was Clare, and as the hour-long interview continued he began to contradict himself, articulating his cause far less successfully than he usually did. All the time Clare kept her eyes glued to his, allowing him no escape from her gaze.

'No, I wouldn't say that gossip was a vice,' Lytton heard himself saying in a voice far more pompous than he intended to use. 'What we try to do on Lytton's Diary is to act as a public watchdog on behalf of our readers.'

'So am I right in saying you would also disagree with Sheridan when he called the newspapers licentious, abominable and infernal?' asked Clare.

'You're quoting out of context again and overlooking, I think, that part of the nature of man is to gossip,' he protested. 'Wherever you get three people you'll get gossip. One to gossip, one to listen and one to be gossiped about.'

'I see,' said Clare. Her expression suggested that she did not see at all.

In the control box Laura watched Lytton with growing despair. He was becoming more uneasy by the minute. Clare Copeland had changed since university. Once a very bright, analytical, but rather shy girl, she had developed into a remorseless interrogator.

In the studio Clare had a copy of that day's Lytton's Diary on the table. One paragraph had been circled. 'Looking at today's edition,' she said, taking her eyes from him for the very first time, 'I wondered if you could justify your story about the ... er ... actress Solveig Lindstrom who, I gather from this item, is about to reveal details of past affairs, details which you, no doubt, hope to print when they are revealed.'

'Well, yes, we possibly will,' agreed Lytton, wishing that she had chosen some other item with which to illustrate her obvious dislike for gossip columns. 'That's the nature of our job. We're there, I think, to act as a public scolding device, a ducking stool, if you like, for those who transgress the simple laws of society.'

'Oh dear,' thought Laura.

Clare Copeland smiled at Lytton and pushed the newspaper away. 'So you really think you serve a public function, do you? You believe that we need gossip columns.'

Lytton put on his patient expression. 'I think,' he said slowly, 'that like it or not we live in a society which is obsessed with glamour. And if, from time to time, I can occasionally burst that chimera of illusion then I may just be not completely wasting my time or the time of my readers.'

'I see,' said Clare. 'You wouldn't say, then, that the people whose lives you record are a coterie of pampered narcissistic parasites whose greatest achievements have been to get into situations where they can manipulate the media and bask in a self-reflecting goldfish bowl like Lytton's Diary?'

Lytton could feel himself rising to the insults. 'What are you talking about?' he grumbled. 'Do you ever read Lytton's Diary? Day after day, week after week we reveal corruption, greed, nepotism . . .'

Clare Copeland smiled very sweetly. She had succeeded in tempting him into losing his temper. No doubt in her terms the show had taken off. 'Oh, come on now, Neville, surely a man of your intelligence can't be so self-deluding. Isn't it the case that the only things which really interest you and your readers are the sexual peccadillos of the rich and famous?'

'No, of course that isn't true.' Lytton was losing all desire to defend himself, had he been given the chance, which he was not, because Clare Copeland was in full flight as the last few minutes of the programme ticked away.

'And wouldn't you also say, Neville, that fame is an insidious seducer and that you're his lackey? Isn't that what gossip columns and show business interviews are really all about in the tabloid press, stoking the egos of those already basking in their own self-importance? Giving space to rag, tag and bobtail international tripehounds whose lives are remarkable only in their abilities as manic self-publicists?'

Lytton didn't even try to answer.

'Do you seriously contend, Mr Lytton, that the motley collection of ego-worshipping, so-called personalities who people your column are of any greater significance than the public's prurient interest in who they are currently sleeping with? Indeed are you not yourself little more than a sponge who soaks up glamour by association with the famous, and who then squeezes out their trivial secrets in spiced paragraphs? In fact, Neville, are you not an overpaid purveyor of bunkum?'

There was nothing that Lytton could have said. He sat there in silence. The second hand ticked away the last minute of the studio clock as Clare ended the programme. In the control box Laura stared at the floor, while Michelle excused herself and fled to the Ladies to hide.

'Neville, that was marvellous, absolutely super,' said Clare, standing up and pushing out her hand towards him. Out of habit and embarrassment he shook it. Together he and Laura slunk away, too stunned to know what to say to each other.

Dolly arrived at Margot Shelley's house just after four,

having purposely loitered during the drive to hear every word of Lytton's torment. Why he had not made a better attempt at defending himself she could not imagine, but the interview was driven from her mind by the sheer splendour of the Buckinghamshire mansion in which Margot lived. Approached by a sweeping drive, the house was Hollywood-on-Thames style, a sumptuous dwelling built in the thirties when land was cheap and space no object. Getting out of her car, Dolly crossed the gravel drive, past the little stone lions guarding the steps, and lifted the gargoyle head which doubled as a door knocker. A timid, elderly lady, probably once a dresser to Margot, answered the door immediately and led her into a galleried gothic hall, the walls of which were covered in posters and stills of Margot and Hunter in their prime. It was, thought Dolly, a museum. As she gazed around the walls Curtois trotted hurriedly down the wide stairs. 'Hi, Dolly, I'm afraid you're not going to like this, but . . .'

Dolly guessed what was coming. She had been a journalist long enough to know when there was bad news on the way, and stars could be notoriously unreliable. '*Curtois!*' she said threateningly.

'Honest to God, Dolly, I'm sorry, but something's come up. Margot's very, very upset. She can't see you today.' When Curtois was embarrassed his accent became more New York and more gay.

For Dolly this was bad news. 'What happened?' she asked. 'Can't she be persuaded?'

Curtois wagged his permed head. 'I'm sorry. I really am. She's apparently spent half the day in tears and the rest on the phone. I can't imagine who she's talking to.' He already had his arm around her and was guiding her back towards the door. 'I'll call you Monday. We'll be able to do it at the beginning of next week, I promise. All right?'

Dolly had no option but to agree. Sadly she made her way out into the drive.

'Thanks for taking it so well,' said Curtois as she got into her car. 'I'm glad I put you down as a Virgo. A Sagittarian would have flayed me alive.'

Dolly pulled a face at him, then putting her car into gear she swung round and headed back down the drive. She was just about to turn into the road when an old black Rover with a crushed near front wing skidded off the road and raced up the drive to the house, causing her to swerve. 'Hooligans,' she shouted, and promising herself a stiff drink when she got home she turned out of the drive and headed back towards town.

Lytton and Laura went for dinner to Gebler's after the Clare Copeland interview. It was as bleak a meal as any they had ever shared.

'I'm sure it wasn't half as bad as you imagine,' Laura tried to console him.

Lytton stared glumly at her. 'I thought you said she was a friend of yours. What on earth did you tell that researcher about me?'

'I'm sorry, Lytton, honestly. I'd no idea she was going to behave like that. They seemed so keen to have you on.'

'She was keen to make a fool of me.'

'She's a professional broadcaster, Lytton. You're a writer. It was a mismatch. She doesn't have anything against you, does she? I mean she wasn't harbouring any grudges because of something you've written?'

Lytton shrugged his shoulders. 'She's just about the one well known woman in London I've never written about.'

'Well, I don't know,' Laura repeated. Then, getting up, she turned to go to the Ladies. 'I'll see you in a minute.'

Lytton hardly noticed her go, so deep was he into his misery. Nor did he notice Gebler approaching.

'Hey, Lytton.' For once Gebler was speaking in a subdued voice. 'About Solveig Lindstrom writing her
memoirs,' he said. He had obviously read Lytton's Diary
that day.

'What about it?'

'Well, you couldn't put a word in for me, could you?
You know, get me off the hook. Anunziata .... well, I
don't know. She wouldn't understand.'

'Really. You too, Nathan?' said Lytton. It hadn't quite
struck home when he'd had lunch with Solveig.

Gebler wasn't in any mood for banter. 'These girls
shouldn't be allowed to write these books,' he said furtively and, Lytton thought, almost angrily. 'It isn't fair.
If a guy wants to play mommies and daddies with a girl
he shouldn't have to risk reading about himself twenty
years later in some paper.'

Finally amused by someone else's troubles, Lytton put
his hand in his pocket and pulled out a cigar. 'If I were
you, Nathan,' he said, 'I'd plead the Fifth Amendment.'

The volume of Gebler's voice increased with his irri-
tation. 'Okay, go on, laugh. But I'm telling you, Lytton,
she's gonna cause trouble. Believe me.'

Laura did not go home with Lytton that night although
he suggested it. 'Some days are better ended early,' she
explained, feeling that he blamed her for the radio *débâcle*,
and insisted he dropped her off at Notting Hill Gate.
Consequently and unusually, Lytton was alone on the
Sunday morning when Solveig Lindstrom rang his front
door bell.

'Well, this is a nice surprise,' he said when he saw her,
wishing that he had been dressed and shaved. Normally
no one ever called before lunchtime on a Sunday.

'Neville, can I talk to you. Please?' she asked. She was
trembling.

'What is it, Solveig, what's the matter?' Suddenly

174

alarmed, Lytton led her into his sitting-room and sat her down among the Sunday newspapers.

Very quickly, between bouts of tears, Solveig explained. She had been out for her daily jog in Hyde Park that morning when a couple of thugs had approached her and advised that if she didn't stop writing her memoirs she would be very sorry indeed. Someone, they threatened, would be very cross with her if those memoirs ever appeared, but they refused to say who that someone was. When she had threatened to tell the police the thugs had laughed to each other and advised against it. The police couldn't watch her all the time, they had said meaningfully.

Lytton made Solveig some coffee while she told her story. She was obviously very frightened indeed. 'Are you sure you've no idea who they might be working for?' he asked. Solveig shook her head. 'But can't you draw up a short list? I mean it's obviously someone who's afraid his name will appear, isn't it?'

'That isn't necessarily such a short list,' said Solveig quietly.

Lytton sipped his coffee. 'Have you considered doing what they suggest?' he asked.

Solveig was adamant. 'I told you, I have to write this book.'

'But you never explained why.'

'Let's just say I'm a greedy girl who enjoys her notoriety.'

'You can say that Solveig, but you can't make me believe it.'

'It's just something personal, Neville. No one knows. Just me. There's no connection.'

Lytton got them both some more coffee. 'Sorry,' he said.

'No, it's me who should be sorry, coming here and spoiling your Sunday. I didn't telephone because I thought you might not want to see me.'

'I'm always delighted to see you, Solveig,' he said. He was, too. 'Tell me, what are you doing for lunch?'

'You really are a very nice man, you know.'

'Not really,' replied Lytton honestly. 'Why don't you finish your coffee while I go and get ready.'

Leaving her in his sitting-room, Lytton went into the bedroom and closed the door. It was too early for anybody to be in the office so he made a quick call to Pandora at home, asking her to get out Solveig's cuttings as soon as she got there.

'I want to know everything about Solveig from the moment anybody ever heard of her,' Lytton said. 'And I want lists of everyone she's been involved with.'

'Leave it to me,' promised Pandora.

For lunch Lytton took Solveig to the Café des Amis du Vin in Covent Garden, where he plied her with roast lamb and red wine until the events of the morning had become distant. He really felt she ought to call the police but she would not hear of it.

'No, that won't be necessary,' she insisted as they left the restaurant. She had now recovered her spirits completely. 'I'm sure all this can be sorted out. I was just panicking this morning. For heaven's sake, if someone doesn't want his name in my life story I'll just take it out. There are plenty of others.'

So, although it bothered Lytton, that was how they left it, Solveig bright and confident again and promising to be in touch about a possible serialization sale to the *Daily News*.

Lytton did not usually go into the office on a Sunday afternoon, and he certainly did not wish to following his disastrous appearance on 'Clare Copeland Interviews'. But because news of Solveig's memoirs had first been leaked in Lytton's Diary he felt a responsibility towards her.

Solveig's cuttings were spread right across the Diary desk when he reached it, having first had to run the gauntlet of yobbish comments from colleagues around the floor who had heard, or heard about, the radio show.

'How's it going?' Lytton asked David, who was emptying a new file on to his desk.

'Endlessly. Solveig Lindstrom must have attended more first nights than the average Moss Bros suit.'

'What about names?'

Pandora passed him a sheet of paper. 'We've made four lists so far. Probable Lovers, Just Good Friends, Escorts For The Night and Surprises. It's like a *Who's Who* of London's most eligible and ineligible men, isn't it.'

'Quite a collection, aren't they?' It's going to make a hell of a book. Willie Sasdy, Benny Wise, Pinkie Burt ... they're all here. She was a popular girl.'

Across the table Dolly was going through the picture files on Solveig. There were swimsuit photos, bikini ones, mini-skirt ones, stills from films, supermarket openings and hundreds of first night appearances. 'That's interesting. I never knew Solveig Lindstrom was in *Juniper and Lamplight*,' she remarked, examining an old publicity still.

'What's that?' asked Pandora.

'*Juniper and Lamplight*. Hunter Lombard's last picture. Margot Shelley produced it. It was never even released it was so bad.'

She passed Lytton the photograph. It showed a delightful Solveig in a maid's uniform, but with a skirt hardly more than a couple of inches lower than her bottom, being cuddled by a very suave, smoking-jacketed Hunter Lombard.

'Small world, isn't it?' said Dolly. 'This picture must be a collector's item ... Hunter Lombard cuddling someone other than Margot. The legend is that they were a hundred and ten per cent devoted to each other, isn't that right, Lytton?'

'I imagine Solveig's the sort of girl men find easy to cuddle,' mused Lytton.

There were no easy answers in Solveig's cuttings. One by one Lytton let his staff go, as Norman came and took over the business of the next day's page, most of which had been written the previous Friday. Lytton stayed at his desk, making endless lists of names. It wasn't only that he wanted to know who had threatened Solveig. He was also puzzled as to why she should have decided to write a kiss-and-tell book. It was so unlike her. At midnight he went home, none the wiser but with some inconsistencies buzzing in his brain. Something had happened to Solveig in 1967. For some reason she had disappeared off the first night circuit for nearly a year. And there was no explanation for it. It wasn't much, but it was certainly puzzling.

If you want to know anything about movies and movie stars in London there are only two places to go. Over at *Screen International*, Peter Noble knows and is liked by everybody. But Peter is a gentleman. For the real mean-mouthed gossip Lytton chose an alternative source, Galleon, the keeper of a film stall in Covent Garden. Galleon was a wretched man, a real cine-buff who resented the fact that he had never been able to find an appropriate niche for himself in the film world and who had, therefore, invented one. In Paris Galleon would have been one of those respected cineasts who populate the Left Bank with their stalls and stills, but in London he was simply a curiosity, tolerated by a nation which has no love for the cinema and little tradition of film as an art form. Galleon's stall sold film memorabilia, often at absurdly inflated prices, for tourists to whom cinema was more than simply a bag of popcorn and a quick cuddle. On Galleon's stall were generations of film magazines, costumes, soundtracks, props, stills, books, postcards and sweatshirts. The stall was called the Hollywood Hills.

'Well, Neville Lytton, friend of the stars,' sneered Galleon, when Lytton called at the Hollywood Hills the following morning. He was wearing a *North by Northwest* sweatshirt.

'How are you, Galleon? How's business?' asked Lytton, picking up a second hand copy of Norman Mailer's book on Marilyn Monroe.

'Can't complain. What are you looking for? A signed photo of Irving Thalberg, Alec Guinness's stick from the *River Kwai* or James Dean's stand up collar from the party scene in *East of Eden*?'

Lytton came straight to the point. 'Solveig Lindstrom,' he said.

'Oh deary me. The Third Division South. Solveig Lindstrom. Hardly even a starlet,' coughed Galleon. He was a big and ungainly man with a bronchial chest.

'But still a name to conjure with. The time I want to know about was some time ago. 1967. July. D'you remember? Bells, beads and kaftans. What was Solveig doing then? Any idea?

Galleon lit a Gauloise. He enjoyed being tested like this. He would have been certain to win on 'Mastermind' if contestants were only questioned on their specialists subjects. Unfortunately, though, he knew nothing about anything other than film. 'Can you give me a clue?' he asked.

'Our cuttings have her appearing in the never to be released *Juniper and Lamplight* in the March, being signed up for the lead in *A Sunday Kind Of Woman* in the May and then dropping out because of ill health in the July. What I want to know is exactly what was that ill health. It put her off the map for over a year.'

Galleon flicked his ash into the gutter and served a teenage girl with a picture of David Bowie. 'I remember what the whispers said it was, but ...' He went silent.

Lytton knew the form. He cast his eyes over the stall. 'How much are you asking for that *Genevieve* clapper board?'

Galleon picked it up, shaking his head wickedly. 'Oh, I couldn't sell you that,' he said. 'Couldn't part with such a sacred souvenir of the British boom years.'

'Fifty quid,' offered Lytton.

Galleon's mouth dropped open. 'What? Right! Done,' he said quickly and wrapped it up. The clapper board was almost certainly fake and worth at the most five pounds. He handed it across to Lytton, who took five ten pound notes from his wallet.

'So, what d'you know?' asked Lytton.

'Well, I didn't believe it then, and I don't believe it now, but the word at the time was that Solveig was having a baby. That was why she dropped out of *A Sunday Kind Of Woman*. Just before they started shooting, wasn't it? Robin Blanche stepped in at the last moment. Now there's a name to forget.'

Lytton wasn't interested in Robin Blanche. 'But Solveig, what happened to her, and the baby?'

Galleon shrugged. 'She went into purdah, and everyone forgot about her for a while. When she came back there was no baby, was there? You don't have to believe it. I don't. It's probably just malicious gossip. Blondes have that effect, you know. They bring up the bile in people.'

Curtois came back to Dolly with a new date for the interview on the Monday morning. Margot would see her that afternoon, she was told. So dropping everything, she grabbed her tape recorder and raced down to Buckinghamshire where Margot, dressed in flowing chiffons of pink and lilac, led her into a sitting-room as comfortable as a tea cosy. It was, thought Dolly, the most hideous room she had ever been in. Everywhere there were mementos of another time and photographs of Hunter Lombard, against a background of awful, sumptuous, super-rich, thirties suburban style. Dolly had intended to ask all kinds of tough, needling questions which would have led Margot to betray herself. But Margot was too old a hand at being interviewed. She dictated the pace and the content.

'So you see, dear, although Hunter has been gone all these years I've never felt alone,' she gushed. 'Quite the contrary, in fact, I still talk to him every day, because I know he's there listening to me and answering me when I need some guidance. That's what I mean by immortality.'

'But surely there must have been moments in your marriage when you had quarrels, like everybody else?' asked Dolly.

Margot smiled as though dealing with an imbecile who could not understand the simplest facts of life. 'No, dear. You see we aren't normal people ... there I go again, talking about Hunter as though he's still here. But we were never normal. That's why our fans love us so. We were the epitome of married love. Are you married, my dear?'

'Er, no, no I'm not,' replied Dolly, not daring to mention her partner from *The Guardian*. She was sure Margot would not approve of people living in sin.

'No, well, you probably wouldn't understand then, I don't suppose,' Margot said, before adding darkly, 'I wouldn't leave it too long, though, if I were you.'

Dolly flinched under the older woman's condescension, but tried for one last question. 'I'm sure this won't arise for many years, but, I wonder, what kind of epitaph would you choose for yourself? Perhaps a line from a film or a performance which was very special to you?'

Back came the reply Dolly had feared. 'No, no film. No performance. Nothing like that. Just Hunter. My epitaph should read: "Together at last: the immortals".'

At that point Dolly leaned forward and switched off the tape recorder. She had heard enough.

'Well, what d'you think?' asked Curtois as they left the mausoleum which Margot called home.

'Quite frankly, I think she's a pain in the neck,' replied Dolly. 'I dunno how you can stand working for her.'

'She's a good account. Someone's got to pay for my lifestyle.'

'You mean you're a mercenary. I should have guessed.'

'That's right. Just like you. Anyway, you're quite happy with what you got, are you?' They were walking back across the gravel to Dolly's car. Parked alongside was the black Rover which had nearly hit Dolly on her previous visit. A bulbous headed man with a beer paunch was tinkering with the engine. Idly Dolly wondered how the very distinctive body damage to the front wing had been caused.

'I imagine I'll be able to cobble something together to further the legend,' she said, turning back to Curtois.

'You won't embarrass me, will you, Dolly?' he asked.

'Don't worry. Our acting editor's got a soft spot for the monochrome myth. Her reputation's safe with us.'

It was indeed. Dolly wrote a dull thousand words still half hoping that it might be given a page of its own, but Charles quite rightly consigned it to the Diary page, cut by half where it helped fill what would otherwise have been a very bleak night.

'Very nice, Dolly, very nice indeed,' Charles complimented as he returned the Diary page proof to Norman for checking.

'Actually it's rubbish,' she said, staring bleakly at her decrepit old typewriter.

'But stylish rubbish,' came in Lytton supporting her.

Charles didn't care what kind of rubbish it was. 'Any word on sexy Solveig yet?' he asked Lytton.

Lytton shook his head. He had been trying unsuccessfully to get hold of Solveig by telephone all day. 'Not yet.'

'Well keep at it,' encouraged Charles and moved away to encourage somebody else.

'Patronizing little sod,' murmured Lytton, and began to put his things away.

'Fancy a drink?' asked Dolly. It was a dry, bright summer evening.

Lytton hesitated. 'I'd like to,' he admitted, 'but I think I ought to call on Solveig on my way home. Just to make sure she's all right.'

Dolly didn't believe him. 'Oh really?' she smiled.

'Well, yes. Look, why don't you come along, if you've nothing better to do?'

'As your chaperone?'

'Don't be silly. But you never know, a woman's intuition may be able to help. There's something very odd going on there. Perhaps lots of things.'

'Okay, if you're sure I won't be a gooseberry,' said Dolly and followed him out of the office.

Solveig lived in a small mews flat over a lock up garage in Knightsbridge. 'Dinky little place, isn't it?' sniped Dolly, as Lytton parked his car in the wysteria and passion flower clad street. 'I would have thought she'd have needed at least a multi-storey car park to accommodate her legions of admirers.'

'I love a woman who can disguise her jealousy,' said Lytton, and led her a few yards up the street to Solveig's flat where he rang the door bell. There was no answer, but surprisingly, the door was slightly ajar. 'It looks as though we can let ourselves in,' he said, and, pushing open the door, stepped inside.

Dolly, who was lingering behind him, was puzzled by something. She was sure she recognized the car parked outside Solveig's flat. It was a black Rover. Then she noticed the stoved in front near wing. 'Hey, Lytton,' she began, as she hurried after Lytton up the stairs. She was never sure whether he heard her or not, because at that very moment two very large men came bulleting down the stairs, pushing past first him and then her in their haste to get out.

'Hey, watch out,' shouted Lytton angrily. The men

ignored him and raced out of the door. Excited, Dolly turned and ran down the stairs in time to see them jump into the Rover and race away down the mews, narrowly missing Lytton's parked car. Dashing back into the building she hared after Lytton. The door to Solveig's flat was open. It might once have been a dinky place, but it was now wretched, pictures torn from frames, cushions burst open, books and papers all over the floors, a lifetime's belongings smashed and broken. She found Lytton comforting Solveig in the bedroom.

'They didn't hurt you, did they?' he was asking her.

'No. They didn't hurt me,' she said. 'But they took my manuscript. All my work. They wouldn't listen to me. I wanted them to tell me who they were working for. I would have taken his name out. But they wouldn't say. They told me that if I wrote it again they would kill me.'

'And you've still no ideas who sent them?' asked Lytton.

'No. No idea.'

Dolly moved forward into the room. 'I think I know who sent them,' she said.

They met Curtois in Margot Shelley's drive. Solveig drove down with Lytton, a photographer went with Dolly and Curtois made his own way. 'Hey, what is this?' he asked as he jumped out of his car to be met by Lytton's welcome party.

'Sorry, captain,' said Dolly. 'The paparazzi were Lytton's idea. You're her to see fair play.'

He turned to Lytton. 'What the hell's going on?' he asked. 'You can't just turn up here like this. Margot's an old lady, virtually a recluse. The shock could kill her.'

Lytton looked sceptical. 'Not from what I hear,' he said, walking across to the front door and ringing the bell. The maid who had probably been watching from the window, appeared almost immediately.

'Hello,' smiled Lytton. 'Mr Curtois would like a word with Miss Shelley. We'll wait in the hall,' and stepping past her he led his entourage into Margot's folly.

'I'm sorry, I can't allow you to come in,' she protested, but made no attempt to stop them. 'Who are these people, Mr Curtois?'

Seeing his account with Margot dissolving in front of him, Curtois turned on Lytton. 'I'll report you to the Press Council for this. You can't go storming into people's private houses.'

'Oh shut up, Curtois,' responded Lytton. Then turning to the maid he said in his politest tones, 'I wonder whether you might be kind enough to tell Miss Shelley that we're here.'

A voice from the gallery drew everyone's attention. It was Margot, looking extraordinary in a long pink house-robe and with her hair blown up on top of her head like a cauliflower gone to seed. She was standing on the gallery at the top of the flight of stairs. 'There's no need to do that. Here I am. What would you like me to do for you?' she said and began graciously to descend the staircase, rather, thought Dolly, as one always imagined Anne Boleyn behaved when she walked to her execution.

The photographer, sensing the theatricality of the performance, immediately began snapping away at her, which must have pleased Margot because she turned to his camera and smiled.

'Margot, I really can't advise this.' Curtois tried to put himself between Margot and Lytton, but she would have none of it.

'Well, don't, then, you horrid little man,' she said imperiously, and turned to address Lytton. 'Now what is all this about? You look like a delegation from my fan club. But I know you can't be. You're far too smart for that.' She examined Lytton closely. So far she had not noticed Solveig who was standing well back by the door.

'I recognize you, don't I?' she said to him. 'You're that chappie in the newspaper, aren't you? And very handsome you are, too.'

Lytton smiled. He enjoyed compliments, even those which came from half-baked old ladies who had never said an honest word in their lives. 'Well, yes, thank you,' he said, 'but I'm afraid I'm here on rather serious business. You see, this young lady – he indicated Solveig, 'believes that you or your employees may have something which belongs to her.'

Margot looked across the room to Solveig. She recognized her immediately. Turning at once to her maid she snapped, 'Claire will you get Marshall and Parker.' She then turned back to Lytton, her demeanour now the tough, iron lady of film. 'If you think you can intimidate me you're quite wrong, you know,' she snarled, a real Bette Davis. 'She'll tell you that.' She pointed at Dolly. Then, turning on Solveig, she became venomous. 'As for her ... How are you, Solveig? Still peddling it about are you? Or are you finding it hard to get buyers these days?'

Solveig retained her perfect dignity. 'I'd like my manuscript back, please,' she said.

Margot was very amused. 'Manuscript?' she chortled. 'Now why would you think I might have your "manuscript"?'

Solveig looked at Lytton for support. He nodded. 'Because of Hunter and me and what you think I might have written.'

The humour left Margot's features. She became Joan Crawford. 'You little slut. I despised you then and I despise you now. Hunter never wanted you –'

'He did,' broke in Solveig, drowning the older woman. 'He wanted to leave you but he was afraid. Every time he tried you threatened to commit suicide. You made his life a misery.'

'What?' How dare you say that. Are you mad? We were

the immortal couple. He worshipped me.' Gloria Swanson was back.

Dolly was switching from one to the other. This was more like the kind of show business she wanted to write about. Real life melodrama: it was hilarious.

'He was weak,' replied Solveig. 'You turned him into your toy.'

Suddenly, remembering again that she had an audience, Margot's performance changed. From Gloria Swanson she went into a passable imitation of Vivien Leigh trying to woo Clark Gable. She played the weak and helpless woman. 'It isn't true. She's trying to destroy me. Don't listen to her.'

'Lytton, this has gone far enough,' interjected Curtois, but he was interrupted by the arrival of two very burly and unpleasant looking spivs, Parker and Marshall.

'I want you to chuck this lot out,' ordered Margot, now more like Mae West.

Parker and Marshall didn't move. Instead Lytton began to smile. 'Hello, Al,' he said. 'Fancy seeing you here. I heard you were out again. Does Dickie know you're doing a spot of freelancing?'

'Get rid of them. D'you hear me?' thundered Margot, but no one listened to her.

'I'm sorry, I didn't recognize you on the stairs at Solveig's place,' went on Lytton. 'You made an awful mess, you know. I can't imagine what Dickie's going to say when I tell him what you've been up to.'

Parker, the tougher of the two, scratched his bald spot. 'Leave it out, Nev,' he said, and then gesturing to his colleague, slipped quietly from the room.

'Well, Margot ...?' said Lytton.

Again a transformation took place as she became the defenceless woman, and sank down in semi-faint on to a low sofa. 'How can you be so cruel to me?' she sobbed. 'I'm just a lonely woman. It isn't easy, you'll discover,' she said looking straight at Dolly. 'A woman without a man is like a ... like a ...' She trailed away. She had forgotten the words.

'Like a boat without a sail,' helped Dolly, then looking at an astonished Lytton, she added, '*Almost Tomorrow*, 1944. She played a war widow.'

Margot turned to Lytton. Now she was pleading, and for the first time, he guessed, she was playing no one other than herself. 'For the past fifteen years all I've ever wanted was for Hunter and me to be remembered,' she said. 'If you print any of what this woman tells you you'll be robbing us both of immortality. Could you be so cruel?'

Lytton looked at her for a long moment. She was suddenly pathetic. 'Only the gods are immortal, Margot,' he said. 'What d'you think, Solveig ...?' But Solveig had left the house.

Lytton found her standing by the car. 'Are you all right?' he asked.

She nodded. 'It isn't much fun, is it?'

'I wouldn't worry too much about Margot Shelley, if I were you. You don't become a legend without a great deal of lacquer-coating. She'll bounce back. You'll see.'

A voice from a side door interrupted them. It was Parker. He was carrying Solveig's manuscript. 'No hard feelings,' he said. 'Sorry about the mess. We'll be round tomorrow to tidy up for you. All right, love?'

Solveig smiled a thank you and took the manuscript from him.

'Now perhaps we'll be able to read the unexpurgated story of Solveig Lindstrom and Hunter Lombard,' said Lytton.

'No,' replied Solveig.

'No?'

'That was the one thing I haven't written about. It was my little secret.'

'So all of this was for nothing?' Lytton was beginning

to feel very bored by these particular kiss-and-tell memoirs.

Solveig nodded.

'Honest to God, Dolly, that's the last time I fix your stars for you,' said Curtois, as Dolly and the photographer got into her car.

Dolly smiled at him. 'Curtois, if only you knew how happy that makes me.'

Solveig explained everything to Lytton the following day during a long walk along the banks of the Serpentine. She liked that part of London, she said, because she enjoyed watching the children playing there with their sailing boats. 'I don't know whether I really loved Hunter,' she said. 'I thought I did then. I suppose that was the last time I ever thought I was in love. He was so much older than I was, but I always felt he was very innocent. He made me want to protect him. I used to think I'd be able to take him away and give him something in life worth living for, but it wasn't to be. He used to play all those very self-confident parts, but he was really very fragile. On the outside he was smiling, but I think he was crippled inside.

'When I became pregnant he was so thrilled. We made all kinds of plans. My career was just starting, but none of that seemed to matter anymore. We were going to move back to Sweden. But then Margot found out, and Hunter just crumbled. She could always control him. He wasn't there when our baby was born. She'd taken him off on an American tour. I suppose I'd always known she would win. I never saw him again. When I realized it was over I began to make plans to have the baby adopted. I didn't think I'd be able to keep him ... I suppose, really, I didn't want him. But it was decided for me. He died when he was five days old. For months I felt as though I was being punished for being selfish, as though the baby had been made to pay, do you understand? But time heals. In some ways. After a while I tried to put it all behind me and get on with my life again. And I suppose I thought I had done.'

'But why the memoirs?' asked Lytton. 'Why do you suddenly want to tell everyone about yourself?'

Solveig smiled. 'I'm middle aged, Neville. Turned forty. All of a sudden life seems to have been a very long waste of time. I want to put something back: give something. I've no real money. I was never clever enough to keep anything from all the men I've known. But my life story must be worth something, mustn't it? I can think of one or two very worthwhile charities that could do quite a lot with a hundred thousand pounds, can't you?'

'Charity?' breathed Lytton. 'You're doing it for charity.'

'Sorry,' said Solveig. 'Have I disappointed you?'

The editor came back from holiday lightly tanned and in good spirits, and roundly congratulated everyone on surviving well during a particularly difficult August. He had, however, some bad news for Charles and Lytton. He had considered the Solveig Lindstrom memoirs, and, although he had found them very interesting, he had decided not to publish them. 'They're too spicey, for us, Neville,' he said, before adding, 'but I have heard that the *Sunday News* is prepared to pay a hundred and fifty thousand pounds for them, so the lady shouldn't be going hungry this winter.'

'A hundred and fifty thousand,' repeated Neville. That was certainly going to be very helpful to one of Solveig's charities.

He was still chuckling to himself about Solveig's good fortune when he reached the Galley Proof, but his smile faded when he heard the unmistakeable voice of Clare Copeland lashing into him once again, courtesy of Henry Field's ghetto-blasting tape recorder.

'Oh hello, Lytton,' laughed Henry, as the rivals faced each other. 'I was just treating all our colleagues to something one or two of them might have missed.' Then pulling out a handful of cassettes he passed them round the bar. 'Take one, they're free,' he giggled. 'Neville Lytton on "Clare Copeland Interviews". The radio moment of the decade. Play it to your friends and relatives. You could even give one to God with my compliments,' he said to Dolly. Finally he came back to Lytton. 'Just in case you think I've forgotten you, Lytton, fear not.' And taking one out of his pocket he handed it to Lytton, complete with a little pink bow. 'I hope you have many happy hours playing it to yourself in your old age. No, go on, take it. I can make plenty more.'

Lytton accepted the tape. Henry was actually being very funny. 'You really are a disgusting, slimy creature,' he smiled.

A voice at his side drew his attention away from Henry. It was Michelle, the researcher from 'Clare Copeland Interviews'.

'Ah, the serpent in skirts,' he greeted her. 'What are you doing here?'

'I actually came to say I'm sorry. I've decided to leave Clare Copeland,' said Michelle.

'Oh really!' Lytton looked bored.

'I've also got something to tell you. You'll perhaps think I'm being terribly disloyal and an awful gossip and everything, but Clare –'

Lytton stopped her. 'Tell me. Are you about to dish the dirt on Clare Copeland?' he asked. 'And is that dirt going to make a wonderfully vicious item in Lytton's Diary?'

'I'm afraid so,' said Michelle.

Lytton's face spread into a very large smile. 'Right then,' he grinned, 'why don't you sit down here and tell me all about it? This is something I really want to enjoy.'

Chapter Six

Come-
Uppance

Lytton was delighted when Wesley told him that he had given up his plans for going into the print and decided instead to become a journalist.

'That's a very wise decision,' Lytton told the boy as they climbed the stairs from the coffee machine one afternoon. 'What made you change your mind?'

'You did,' said Wesley.

Lytton was very flattered. 'Oh really. That's nice to know.'

'Yes, well, I reckoned that if you can do it anybody can.'

Lytton had to be amused. 'This is true, Wesley. But let's keep it quiet, shall we, or they'll all be at it.'

Lytton made his way across to his desk chuckling to himself and laid the proof of the next day's Diary page on Norman's desk. It was a particularly attractive page, and both Norman and he were pleased with it. THE LADY, THE MOONIE AND A MIDSUMMER NIGHT'S MADNESS, ran the headline.

'This should keep the punters happy,' smiled Norman. There was nothing to beat sex when it came to pleasing the readers, in Norman's opinion.

The lawyer, however, was less certain. As Lytton and Norman skimmed through the page looking for literals he stalked across to them, Lytton's copy in hand. 'We're taking a bit of a chance here, aren't we, if this Moonie blighter isn't the child's father?'

'I don't think so,' Lytton replied. 'We don't actually say that he is. It's more of an implication. He is the father, anyway. You aren't going to stop the story are you, Colin?'

'If you're so confident, I'm not. Just making sure,' he fussed, and hurried away to query somebody else's work.

Down the table Norman and Dolly exchanged glances. 'One thing about Lytton,' Norman said. 'He isn't afraid to have a go, is he?'

'Some might think he goes looking for trouble,' said Dolly, and pulled the cover on to her typewriter at the end of another day.

Wesley got a ride across town to the West End with Lytton that evening. He was going to a special screening of a new American ghost movie at the Rank screening room in Mayfair, which happened to be not very far from Lytton's destination, the bar at the Dorchester where he had promised to meet Catherine at six-thirty.

Since lunch at the cottage Lytton had not seen Catherine, although they had spoken several times by telephone. Now he had received another summons and rather dreaded what might be in store for him.

He found her sitting at a corner table and reading a Penguin book on the middle ages, while the pianist played variations on 'As Time Goes By'. Lytton always liked the Dorchester at this time of day, the happy hour, filled as it was with adulterous twosomes making plans and promises which would never be fulfilled. You never knew who you might bump into.

'You know, if you weren't my wife I really would fancy you something rotten,' he said, as he sat down.

Catherine wasn't quite sure how to react. 'Oh, that's nice. Or isn't it? I'm not quite sure.'

'I think I intended it as a compliment,' Lytton decided, and then, believing that attack was the best form of defence, he said. 'How's that little turnip you sleep with?'

Catherine responded with characteristic patience. 'My lover is very well, thank you, and wishes to be remembered to you. He's going to Albuquerque tomorrow to lecture on the bubonic plague.'

'Lucky Albuquerque,' scoffed Lytton. 'What about you, the country still agreeing with you?'

'Well, funnily enough,' said Catherine, as Lytton ordered the drinks, 'you asked on the right day. There was high drama in the village, this morning.'

'Go on, poleaxe me, someone stole the parish pump.'

'No, seriously. It wasn't funny. A gang of skinheads began picking on the chap who owns the local supermarket. He's Indian or Pakistani or something. They were vile. Frightening, actually. I was quite scared for a minute.'

'There you are, you see,' said Lytton, not particularly interested in what happened in village grocery stores, 'and you thought your country people were better behaved than us city folk.'

Catherine smiled. 'Well, actually, this lot weren't local. Apparently Hal Rimmer has got them on some toughening up course in the grounds at Staffes. They had some really unpleasant minder come and take them away. It was thrilling stuff I'll tell you.'

'I never thought of Hal Rimmer as a social philanthropist,' said Lytton. Hal Rimmer, or Lord Henry Rimmer to use his title, was the only son of one of the few aristocrats to have combined breeding with financial wizardry, and had inherited a very large estate in Sussex at an age when most young men were struggling to buy their first motor car. Since then Hal had been a regular fixture in night clubs, at races and at various flesh spots around the world, having little to do with his life, and seemingly few inclinations other than self-gratification. Now in his mid-thirties, Hal was obviously getting over his arrested adolescence.

'The locals don't see him as a social philanthropist,

194

either,' said Catherine. 'They're really fed up in case he invites the skinheads to his annual bash.'

Lytton took an envelope from out of his pocket and scribbled a reminder to himself. 'I'll get someone to look into it,' he said, vaguely. 'You never know. Anyway, what bash is this?'

Catherine shrugged. 'Usual sort of thing. Once a year Hal has a party for his pals and the estate workers. I'm invited as a village tenant, but I'm not going. It's really gross. You'd love it.'

Lytton turned down the corners of his mouth. 'Wouldn't I just,' he grimaced. Then he smiled. Catherine looked wonderful. Not sharp and aggressive, like so many women he knew, but warm and clean and very pretty. 'You know,' he said, 'it really is very nice to see you again. A real treat.'

Purposely Catherine picked up her glass. It was the act of someone not keen to become too pally. Lytton recognized it instantly. 'I know this is a delicate subject with you, Neville,' she said, 'but I really do think we should finalize things.'

'Sorry?' Lytton looked perplexed.

'I mean I'm starting divorce proceedings next week,' said Catherine flatly.

'Oh, I see,' Lytton nodded to himself. 'Talk about hitting a man when he's down.'

Catherine was astonished. 'You aren't down. I've never seen you so up. Your career is blossoming, you've got a string of girlfriends, you're richer than ever you've been in your entire life, people talk about you, you were even the star on "Clare Copeland Interviews" ...'

'So why are you so keen to get rid of me?' demanded Lytton, anxious to get off the subject of Clare Copeland. 'I don't understand. You married me when I was penniless, jobless and homeless, and now that at last things are beginning to look up you take off with some fly-by-night academic who would bore the stars out of the sky.'

'That isn't fair. Tom isn't boring.'

'Not boring? Is the grass green? He's the most boring man of the century.'

Catherine listened quietly and without offence. She had heard all of Lytton's hyperbole before. 'He's very intelligent,' she said.

'Of course,' agreed Lytton. 'Why else would he have stolen you away from me?'

'He didn't steal me. I was going anyway.'

'How long's the swine away for?' asked Lytton.

'Three weeks.'

Lytton grinned. 'What are you doing for dinner tomorrow night?'

Catherine shook her head. 'Neville, I mean it this time. I'm divorcing you. I really am.'

Lytton's face fell into an expression of despair. 'Oh well,' he said unhappily, 'I suppose I'd better drown my sorrows.' Holding up his hand he summoned the waiter. 'The same again for my wife, please, and a hemlock and soda for me.'

Catherine giggled.

Lytton chose David Sellier to investigate the Hal Rimmer story, suggesting that he nip down with a photographer to see if they could get a shot of the lads doing their PT against a backdrop of an English country house.

Unfortunately for David the photographer was a whining little character called Neil, who had come to Fleet Street via a good contact in the dark room, and was pitifully low in news sense. 'It's all a bloody wild goose chase, if you ask me,' he complained as he and David drove into the Staffes estate.

David had been afraid that there might have been someone on the gate but they entered through the stone archway without impediment and began to tour round the side of the house towards the stables at the back. 'Oh, I dunno,' he said, grateful for a day out of the office. 'It isn't that bad. "Skinheads at the manor", "country folk up in arms", "loutish invasion". I've chased wilder geese.'

'Jesus, what's that?' broke in the photographer.

David stopped the car alongside a large wooden effigy of a crusader which had been erected in front of the house. 'Vicious looking beggar, isn't he?' said David, running his eyes over the sword and helmet that the crusader wore. 'He looks like some sort of totem pole. I'd get a couple of snaps of him, if I were you,' he prompted.

Grudgingly the photographer pulled his camera out and took the required pictures. Then, as David drove along the lane, he turned his camera on to the house. 'One thing about the aristocracy, they do have style. It makes you wonder how anybody could ever become so rich, doesn't it?'

David glanced at the house. It was a particularly attractive example of eighteenth-century extravagance, neo-classical in design and no doubt incredibly expensive in upkeep. 'In Hal's case a distant ancestor had the foresight to lend his wife and daughter to one of our glorious monarchs,' he said. 'After that the bastards never looked back, if you get my meaning.'

They had reached the stable block and, parking the car, they climbed out. A door from an outhouse adjoining the big house opened and five skinheads emerged. They looked, thought David, as gruesome a tribe as he had ever encountered. The leader was wearing a T-shirt with a Union Jack plastered all over it, while the rest wore various uniforms of thuggery, some bearing the cross of St George, a couple of others the swastika. Their hair was regulation skull scraped, and tattoos defaced the skin on their arms. Quickly the skinheads made a ring around David and the photographer.

'Hello, we're from the *Daily News*, and we were wondering exactly what kind of training course you chaps are on down here?' David smiled enthusiastically around him. Their eyes met his with a dull menace. He was not at all sure now that it had been a terribly good idea taking a day out in the country.

Another door opened and an athletic, older man of about forty, wearing army fatigues but without the insignia of rank or regiment, joined them. This must be their minder, remembered David.

'I'm afraid we've nothing to say to the press,' the man in fatigues said. 'Goodbye.'

'But we understand that Hal has –' David never expected to get any story without a struggle.

'I said "goodbye",' he was told again.

Sensing that they might not be staying very long the photographer raised his camera and took a couple of shots of the skinheads and their minder.

One of the skinheads moved forward. 'If you want that camera stuffing down your throat, mate, you just carry on,' he snarled. The photographer allowed the camera to drop.

'This your car, mate?' another one asked, and then very casually bent back the radio aerial into an inverted U shape.

'Hey, watch that,' shouted David. The skinhead grinned, spat on the ground and then moved away.

'Lord Henry doesn't encourage trespassers,' the older man said evenly. 'This is a special youth training scheme and these young men have work to do. I'd go now if I were you.'

David didn't need any second bidding. Returning to the car (the photographer was already inside, winding up his window and locking the door), he climbed in and drove away, leaving the skinheads grinning among themselves.

*

198

Lytton was not particularly surprised to receive a writ for his story about the Moonie and the Lady. It was the sort of piece that any self-respecting husband had, at least, to do a spot of sabre-rattling about. That was what usually happened, anyway, when husbands read accounts of their wives' infidelities. No matter how well known or how much condoned, few husbands liked to see a newspaper print an account of their being made a cuckold without making some kind of gesture: a gesture which nine times out of ten was never followed up and quickly forgotten.

What Lytton was surprised by, however, was the editor's attitude when he summoned both Lytton and the lawyer in to see him.

'It all seems pretty clear to me,' Cruickshank mused. 'Bickersfield is threatening fire and brimstone for implying that the child his wife is carrying is the result of her liaison with a mad Moonie who came to the door asking for donations.'

'She virtually said as much,' Lytton reminded him. She actually *had* said as much, but he was being a gentleman – after a fashion.

'Which she now denies,' chipped in the lawyer peevishly. 'I did point out last night that –'

Lytton was in no mood for fencing words with him. 'You mean, you told me. So you did.'

The editor lifted his palms to them both, indicating that there was nothing to fall out about. 'I'm not blaming you, Neville,' he smiled agreeably. 'This is an occupational hazard which any good columnist runs. But I'm afraid our chairman isn't very amused. He thinks the story was an error of judgement, and wants it settling as quickly as possible.'

Lytton didn't understand this. 'You mean he wants us to say we made a mistake and to pay up?' he asked.

'Something like that.'

'But the story's true. We can't do that,' protested Lytton.

'We can't be one hundred per cent certain of that,' came in the lawyer.

Lytton felt his hackles rising. Colin was a disagreeable fellow at the best of times, most lawyers are. But when he was playing at being a clever dick he was positively enraging. 'The story's true, believe me. I'm not going to apologize for getting something right,' he insisted.

There was a short silence. Lytton glared at the floor and the lawyer looked to the editor for guidance. Cruickshank took off his glasses. 'If you don't mind my saying, Neville, you can be very naïve sometimes. You've got to choose your battlegrounds in this life,' he said firmly.

Lytton wasn't satisfied. 'But if we give in over this we'll be giving in all the way along.'

'A compromise now could possibly save us a great deal of money later,' warned the lawyer.

Lytton ignored him. The editor shuffled his papers on his desk: 'I'm sorry to have to ask this of you. I really am.'

There was no point in arguing the matter. Lytton could see that. He walked out of the room without another word.

'He's right, of course,' Cruickshank reflected as the door closed after him. 'We should stand by our story. But the survivors in this game sometimes have to choose which story to stand by.' He put his glasses back on and instantly became business-like again. 'If you could phrase the usual apology line, Colin, we'll find a hole somewhere for it tonight.'

The lawyer nodded and followed Lytton out of the room.

It was never easy being an editor, considered Cruickshank, when he was alone. Keeping the peace between litigious husbands, social-climbing proprietors and ambitious writers was a juggling feat of skill and not a little diplomacy.

Over on the Diary desk Lytton was using absolutely no diplomacy at all as he gazed derisively at the four thin paragraphs David had offered as his story on the skinheads. Alongside stood the photographer with a couple of undistinguished pictures. 'What d'you mean, that's all?' shouted Lytton, so loudly that people on the reporters' desk looked across to see what the row was about.

David blushed at being given a public roasting. 'They wouldn't talk,' he muttered apologetically. 'There was this bloke there ... his name's Maxim apparently ...'

'Well there must be some reason why Hal Rimmer has taken to letting his property be overrun by skinheads. Did you talk to him? Or the estate manager? Or any of the staff in the house?' No one had ever seen Lytton so angry. Around the rest of the Diary, reporters kept their heads down and got on with their work.

Vainly David tried to salvage something of his reputation as a reporter. 'A chap in one of the village pubs, he was telling us about Maxim, he said that everyone was really fed up with them ...'

'Dear God,' groaned Lytton, 'a hundred and fifty miles round trip and all you come back with is four paragraphs and a claim form for a twisted aerial.'

'There were four of them,' butted in the photographer.

'I wasn't asking you to go to war,' snapped Lytton and took his pictures from him. They showed the skinheads and the house. 'Was there really nothing else?' he asked.

'Well ...' The photographer looked hesitantly through his roll of contacts. 'There was this.' He showed Lytton a picture of the crusader effigy.

Lytton stared blankly at it. 'You'd better get this blown up and let me have a decent print of it,' he said, 'seeing as you came back with nothing else worth printing.'

Quietly David and the photographer melted away from him.

Lytton was not happy. A few days ago he would have overlooked this shoddy attempt at reporting by David but all of a sudden life was getting on top of him. First Catherine wanted a divorce; then the editor had decided against him in the Lady and the Moonie story, and then there was the problem with Laura. Or was it a problem? He couldn't be sure, but it was certainly having an unsettling effect upon him.

He met her for lunch in Mother Bunch's, an alternative haunt to the Galley Proof. At least here they wouldn't be bothered by Henry Field and his chums.

'Well, you have to admit, it's a good offer, isn't it?' she said. 'I mean I'd be a fool not to consider it seriously, wouldn't I?'

Lytton pretended to shudder. 'But New York? It's so far from anywhere. Virtually the back of beyond,' he lamented.

Laura had to be amused at his absurdity. 'You mean it's a long way from you.'

'I really don't think you'd like it there, you know. Not to live,' came back Lytton. 'It's all right for a visit. There's nowhere nicer for a couple of weeks in September. By the way, did you know there are five women to every one man in New York now?'

'I know that's a lie,' smiled Laura.

'Why d'you want to go, anyway?' he asked. 'I don't understand.'

'I don't know. I suppose I feel it's about time I spread my wings. Put my toe in the melting pot, or something. Everything I do now seems so predictable. Career, social life ... even you and me.'

Lytton grinned ruefully: 'You've already made up your mind, haven't you?'

'Nothing's as easy as that,' she replied. 'But it is tempting.'

'Yes, I suppose it is. Shall we have another bottle and tempt ourselves back to your place for the afternoon?'

'Don't be silly. I've got work to do.' She stood up. 'Shall I see you over the weekend?'

'Oh yes, I suppose, so,' he said glumly. 'If you like.'

She leaned forward and kissed him on his forehead. 'Of course I like, you silly man,' she cooed, and then hurried back to the office.

Miserably Lytton ordered himself another half bottle of claret and set about downing it alone. It was years since he had been so depressed.

That was how David found him, feeling sorry for himself and getting drunk. 'Laura told me you were in here,' the younger man said, 'I'm sorry I cocked up yesterday.'

'What? Oh, don't be silly,' replied Lytton, and, tapping a waitress on the arm, cadged another glass. 'Sit here and help me finish this. I'm sorry I was so sharp with you. I think I'm becoming crabby in my old age. All of a sudden I seem to be getting the bum's rush wherever I turn. Life's a funny thing, David. One minute you think you have complete control and you're hitting all the buttons perfectly. And the next you're a fraction of a second out and the whole damn thing starts backfiring all over the place.'

'I'm not sure that Hal Rimmer was a backfire.' David poured himself a very generous helping of wine. 'I know I didn't come back with much yesterday, but I've just been making some inquiries, and it's altogether beginning to sound as though Young Hal might be mixing with some very odd company.'

'And the skinheads?' asked Lytton, his face clearing.

'Heaven knows where they fit in. But I think we should find out.'

'That's better,' grinned Lytton, and kicking away a pile of sawdust by his foot he stood up.

'I should warn you, though,' said David as they made their way out of the bar, 'there may be a snag. Hal's father has massive business interests in Australia ...'

'And ...?'

'He and Wayne Monroe are hand in glove all over the

203

southern hemisphere. The word is that the Rabid Dingo would like him on the board of the *Daily News*.'

'Really! Well, that can't be our concern. We just chase the stories. It's up to other people with other motives to spike them.'

That afternoon Lytton held one of what David liked to call his group gropes, in which the entire Diary staff chipped in with whatever information on a certain person was available, and Lytton tried to grope his way to an understanding of that person. The subject under discussion was Hal Rimmer.

'He's as rich as Croesus and as thick as a brick,' said Pandora. 'He was at Eton with my brother.'

'He would be,' mouthed Dolly.

'He isn't the horsey Rimmer is he?' asked Jenny.

'That's his father, Billy the Kid. He's a very powerful chap. I suppose Hal must be a bit of a disappointment to him,' Lytton explained.

'That won't prevent him from going for our throats if we try to make a monkey out of him,' came in Norman.

'This is true,' Lytton agreed, picking up the photograph of the wooden crusader. 'I wonder who this chappie's supposed to be.'

David hadn't spent half a day sitting in the pubs near Staffes without learning something. 'If you had an invitation to tomorrow's party you might be able to find out,' he said.

Lytton smiled.

Hal Rimmer's garden party was the sort of occasion Lytton would normally have avoided like the plague, being basically an excuse for Hal to show off in front of the families of his estate workers and smart friends from town. Once, in a bygone age, intended as a social gathering where gentlemen and workers could rub shoulders happily in pursuit of country games, the Rimmers' recent parties had never succeeded in being anything other than occasions when Hal's family could happily patronize their tenants in the name of fun. Elsewhere in England fashions had moved on and outlawed such anachronisms as cricket games of Gentlemen (Hal's friends) versus Staffes (Hal's workers). But down there in Sussex social progress would always limp so long as Hal Rimmer and his family owned their estate, most of the village and much of the surrounding countryside.

Not that the Rimmers didn't push the boat out on these occasions, providing food and drink in abundance and inviting everyone who might have some claim to patronage. But, although there was some degree of joking rivalry between the different castes of guests, few would ever be able to say that they were really comfortable. That was not what Hal wanted. Thus three separate encampments could be identified on the wide lawn and terrace where tea was served that Saturday afternoon. There were the London people, well dressed, well heeled and well spoken; there were the estate workers and their families in their best Burton suits and Marks and Spencer shirts, enjoying this day when they could wig the boss; and there were the village people. Once, no doubt, the village people had not been very different from the estate workers, since most were the Rimmers' tenants. But if social progress had not reached the estate it had certainly penetrated the village, where weekend cottagagers from London, with jobs in advertising and property, had now encamped en masse alongside the older generation of country folk. And to them Hal's annual garden party was an affair of much importance in their social calendar.

Neither Catherine nor Lytton fitted naturally into any of these groups, but Catherine was a tenant and had been invited, and to Lytton this was an advantage not to be missed. 'It's so nice to be out with you again,' he complimented her as they strolled together around the gardens.

'You're not "out with me", Neville,' Catherine corrected. 'I'm simply doing you a favour by being in your presence at the same appallingly patronizing party. And one more jibe like that and I won't be. I can't imagine what Tom would say if he knew I was here. He'd be appalled ...'

'Well, well, look who's here, the poor man's Dickie Davies,' a familiar voice broke into her worries. Marching towards them, wearing a blazer and a pair of cricket flannels was Henry Field.

'I thought you said this was an exclusive do,' murmured Lytton to Catherine. Then turning to Henry he added, 'Hello, Henry, get you down to play the village idiot, did they?'

Henry ignored the insult. 'And Catherine, too. My word, this is a nice surprise. Are you two planning a revival of the old marital double-spread or something?'

'I'm a local in these parts, Henry. What's your excuse?' said Catherine, ignoring the question.

'Well, promise you won't laugh, but I'm only here for the cricket. Charlie here dragged me in at the last minute. I was out first ball.' He nodded towards a dapper young man who was walking past carrying a couple of pints of ale.

Although Lytton would never admit it, he was not displeased to see Henry on that particular day. At least he had something in common with Henry and could understand what he was about. Although he recognized several of the upper-class faces wandering around the grounds, and admired several of their wives, he was like a fish out of water in the country. He was a town bird through and through, as was Henry. So for the first time in months he and Henry chatted aimiably, both grateful for each other's company. And despite everything she said, Catherine, too, enjoyed the banter of the two arch rivals.

There was to be a dinner and dance in the main hall of Staffes in the evening, but in the late afternoon Hal Rimmer ascended the small rostrum at the end of the terrace to select the winners of the Staffes All Comers raffle. He was a handsome man in his thirties, although he looked younger, and was blessed with a casual assuredness.

Lytton and Henry watched him choosing the winners from the lawn. It was a simple system. A pretty girl, the belle of the village, in a T-shirt she must have borrowed from someone several sizes smaller than herself, held a large hamper into which Hal plunged his fist, all the time keeping up the friendly, cosy chatter of a man among friends and dependents. He was, thought Lytton, paternal in the way he addressed the estate tenants, although he was considerably younger than a great many of them.

'It's at times like this that I wonder whether things were not a lot easier when everyone knew his place in the world,' said Henry, watching Hal joking with the farmhands.

'And which particular position do you think you'd be occupying, Henry?' asked Catherine.

Lytton stepped in: 'I wouldn't answer that, if I were you. At least not in front of a lady.'

When Henry went in search of another drink Catherine said: 'Isn't it time you two patched it up?'

'No,' replied Lytton, but his mind was hardly on what she had said. Five skinheads were making their way across the lawn and on to the terrace accompanied by the man in army fatigues known to David as Maxim.

'There you are, what did I tell you?' said Catherine. 'Gosh, they look almost smart today.'

'I'd hate to see them when they're not smart,' shuddered Lytton. To him they looked revolting, but, he noticed, there were no signs of any swastikas or Union Jacks.

On the rostrum, Hal had reached the star prize of the afternoon. Having handed out a hair dryer to a bald man, a tennis racquet to an old lady and a sack of potatoes to a couple of debby-looking girls, he now dived into the hamper one last time to discover who had drawn the extremely large wheelbarrow. 'And the winner is, yellow, ninety-nine,' he announced. 'Who has yellow ninety-nine?'

At the end of the terrace a hand went up. It belonged to Maxim. 'Over here, Hal,' he called.

'Marvellous, well done, Max.' Hal was roaring with laughter. 'For those of you who don't know him yet, let me tell you that Max is a very great friend and a wise adviser. Come on up here, Max, and get your wheel-barrow.'

'What do you think? Was this worth coming all this way to see?' asked Catherine as Lytton watched Maxim trot through the crowds.

'Oh yes. Very well worthwhile.' Lytton gazed hard and long at Maxim.

A few moments later Hal, now mingling with the crowd and being congratulated on his choice of gifts, spotted Lytton. 'Hello, Neville. This is a nice surprise.'

'I wonder, am I mistaken or might I have met your friend Max somewhere before?' asked Lytton, still trying to place the face.

Hal shrugged, apparently disinterestedly. 'I really haven't the foggiest idea,' he said. 'Enjoy your day.' And he strode away across the lawn to talk to his friends.

Catherine and Lytton might well have left at that point (Catherine actually suggested that it would be a very good idea if they did) but Lytton had still not seen enough, so they took a long walk in the grounds, played a happy game of croquet against Henry and the wife of his cricketing chum, and ate a dinner of roast venison off paper plates in the conservatory. And then, hands washed, and not a little weary from so many hours' drinking, they made their way with the other guests to the hall where a local pop group played while the guests danced. Lytton had never been one for shaking his limbs, but he did try, and while all the world danced frenziedly around him, he and Catherine waltzed sedately around the periphery of the floor.

'Have you seen all you wanted yet?' asked Catherine as the clock edged towards ten-thirty.

Lytton, who was now actually enjoying himself, held her close, his eyes watching everything and everyone. 'Not quite,' he whispered. 'Just do me one last favour, will you? Keep the opposition occupied for a few minutes and I'll give you as many divorces as you want.'

'Darling, you say the sweetest things,' she murmured, and reaching up she kissed him in mock gratitude.

Unknown to either of them, a photographer who had been earlier taking photographs of the party games happened to be standing close to Henry, and, at his suggestion, caught the kiss on celluloid for posterity.

'Come on, Henry, just one dance, for old time's sake,' called Catherine, and Henry, whose own wife had decided not to come down for the day's festivities, leapt to her side.

'Sorry, Lytton, looks like I win again,' he chortled, as he took Catherine into his arms and danced away across the floor.

'Of course you do, Henry,' smiled Lytton, and slipped out of the hall.

Lytton had no clear idea what he intended to do but he had earlier noticed several of the younger men following Hal out of the hall, leaving their wives and girlfriends to chat alone. Curious to know where he had gone and what had happened to Maxim and the skinheads, he made his way quickly up the main staircase into the interior of the house. There was something extremely odd about the presence of the skinheads at Staffes, an opinion he

209

manifestly shared with the tenants who had given the boys a very wide berth. And as the day had progressed he had become increasingly certain that Maxim was not the real name of the man in army fatigues.

He might have missed Hal's fund-raising activities had it not been for a little show of petulance on the part of the host. As it was Lytton was attracted to the slightly open door of the library by the waspish chastisement which Hal was bestowing upon one of his younger friends. 'Come on, Nick, you can't start backing out now,' he heard him bark angrily.

'I'm not backing out. I just feel that I'd like to know where my money's going to be spent before I make any more donations,' came the reply.

Lytton moved forward and peered through the crack between the door and the frame. Hal was sitting at a table, surrounded by half a dozen of his smart London friends. On the table stood a small crusader, a replica of the one in the grounds. Maxim leaned against the fireplace.

'You can be certain we make the best possible use of funds,' Maxim said, staring deeply at the young man.

A less cautious young blood spoke up next, chucking a cheque across the table towards Hal. 'Here's my bit, anyway,' he said 'And cheap at twice the price, say I.'

Nick the unready gave in and took out his own cheque book. 'Okay, I'm sorry. I was being silly,' he muttered.

Hal looked at Maxim. 'The movement won't forget this, Nick,' he said.

Outside in the corridor, Lytton tiptoed away from the library and moved stealthily along another corridor towards the rear of the house. That was where he figured the outhouses must be situated. Going down some steps he discovered a short balcony off which were several doors. Gently he pushed one and peered inside. It was a small dormitory. A few paces further along he came to another room. Emblazoned on the door was a cardboard cut-out of the crusader. Gently he opened the door and looked inside. It was a small print room, with banks of paper, a photocopying machine and piles of home-made magazines. Quickly Lytton stuffed one into his pocket and, hearing voices, hurried back towards the main hall.

As he turned a corner he almost walked into three of the skinheads. 'Oh, sorry,' he apologized. 'You wouldn't, by any chance, know where the guests' cloakroom is, would you? I seem to have lost my way.'

'Well it ain't up there, mate,' came the sour reply.

'Ah, I see, jolly good,' burbled Lytton and hurried on.

Lytton showed Wesley the magazine he had taken the following morning. It was called *Patriots* and had as its emblem the crusader. On the cover was a photograph of a gang of black boys beating up a white policeman. The headline ran REPATRIATION NOW: ENGLAND FOR THE ENGLISH.

'What d'you reckon?' Lytton asked the boy.

Wesley sniffed. 'Not a lot. These geezers aren't worth writing about, are they?'

'No, they aren't, in the normal course of events,' replied Lytton. 'But when someone like Hal Rimmer becomes involved, that's different. He has enough money to make them into a very sinister and troublesome little gang of thugs.'

Then, turning to the Diary writers, he allocated tasks. Pandora was to find out everything she could about Hal and his friends, Dolly was to pursue the British Patriots' Party, publishers of the magazine (Lytton wanted names, backers and addresses), while David's job was to discover everything he could about Maxim. Lytton had still not placed the face.

While he was instructing the staff his telephone rang. It was Catherine. He told Jenny to say he would call her back.

'Was she upset?' he asked, holding the phone before daring to dial.

'She didn't sound very happy. She'd read it.'

Lytton put the phone down without dialling. At that moment Laura went past him on her way to her desk. 'Have you seen Henry Field's column today?' she asked.

Of course Lytton had seen it.

'At least I now know why you weren't able to see me on Saturday night.'

Lytton really didn't have time for these little tantrums. 'Oh, come on. You know it's all nonsense. Henry's got the wrong end of the stick again.'

'So have I,' replied Laura, and walked on.

Lytton caught up with Henry in the Galley Proof at lunchtime. He was very cross. 'D'you mind telling me what you're playing at?' he demanded, slamming a copy of the *Daily Post* down on top of the bar. At the bottom of Henry's page was a photograph of Lytton being kissed by Catherine and a short paragraph in bold type.

'I couldn't resist it,' smiled Henry happily.

'But it isn't true. Catherine and I are not "starting out again". There has been no "reconciliation". We were not like "two young lovers" on Saturday evening, and divorce plans have not "been shelved". Where did you get all this from?'

Henry passed Lytton a drink. "You know that chaps in our position are allowed to read between the lines a little bit.'

'But this was complete fiction! You never did this when you worked for the *News*.'

'Well, no, but we at the *Post* have a less literal attitude towards news these days. We like to get to the spirit of the matter. Facts can sometimes mislead. It was only a joke.'

Lytton scratched his head. 'I don't understand you, Henry. It isn't usually the habit for one newspaper even to concede the existence of another, let alone print a picture of a rival columnist. What's going on?'

For a moment Henry looked embarrassed. 'To be honest, I had such a nice time chatting with you at that terrible party on Saturday and enjoyed the croquet so much – Catherine really is a wonderful woman – that I thought it was about time we forgot all our differences and made friends again. We were quite chummy once, remember?'

Lytton looked mystified. 'No, I don't think I do.'

'You know, when chaps get to our age they value their friends. I know we're rivals, but why don't we bury the hatchet and start behaving like old pals again? What d'you say?'

'Well, yes, I'd like to bury the hatchet, Henry. Honestly, I would. But preferably in the back of your skull.'

David, anxious to make amends for his poor start on the story, uncovered the reason why Maxim looked so familiar during a marathon search of the cuttings library. It was all in a yellowing press report from the *Daily Post* written by a young reporter called Neville Lytton, dated 1968. He showed Dolly. ARMY DISMISS RACIST INSTRUCTOR, the headline read and below was a picture of Maxim taken fifteen years earlier. 'Apparently friend Maxim was known as Bernard Goodenough then. The army kicked him out for delivering racist magazines to a housing estate near Catterick. He was PT instructor. So, if you're still struggling with the Patriots' Party, I think the name Goodenough might help. Apparently he now operates from a gymnasium over a pub at Catford.'

'Catford doesn't sound much like Hal Rimmer's territory, does it?' Dolly mused.

'It's a cover,' explained David. 'They use it as a recruiting centre for the troops. Politics makes strange marriages, doesn't it?'

Lytton presented the story to the editor the following day. Cruickshank read it very slowly, marking certain paragraphs with a ball point pen as he went. 'There's no doubt about it, it's a hell of a story,' he agreed, 'if we can get Hal Rimmer to own up to it.'

Lytton frowned: 'He'll never do that. He isn't a complete fool. We don't need him, anyway. The bare facts of his involvement are pretty damning in themselves.'

'And pretty damning for us too if our chairman isn't convinced by them.' The editor was being uncharacteristically cautious.

'But I *saw* what went on,' insisted Lytton. 'I saw the photocopying machine they use and we've checked exhaustively. This bloke Max *is* Bernard Goodenough and he does run the Patriots' Party. And a violent lot of louts they are too, by all accounts.'

The editor put the copy down on his desk. 'Unfortunately, Neville, your checking has been so thorough that Hal Rimmer and his pals are now well alerted to the fact that you're on to them.'

'That was a risk we had to take,' Lytton explained. There was no way that inquiries of this nature could be made without it getting back to the subjects of those inquiries within minutes. For a day and a half the entire Diary team had been phoning anyone who knew Hal or had anything remotely to do with the Patriots' Party.

'That may be so,' the editor agreed, 'but it's given Young Hal the opportunity to use all the pulling power he's got to keep his name out of the paper.'

'You mean the old man has been on to Monroe?' asked Lytton.

The editor nodded unhappily. 'That's how it looks from here,' he said, and then added, 'it might be easier for us all if Mr Monroe were a journalist. He doesn't understand anything that doesn't add up on a balance sheet.'

'When Monroe bought the paper he made a public declaration that he didn't wish to influence the editorial content in any way.' Lytton was astonished that he and Cruickshank should be even having this conversation.

'Every time any rich man buys a newspaper he promises not to interfere. But they always do,' said the editor. 'They can't help themselves. What's the point in owning a paper if you can't influence it and make it work for you.'

Lytton could feel the argument slipping away from him. 'That doesn't say an awful lot for the freedom of the press, does it?' he replied bitterly.

If there is one thing that editors do not like to be reminded of, it is the notion that they are being derelict in their duty to defend the so-called freedom of the press. The expression of sympathy which Cruickshank had worn throughout the meeting was wiped from his face. He slid the sheets of copy back across the table. 'I'm sorry, Neville,' he said. 'This isn't firm enough. Even if Hal Rimmer weren't the son of the chairman's closest friend I wouldn't run it. You'll have to get some more if you want to get that into the paper.'

Laura found Lytton sitting at his desk at ten-thirty. She had been finishing a feature on the perils of promiscuity. Lytton was staring into space with his rejected story on Hal Rimmer lying in front of him. 'Penny for them,' she said as she reached him. 'D'you want to buy me a drink?'

Lytton looked at his watch. 'It's a bit late now, isn't it? Besides, I thought we weren't friends any more.'

Laura ruffled his hair. 'Of course we're friends. What were you thinking about?'

Lytton shrugged uneasily. 'Oh, I dunno. Nothing. Everything. Fleet Street. Newspapers. Nothing important. It's just that if this Hal Rimmer story doesn't get in, if it's stopped for fear of embarrassing Wayne Monroe, or the board, or Hal's father, I think I'll have to resign.'

'Hey, steady on, Lytton.' Laura had never heard him

speak like this before. 'It isn't life and death, you know. It's only a story.'

Lytton laughed. Laura's basic professional attitude could always be counted upon when questions of journalistic ethics arose. 'Come on, let's go in search of that drink. Somewhere must be open,' he said, and getting up he took his raincoat off the peg and walked with her out of the office.

It was a mild, damp, autumn night and Fleet Street was busy with the diesel rattle of the vans as Lytton and Laura walked west towards the Strand. 'Do you ever wonder if you did the right thing becoming a journalist?' he asked.

Laura laughed. 'Is my copy so appalling?'

Lytton smiled. 'I was just thinking, Wesley's decided he wants to become a reporter, but he's such a nice lad. He still believes newspapers are full of news.'

'Oooh, you cynic.'

'You know what I mean,' persisted Lytton. 'You and I spend our lives repackaging publicity material and rewriting hand-outs from everyone from the Government upwards.'

'Except for stories like the Hal Rimmer one. That isn't exactly repackaging publicity.'

'And I can't get it into the paper.'

'You will though.'

They had reached their cars which were parked on a steeply inclined street which led down to the Thames. By coincidence they had parked within a few feet of each other when they had arrived at work that morning.

Lytton waited while Laura searched in her bag for her car keys. 'You weren't really cross about Catherine, were you?' he asked.

Laura smiled. 'Irritated,' she said, shaking her head. 'I didn't believe it, but I didn't like to read it either.' Gently she took the lapels of his raincoat in her hands.

'Look, about New York, I've made up my mind. I'm going to try it for six months. Is that all right?'

'Would it make any difference if I said no?' he asked.

'If I don't go now I never will.'

Lytton nodded. He understood. 'I know. I just wish I could go, too. Chuck it all in here and start again where there are no Wayne Monroes, no terrified editors, no Henry Fields ... no Fleet Street, I suppose.'

'You don't,' said Laura. 'Not really. You wouldn't last five minutes, Lytton. You need Fleet Street. You live off the hustles and tussles, the bitching and the rivalry. They're your lifeblood. You're a hundred per cent Fleet Street man, and you're going to have to accept it.'

'I'm going to miss you.'

'Of course you are. But in the meantime you're going to nail Hal Rimmer and his pals to their Patriots masthead good and proper. Okay?'

'I'll do my best.'

Laura opened her car door. 'What d'you think? Your place or mine for cocoa?'

'Cocoa,' smiled Lytton. 'That's something else I'm going to miss.'

Lytton and David drove down to Catford the next day, Lytton's enthusiasm for the story reactivated after Laura's cocoa and sympathy. Lytton had intended to visit the gymnasium alone but David, having had one not too pleasant brush with the forces of the Patriots' Party, insisted upon accompanying him.

They found the place easily, a side entrance to a back street pub. Together they climbed the dank Victorian stairs into the gymnasium.

It was a larger room than Lytton had expected, complete with three-quarter-sized boxing ring, punchbags, medicine balls and considerable equipment for weight training. But there was another aspect to the place. Hung on the varnished panelled walls were a variety of Patriots' Party posters and emblems, including several of the crusader.

The gym was not empty when Lytton and David entered. In one corner a blond, muscular boy of about eighteen was working steadily at improving his body and much tattooed arms, lying on his back pumping iron. Unaware of their presence, he pumped on as Lytton and David looked around.

'Just about the only thing missing here is the swastika,' said Lytton glancing around the walls.

David viewed the muscle boy with some caution. 'Let's make sure we don't get on the wrong side of that fellow,' he whispered.

Oblivious to their presence and consumed completely in his narcissism, the boy worked on.

'Well, well, well ...' Lytton had stopped by the large fireplace. Standing along the mantelpiece were a row of framed photographs, a rogues' gallery of all the Patriots' Party hierarchy.

'Hey, what do you two want?' The muscle boy had become aware of their presence. Lytton turned towards him, leaving David by the fireplace.

'We were wondering –' he began, not knowing quite how to finish.

He didn't have to. A voice from the door, shrill and angry, finished his reply for him. 'I think they're probably looking for me. Isn't that right, Neville?' Hal Rimmer, accompanied by Maxim, walked into the gym.

Always ready with a bluff, Lytton smiled widely at them both. 'Ah, yes, I was wondering whether we might have a little chat,' he said brightly, but his tone faded as three of the Staffes skinheads followed the two leading Patriots into the room, 'about your involvement with the Patriot Party.'

'You never give up, do you,' said Maxim moving towards him.

'I'm sorry?'

Maxim looked at David. 'Nor you. You've already had one warning off. Have you forgotten already?'

David stayed by the fireplace. He didn't answer.

Lytton turned on Maxim. 'Perhaps you'd like to tell us how the Patriots' Party operates, Mr Goodenough. This is your training centre, isn't it?'

Maxim leant against a punch bag. 'This is a gymnasium. We teach our lads to look after themselves in here. 'D'you want one of them to give you a demonstration?'

A couple of the skinheads laughed. Lytton ignored them. 'How much have you contributed to the Patriots' funds, Hal?' he asked.

'Who said I ever did?' Hal answered casually.

'How did you find us down here?' asked Maxim. 'I thought you only mixed with toffs.'

Lytton was concentrating upon Hal. 'It takes all types to make a party, doesn't it, Hal.'

'You'll never be able to print any of this, you know,' Hal replied. 'My old man's got Monroe in his pocket.'

'You can be so certain?' asked Lytton.

'Yes,' grinned Hal.

Lytton shrugged. 'You may be right. We'll see.'

Noticing that David was still loitering by the fireplace, Maxim turned on him. 'And what about you, the organ grinder's monkey? Are you gonna help your mate? We should have duffed you up the first time we saw you, you bleeding little creep.'

David still didn't answer. Lytton noticed that he seemed to be blushing.

'What I don't understand is what you and your pals see in this half-baked troop of bother boys, anyway,' he said to Hal, drawing the fire away from David. 'Even an idiot can see that they're nothing more than a gang of simple-minded hooligans.'

The muscle boy began to move towards him. 'Here,

219

mate, you wanna watch your mouth. You could get into serious trouble talking like that.'

Maxim put out an arm. The boy dropped back.

Lytton smiled: 'Thank you. But doesn't that illustrate my point precisely,' he said to Hal. 'Their only weapons of debate are their fists and their boots. They're pathetic. Look at all this ... emblems, flags everywhere, like some sort of museum for madness. How many members do you have, Max? Fifty, a hundred, two hundred?'

'There are more members than you'd think,' said Hal, unable to resist rising to Lytton's challenge. 'Your kind have run things for long enough in this country. Always sneering at everything and everyone. And look at the mess you've got us into. Well, it's going to be our turn again soon: you'd be surprised how much backing we're getting. Take a good look around you. This is only the start. With the money we're raising –'

'Hey, careful, Hal,' Maxim broke in. He was looking anxious.

But there was no stopping Hal. 'Don't "Hal" me,' he snapped. Then turning back to Lytton he said, 'With the money we're picking up now, the new members, the connections, we're going to blow away people like you. Your lot won't know what's hit them.'

'Spoken like a real crusader,' mocked Lytton.

Over by the fireplace, David coughed. 'Er, Lytton,' he said, 'I think perhaps we ought to be making a move.'

Maxim looked relieved. 'That's right. You get him out of here before he gets himself into serious trouble. He's liable to get himself killed.'

'Come on, Lytton, let's go,' urged David, anxious to get out.

'Thank you for being so co-operative,' Lytton scoffed at Hal, and together he and David slipped out of the gymnasium. At the top of the stairs Lytton stopped and put his ear to the door.

'How many times have I told you we don't talk to the press,' screamed Maxim at Hal.

'Don't worry,' muttered Hal, 'Lytton won't ever be able to write any of this.'

It was only when they were back in the car that Lytton understood the reason for David's haste. From inside his jacket David produced one of the framed photographs which had been standing on the mantelpiece. The picture showed Hal and Maxim linking fists in front of a poster of the crusader. Scrawled across the photograph was a message. It read: 'To my brother in Patriots, Maxim. Together we shall overcome.' And it was signed by Hal Rimmer.

Cruickshank called Lytton in to see him just before going for dinner at seven o'clock. He was studying the revised story on Hal Rimmer. On the desk was the photograph of Hal and Maxim. 'Well, you've really put me on the spot this time. You say he's confident that we won't run it, eh?'

'That did seem to be the general notion,' Lytton replied.

Cruickshank sighed. 'You know, when an editor gets a story like this he can do one of two things. He can throw caution to the winds and print it because he believes it an important issue which should be broadcast widely, or he can seek advice from those who employ him and own his newspaper. In my opinion, since this story is already of very great interest to our proprietor ...' he paused momentarily '... I think our best course of action would be to run it right across page one tomorrow.'

Absurdly Lytton found himself playing the devil's advocate. 'You don't feel that Mr Monroe –' he began, but Cruickshank stopped him.

'Mr Monroe signed a declaration that he would not be interfering in editorial matters. And nor will he, if he isn't given the opportunity. He can complain all he wants once the story is in the paper.' He smiled. 'Well done, Neville.'

Catherine was waiting for Lytton by the ticket barrier at Waterloo Station. She had tried several times to reach him since Henry's story of their day at Staffes had been published, but Lytton had purposely avoided her. He didn't want to know what he thought she had to tell him. He was reconciled to the idea of Laura going to work in New York. She had only ever been a part-time girl-friend anyway. But Catherine had been for keeps. He didn't want to discuss divorce proceedings, or even think about them. But with his story about Hal Rimmer already being set, she had phoned and asked him to meet her for an urgent discussion before she took the train home. He couldn't very well refuse.

'I began to think you were avoiding me,' she told him as they met. 'I've been calling you all week.'

'Yes, I know, I'm sorry, but it's been very busy . . .'

'Neville, I'm having to call off our divorce,' she said, breaking in on him.

'What?' This was exactly what Lytton had not expected to hear.

'I'm postponing it for a while. Bloom and Bolsover think that Henry's little joke has definitely given the impression that we're together again, and they want us both to know that judges have recently become pretty sticky over keeping to the letter of the law in divorce cases.'

'Oh, Catherine, I'd no idea. I'm sorry,' lied Lytton, try-ing not to smile with relief. 'Will Tom be terribly upset?'

'Don't lie to me, Neville. You're tickled pink,' chided Catherine.

'Oh, no . . . well, yes, actually,' agreed Lytton.

'Anyway, I thought you'd like to know,' she said. 'And now I'd better be off or I'll miss my train.'

'I'll walk down with you,' said Lytton, and, buying a platform ticket, joined her on the platform.

'Only you could get away with this,' said Catherine as she climbed the steps on to the train.

Lytton smiled. 'Look, if Tom's still away in Albuquerque, why don't we have dinner some time next week and discuss things?'

Catherine leant through the open train window and kissed him on the forehead: 'Don't push it too far,' she smiled.

And nor did he. Waving goodbye as the train pulled out, Lytton walked contentedly back along the platform and then took a taxi back to Fleet Street. He called in the Galley Proof but, not finding anyone to chat to, decided not to stay for a drink and popped back into the paper to pick up a copy of the first edition. He was very pleased with what he saw. The front page headline read LORD WHO BACKS RACISTS. It was an exclusive by Neville Lytton, complete with stolen photograph of Hal and Maxim. On the Diary page were several further stories about Hal and the Patriots.

Tucking the paper under his arm, Lytton bade goodnight to Norman and, leaving the office, set off back towards his car. All things being equal, he thought, he had a great deal to be happy about.

He had again parked the BMW on one of the narrow little streets leading down from the Strand to the Thames, a quiet spot popular among urban lovers who sought its seclusion as a place to meet in their parked cars. But tonight there were no lovers.

Lytton had almost reached the BMW when someone called to him from a doorway. 'You wouldn't, by any chance, know where the guests' cloakroom is, would you? I seem to have lost my way,' mimicked the voice.

Had he had time to think about it and recognize his own words being thrown back at him, Lytton might have seen the danger. But there was no time. As he turned to see who was speaking a knee came up into his crotch, and, as he buckled in pain, a shaved head butted him viciously under the chin. He went down immediately, his arms flailing about him as he tried to stop the force of the blows being rained on him by the five skinheads. He hit the pavement with a bounce. As his eyes opened and closed he saw the face of Maxim staring down at him while the boots of his troops went to work, kicking him between them like a rag doll.

'Never underestimate the power of the press to get you into a great deal of trouble, Mr Lytton,' spat Maxim as he delivered a final vicious kick into the fallen man's kidneys.

For a long time after the attack Lytton lay spread across the pavement, his face down against the flag stones. He hurt everywhere, too much to move. He had hardly seen his attackers. But he knew what had happened. The blows which struck him had been aimed by the thugs from the Patriots' Party. But Lytton knew that throughout the length and breadth of London there were those who would not sympathize with his sufferings. In their opinion Neville Lytton, the snooper into private lives, the trader in rumours and the peddler of secrets, would have received his come-uppance.